A STRANGER IN WYNNEDOWER

by

Grace Greene

A Virginia Country Roads Novel

Books by Grace Greene

Stories of heart and hope ~ from the Outer Banks to the Blue Ridge

Emerald Isle, NC Stories
Love. Suspense. Inspiration.

BEACH RENTAL (Emerald Isle novel #1)
BEACH WINDS (Emerald Isle novel #2)
BEACH WEDDING (Emerald Isle novel #3)
BEACH TOWEL (short story)
BEACH WALK (A Christmas novella)
BEACH CHRISTMAS (A Christmas novella)
CLAIR: BEACH BRIDES SERIES (novella)

Virginia Country Roads Novels
Love. Mystery. Suspense.

KINCAID'S HOPE
A STRANGER IN WYNNEDOWER
CUB CREEK (Cub Creek series #1)
LEAVING CUB CREEK (Cub Creek series #2)

Single Titles from Lake Union Publishing

THE HAPPINESS IN BETWEEN
THE MEMORY OF BUTTERFLIES

www.gracegreene.com

Kersey Creek Books
P.O. Box 6054
Ashland, VA 23005

Cover Design by Grace Greene
Trade Paperback & Digital Release: November 2012
Large Print Version Release: August 2014
ISBN-13: 978-0-9884714-7-4

DEDICATION

This book is dedicated to families—first born, middle child, baby of the family, parents and those who perform the role of parenting, grandparents, extended family, ancestors and generations yet to come. Through a miracle of 'heart chemistry,' our loved ones and memories make the places and structures in which we live, our HOME.

HOME. It isn't necessarily under one roof, but rather a place represented by the capacity of our hearts, a place that isn't truly home without the people who matter to us. HOME is the place for which you'll risk everything to keep it and the loved ones who fill it, safe and sound, and they'll do the same for you.

It takes some of us a little longer than others to find our HOME, but when you do, you know it. And that's my wish for my readers ~ may you find your true HOME and be blessed by the treasure within.

ACKNOWLEDGEMENT

My love and sincere appreciation to my husband and family for their support—you are my HOME.

A STRANGER IN WYNNEDOWER

Love and suspense with a dash of Southern Gothic...

Rachel Sevier, a lonely thirty-two year old inventory specialist, travels to Wynnedower Mansion in Virginia to find her brother who has stopped returning her calls. Instead, she finds Jack Wynne, the mansion's bad-tempered owner. He isn't happy to meet her. When her brother took off without notice, he left Jack in a lurch.

Jack has his own plans. He's tired of being responsible for everyone and everything. He wants to shake those obligations, including the old mansion. The last thing he needs is another complication, but he allows Rachel to stay while she waits for her brother to return.

At Wynnedower, Rachel becomes curious about the house and its owner. If rumors are true, the means to save Wynnedower Mansion from demolition are hidden within its walls, but the other inhabitants of Wynnedower have agendas, too. Not only may Wynnedower's treasure be stolen, but also the life of its arrogant master, unless Rachel can save them.

A STRANGER IN WYNNEDOWER

Chapter One

Rachel Sevier stared at the monstrous stone house, and its rows of blank, dirty windows stared back.

She'd driven from Baltimore to Virginia, to this area called Goochland. After leaving the interstate, there'd been a pocket of shiny new construction—a small shopping center and houses—but that snippet of civilization was quickly gone and then she was deep in the woods.

Jeremy had given her directions: drive until the trees crowd in close and the road looks like it's about to end, then keep driving. She had.

Wynnedower Mansion, built of gray stone and mellow wood, looked out of place, as if a giant hand had plucked it from the gently rolling hills of England, dropped it into this clearing, and left it to rot amid honeysuckle vines and Virginia creeper.

Not quite what she'd expected. To her, the word 'mansion' meant something a little more upscale.

Gnats swarmed in the humidity. Rachel shooed them away. Hers was the only car here, and there was no one else, including Jeremy, anywhere in sight.

Several weeks ago, with graduation barely behind him, he'd told her he was taking a job at Wynnedower as a caretaker. He already had a real job in Richmond and was supposed to be preparing for graduate studies, but he wanted to be independent. *It's a great deal, Rachel,* he'd said. *No rent in exchange for part-time caretaking.*

Caretaking? Really? She adored her baby brother, six-foot-two, golden-haired and smart—so different from her own appearance that no one believed they were related until they saw their eyes. There was no mistaking their unusual eye color. But handsome or not, he wasn't trained in security and had no handyman skills. The worst of it was he'd stopped returning her calls two weeks ago, right after he told her he'd met a girl. He'd said it in that special way in which *girl* didn't just mean girl— it meant everything bright and shiny and worth living for.

It was a big sister's job to inject reality and practicality and she'd done her duty. He hadn't appreciated it, and it wasn't the first time they'd disagreed, but he'd never stopped talking to her before.

Finally, she gave in to worry and moved up her visit. Luckily, the change in timing worked for her current job and for the new job she hoped to get, but she needed to find her brother before she could get on with her plans.

She tucked her cell phone and keys into the pockets of her suit jacket and locked her purse in the car.

Scraggly bushes obscured the ground level of the house. A wide stairway bypassed that level and led to the main floor. Rachel paused at the entrance. A broken doorbell dangled by a wire. She settled for knocking.

There was no shade on the porch. She tapped her shoe, tugged at the neck of her blouse and fanned the front of her jacket. She should've waited until after she'd arrived before getting into this suit.

The suit was out of place here. Dressy and expensive, it was not in the budget, but it made a bold statement and was perfect for the event she planned to attend in Richmond that evening. She straightened her skirt, brushed off a speck of lint, and knocked again.

No answer. She tested the knob, barely touching it, yet the door swung slowly inward on silent hinges.

The foyer was the size of her apartment living room, but without a stick of furniture or decoration. Ahead, a wide opening led to an even larger room.

She leaned inside and called out, "Jeremy?"

Her voice traveled through unseen rooms and echoed back emptiness.

Rachel stepped inside and eased the front door closed.

As she crossed the bare wood of the foyer her heels clattered. No one had responded to her call; she was surely alone here. Even so, she removed her shoes and tucked them under her arm.

This room was vast and high-ceilinged. The walls were a mess of half-stripped wallpaper and dingy paint, and none of the work looked recent, but the air was surprisingly, deliciously cool. She paused to soak it in. To her right, a wide staircase climbed halfway to the second floor, did a U-turn and continued upward.

Did she dare?

She'd risk anything for Jeremy.

Dark wood balusters led the way. Upstairs, doors and shadowy alcoves ringed a spacious landing. A hallway continued onward, but she didn't follow it because the only light filtered up by way of the stairs. The doors on the landing each presented the same paneled surface with faceted glass door knobs set into cast iron plates.

She turned the knob of the nearest door. Locked. The door directly across was locked, too. She stooped to peer through the keyhole.

A gruff shout jolted her. "What are you doing?"

He was a tall man, broad and unshaven, with long, unruly black hair. His jeans were rumpled and worn, and marred by paint smears. He wore an unbuttoned, wrinkled cotton shirt over a white t-shirt.

Rachel stumbled back a few steps, then steadied herself. She pointed her spiked heels at him. "Who are you?"

The dark hall deepened the shadows beneath his brows, making his face impossible to read. She felt his eyes take in her shoes, her suit, then drop down to her nearly bare feet. She felt even shorter than she was.

"You're trespassing. Get out," he said, his voice rough and uncompromising.

"Is Jeremy Sevier here?"

"If you're a jilted girlfriend, that's not my problem. If you're hunting antiques, you're a looter."

"Looter?" Outrage pushed her fear aside. "I'm his sister. Where's Jeremy?"

"Sister? He didn't leave a note. Get out." He turned and walked toward the alcove.

"Wait, tell me what you mean. He left? Why?"

He looked back and glared. "Ask him when you find him."

"You said he didn't leave a note. What did you mean?"

"What I said. He didn't notify the property management company he was leaving, so unless he sends a postcard from wherever, I don't expect to hear from him."

Fear curled up hard and cold in her belly. "How can you be sure he simply left?"

"What?"

"That something didn't happen to him?"

He moved a few, deliberate steps toward her. "If it did, it didn't happen here."

Past her first shock and with her eyes better adjusted to the low light, Rachel realized that his clothing, though shabby, was clean. She detected a whiff of soap. The wild hair that had looked stringy was actually still drying, and the stubble on his face obscured the strong bone structure.

"Are you the owner?"

He made a rude noise. "Owner? Right." He pointed toward the stairs. "The door is that way. Leave or I'll call the police. Trespassing is a crime." He walked away, dismissing her.

Rachel waited, breathless, disbelieving his behavior and expecting him to return. Her hands fisted. This man was no help. An impediment, that's all he was. And he'd left, arrogantly assuming she'd follow orders, so he was also foolish.

She went to the stairs, but only descended a few steps, then waited as the sound of his footfalls grew distant. If she moved quickly, she could check the other doors before he returned.

The door opposite the alcove was unlocked. It opened. The brighter light straggling in through the grimy window was a welcome sight.

The corded plaid spread on the bed—she recognized it. She'd purchased one for Jeremy years earlier. He'd taken it with him to college, and this one was bedraggled enough to have been in use for a decade, but it was a common style and proved nothing, really.

A comb, a few pennies and a green dry cleaners' tag littered the top of the dresser. Old paperbacks were stacked in a corner. Nothing identifiable as Jeremy's.

Unlike the floor below, the air up here was musty and hot. Rachel tossed her shoes onto the bed. Through the window, she saw her car below. She pushed up on the window sash. It was out of alignment and budged only one stubborn inch. She gained another inch on the second try but left it at that lest she break a nail. After all, she had plans for the evening, plus the job interview in the morning.

Rachel shrugged off her suit jacket and hung it on the door knob. With the door open and the window up a bit, the fresher air made the heat more bearable. The silk shell stuck to her back. She pulled it away from her damp skin.

She searched the room. The closet was empty except for plastic hangers. In the drawers, she found a few socks with threadbare heels and an old pair of jeans. There were so few personal items. Yet this was where she'd expected to find him and she found it hard to give up that idea. Then she hit jackpot—a sweater she'd given him two Christmases ago.

Relief washed over her. She leaned against the dresser, elbows resting on the scarred wood and her face in her hands. Jeremy hadn't been a kid in a long time, but she'd raised him, bandaged his scrapes and fussed at him to do his homework. As he grew and towered over her, she'd worked to support him. He'd always be her baby brother and he was the only family she had left.

The lack of possessions in the room suggested he'd moved out, at least in part, perhaps in haste. Next, she'd talk to his employer—his real employer, not this guy.

Who was this man, anyway? A handyman? A new caretaker? Had Jeremy already been replaced? She slapped the top of the dresser.

A waft of cooler breeze caught her by surprise and caressed her face. She closed her eyes, relishing the relief brought by the stronger draft—until the door slammed shut.

Momentary blankness swamped her. Rachel gripped the edge of the dresser and drew in a long, slow breath. Calmly, she walked to the door, twisted the knob and pulled. Nothing.

"Hello?" She called out in a reasonable voice, then louder, "Hello?"

The man must have opened an exterior door. The air had sucked through like a wind tunnel, pulling the door along with it.

"Hello? Hello?"

She grabbed the knob and rattled it, shaking the door. She added her other hand, getting a firmer grip on the knob and—

Whoa. No need to panic.

She released the doorknob and brushed her moist palms against her skirt.

Breathe deeply. Think it through.

He had opened a door, probably the front door for the draft to have such force. He'd see her car and come back. If not, no problem. She had a phone. She could call for help. She'd deal with trespassing issues later.

Rachel patted her sides. No pockets. No jacket. She turned to the bed, but only her shoes were there. Her jacket wasn't on the floor; therefore, it was on the other side of the door, out of reach, with her phone in the pocket.

She drew in a long, deep breath, closed her eyes tightly and focused, willing it to happen. She visualized that rude man from his dark hair and shirt to the jeans with paint marks and the broken down loafers. He gets angry when he sees the car and realizes she ignored his order to leave. He storms up the stairs. Her red jacket hangs from the doorknob like a flag. He sees it and understands what has happened, that this falling down house has trapped her.

Her heart pounded.

No panic allowed.

She slumped against the door and sneezed.

More than a century of dust, long settled into the sinews of the house, seemed to swell and fill the hot air. Stuffy and a headache-maker, for sure. Now, thinking about heat and dust, she was thirsty, too.

The mattress dipped as she sat on the edge and stared at the door. Perspiration prickled at her hairline, and rivulets trickled down her spine.

She squashed her fear by focusing on reality. This delay jeopardized her evening plans. Time wise, it was a good thing she was already dressed for the reception because, if that awful man rescued her soon, she could still make the museum reception.

Oh, Jeremy. Where are you?

Suddenly she saw what was right in front of

her: a gap of about one-half inch, maybe a bit more, between the door and the floor. Rachel dropped to her knees and peered through the opening.

Her jacket had fallen to the floor.

It was a dark, reddish mound in the dim hallway. If she could snag the material with a hanger, she could pull it, along with her phone, through the gap.

The pantyhose would never survive a sprawl on the floor. They were hot, too. She slipped them down her legs, then folded and tucked them into the top dresser drawer along with the lonely socks, presumably Jeremy's. The scatter rug would protect her skirt from the dirty floor.

Plastic hanger in hand, she lay down on the rug. It scrunched up beneath her. She smoothed it out and tried again. Cheek to the floor, she pushed the hanger through. Slowly, the crook went into a fold. She coaxed the red fabric toward the door.

Sweat broke out in the parts of her body that had been dry until now. She ignored it, as well as the grainy feel of the dirt between her cheek and the floor boards, and focused on the jacket. It slid, making a soft brushing sound against the floor. It came loose, but close to the door. She stretched her fingers through the opening. It was a snug fit and the bottom edge of the door scraped her skin, but lightly. She touched the fabric with the tips of her fingers.

A shadow fell across the jacket.

She held her breath. Why wasn't he saying

anything? Her fingers were sticking out. He had to know she was here. She pulled her hand back, rose to her knees and banged on the door.

"Please, help me. Get me out of here. I'm trapped." Ear to the door, she listened in vain. "Hello? Who's out there?"

She pressed her cheek to the floor and watched as the shadow moved. A floorboard creaked, and then there was nothing except the jacket and that narrow view of the hallway.

Anger bubbled in her veins; the heat in the room faded by comparison. Someone had stood, watching, hearing her pleas for help, yet had abandoned her without a word. Adrenaline fueled her anger. She stretched her fingers forward again, beneath the door, and pushed half of her hand through. Her flesh tore, but she snagged the fabric between two fingers and pulled. The jacket came forward. The red fabric peeked through the gap below the door, but then stopped.

Was it the phone or the keys? She didn't know, didn't care. A tight fit, but they *would* fit. She would *make* them fit.

Rachel grasped the sleeve with both hands and tugged. She half-rose to improve her leverage and pulled harder. On her feet, she gripped the fabric in both hands and yanked for all she was worth. The scatter rug slipped. She launched, feet up and backside down, and smashed onto the floor.

Stunned, winded, coated in sweat, she lay

there gasping to refill her lungs. In her hand, she clutched one red sleeve.

After a few minutes, the pain eased in her lungs and back. She rubbed her face. A coarse film of dirt covered her hands and cheeks.

She'd saved her pantyhose, but the suit jacket—the expensive suit she couldn't afford—was torn and no longer wearable for the reception.

Her eyes burned. She closed them tightly forcing the tears to remain unshed.

She'd hoped to get that job by going to the reception looking fabulously chic. It seemed a great idea while she was sitting amid H-frames stacked with plumbing fixtures and supplies, counting the stock and making plans. The intersection of daydreams and reality was a harsh, smack-you-in-the-face, experience.

Lying there on the floor, she remembered she was resilient. The museum people hadn't been expecting her tonight, and she might have said the wrong things and screwed it up, so maybe it was just as well. Her actual job interview wasn't until tomorrow. After a bath and a good night's rest, she'd make an unforgettable first impression. After she found an inexpensive hotel room for the night. After she got out of this prison.

She needed to think, but first she needed to rest a bit, just long enough to stop her head from spinning, and to get her thoughts together.

Rachel crawled over to the bed and hauled herself up onto the old bedspread. She stretched out flat on her back and tried to imagine 'cold.'

Eyes closed, she envisioned a tall glass of ice water with condensation gathering on the sides. Ice cubes, clear as crystal, filled the glass. She focused on the image and the chill radiating from it cooled her face. She held it, in her mind's eye, and touched it to her forehead, her temples, and sighed.

****

Her head was splitting, and it was dark. Sweat had soaked her silk shell. The fabric had dried and felt pasted to her skin. Rachel raised her hand and heard a male voice say, "Don't move."

Her immediate reaction was to do exactly that, but her limbs felt sluggish. Where was she? Jeremy's room? She remembered. She'd climbed onto the bed.

"Lie still. I have a damp cloth." He laid it across her forehead, and then stepped away. A soft light snapped on across the room. "What happened? Do you need an ambulance?"

"No, it was just the heat."

"Then why didn't you leave?"

Was the man blind? "The door was jammed shut."

"No, it wasn't."

Pushing the cloth higher on her forehead, she raised herself slowly upright and lowered her legs over the side of the bed. Beyond the window was night. What had happened to the day?

"I don't think you should stand yet."

"I fell asleep, that's all."

His hair was disordered, some of it caught into a short ponytail at the nape of his neck. He looked a century out of date. Those dark, heavy eyebrows hadn't improved either. He was probably angry and, honestly, who could blame him?

She asked, "Did you see my jacket on the hallway floor? Or was it the car out front that got your attention?"

"It was the open door. I keep them closed and locked. Your jacket is hanging on the bedpost."

He'd ignored her question about the jacket on the floor. She let it go, too weary to push.

"Thanks for picking it up."

"I didn't. It was already hanging there."

The cool washcloth against her face helped. Was she dreaming? Had she been hallucinating? No. Her legs were bare. She knew what had happened. If this man would lie about a door being jammed, then there was no point in asking why he'd ignored her plea for help.

Rachel pushed off the bed and onto her feet. She handed him the dirty, but neatly re-folded washcloth.

"I'll give you my cell number. If you hear anything from Jeremy, please contact me. I have an appointment in the morning. If there's no word from him by that time, I'll go to the police and file a report."

"The police? A report?" He stopped in the open doorway, seeming to fill it.

"Of course. To file a missing persons report."

"Do you believe he qualifies as missing?"

Her heart said 'yes.' "He's not here, he doesn't answer the phone, and neither of us knows where he is. I have to do something."

"Where are you staying?"

All he needed was her cell number. The creepiness of knowing he'd watched her from the hallway without speaking a word rankled. For heaven's sake, she'd groveled on the dirty floor with a stupid plastic hanger.

"I'll find a hotel in town. Do you have something to write my number on?"

"Just say it. I'll remember it."

In the dresser mirror, Rachel caught sight of herself and every other thought was swamped. Her silk top was stained with dirt and sweat. Her dark hair was frazzled and stuck to her grime-coated cheeks.

Bitter words overwhelmed her self-control. "You act so concerned now. Where was that concern when you stood in the hallway watching me trying to force my jacket through the crack? I'll bet that was quite a show. Did you have a good laugh? Why didn't you open the door?"

He drew back. "What are you talking about?"

"Please. Who else could it have been?"

"Your imagination? Or a trespasser like you?"

She stormed past him, then paused at the

top of the stairs. "What's your name?"

"Call me Jack."

"I don't want to call you anything. I want to know what name to give the police when I file the report."

His face hardened. He crossed his arms. "Do what you have to do. I doubt they'll be interested. Jeremy—is that his name? Jeremy's a grown man and single. He probably moved into town with a girl. There'd be a lot more to interest him there, and maybe he didn't think it was his sister's business."

He held out her jacket. "Don't forget this."

Rachel grabbed it from him and went straight to the stairs. She didn't stop until she reached the bottom where she paused to put on her shoes.

He called down. "Wait, I'll walk you out."

"No thanks." She took the keys from her pocket and entered the night.

Dark. Breathless dark. It hit her like a wall. She stopped. This was not city dark.

An exterior light switched on with a puny glow.

Thanks for nothing, Jack.

Jack? The owner? She wasn't surprised. At some point, she'd figured it out even though he'd denied it earlier. Or had he denied it? Her brain was mush.

She held on to the iron stair rail as she descended. The car was parked a few yards away where she'd left it hours ago.

The lower level of the house, that area

behind the bushes, was black as pitch. It was unnerving to look into the void. No sight. No sound.

Rachel hit the door unlock button on her key fob. Nothing happened. She hit it again and again.

Desperation rising, she fumbled the key trying to fit it into the lock, but finally got it and the door opened. Once in the driver's seat, she pushed the manual door lock. Only then was she able to draw in a deep, cleansing, calming breath.

Refusing to accept the car was dead, she inserted the key into the ignition and turned. Nothing happened. The darker than pitch area ahead of her seemed to swell. It swallowed the world beyond the windshield.

A light flickered from within the bushes.

Too much. It was too much.

Calm down. Think it out, Rachel.

Should she call a tow truck? If she could get to a hotel, she could deal with the car in the morning. But the expense of a cab…costly, either way.

She hadn't dialed information in years. Hoping information was still 4-1-1, she punched the number in and hit dial. No ringing, there was only an unfunny series of beeps. She read the screen. The battery was low. The message suggested charging the phone immediately. What next?

Phone dead. Car, too. The heat. The dirt. The manicure. Tears squeezed from Rachel's eyes. How shallow was it to cry over a manicure? It was the safest thing to cry about. Not her missing brother. Not the events in the house. Not home. Not her aloneness.

If she returned to the porch and knocked on the door, would he answer? Or had he already vanished into whatever cave he hid in when he wasn't frightening lone women and trespassers?

Pull yourself together. You're an adult.

Things happened. Everyone knew that.

Suddenly, she wanted to speak to Daisy, to hear her friend's sympathy and common sense. Daisy would say, 'You just need a bath and a good night's sleep.'

Daisy was right.

She'd deal with one thing at a time.

Tonight, she needed a place to stay and a mechanic or tow truck. She'd call Martin Ballew at the museum in the morning and reschedule the interview for later in the day. He'd understand. Meanwhile, she'd do what she had to do.

The porch light still burned. She removed the keys from the ignition.

Something brushed the side of the car. Her side, but nearer the back seat.

She was overwrought; she pushed away panic.

Consider it rationally. Strip away the emotion.

Rachel closed her eyes and tried to visualize a well-lit, secure hotel room.

Remove the extraneous. Identify the true need.

Something hit the window next to her head. She screamed. A huge shapeless dark mass grabbed at the door, yanking at the exterior handle.

Skirt, heels, and all, she scrambled over the gear shift and to the passenger side seat. Her fingers scrabbled at the door, desperate to exit and forgetting it was locked. She heard a voice, Jack's voice, shouting from the far side, his face close to the glass, wild and scary. Her heart slammed almost through her chest.

"Stop yelling. Are you hurt? Unlock the door."

Should she? It was hard to take that giant step back into sanity. She hit the manual unlock button and opened the passenger door. Sliding out, clinging to the door frame, she yelled at him over the car roof, "You startled me."

"Startled? What do you do when you're terrified? You scared the crap out of me. I thought something was attacking you in there."

"So did I." She sniffled. "My car won't start." She crossed her arms to stop the shaking. "My phone died. Can I borrow yours?"

His hands were on the roof of the car. He thumped them lightly against the thin metal. The porch light edged the side of his forehead, his cheekbones and the long line of his jaw with a narrow glow.

"You can come in and use the phone."

Not back inside. "Do you have a cell phone?

I don't want to put you out."

He laughed rudely.

"I mean more than I already have. I apologize for trespassing, although I didn't believe I was. I thought I was visiting my brother, or looking for him. I should've left when you told me to, but then...."

"But then you still wouldn't know if your brother was here."

"Yes."

"I only have a landline."

He walked slowly around the car, his fingers trailing across the hood. Her knees were quaking, but she held her ground, refusing to appear weak. Afraid? Yes. Hysterical? Maybe. But weak? Never.

He stopped a few feet away and glowered. Her heart raced.

With a small, sardonic bow, he said, "After you."

Chapter Two

Nothing lay beyond the wide arch on the far side of the huge living room.

Rachel froze as she stared at the pitch-dark opening. "Where are we going?"

"The only phone is in my room."

One phone and it was a landline. This man lived in the Dark Ages. "What about your tenants?"

"Tenants? You mean the caretakers? Like your brother? They have cell phones or no phones. There are some old phone lines in the house, but so far you're the only one who has raised the question. And, frankly, you are a—"

"Trespasser."

"Right. Do you want to stand here and discuss it?"

She didn't. She followed him into the dark place. They turned a corner into a hallway. Here, there was light, not much, but welcome. Weak bulbs in sconces lit the back hallway and created deep, distorted shadows that climbed the walls and festered in the corners.

They passed doors on the right and a row of windows on the left, but no moonlight made it through the clouds tonight and there was nothing to see outside. Rachel caught the lingering smell of food. It reminded her of

Daisy's diner and her own, small apartment over the restaurant. She pressed one hand to her midsection willing her stomach not to rumble.

Near the end of the hall, he opened a door and gestured for her to enter. Again, she paused. Following him into his room warred with every iota of common sense she possessed.

"It's here or nowhere," he said.

The lighting was stronger in his room. It revealed old furniture, cheap area rugs and general clutter. A lamp scattered light across a desk stacked with papers and cast a halo on the ceiling. The phone was on the desk. Belatedly, Rachel thought of getting her phone charger from her suitcase in the trunk. A quick unzip would've put it in her hand where, now that she was near an outlet, she could've plugged it in for a fast charge.

"I have a phonebook somewhere." He waved his hand in the general area of the desk. "I'll find it. Why don't you use the bathroom? Wash your face or something."

She should wash her face?

Rachel held her breath, forcing the ungrateful words to stay unsaid. His bad manners didn't justify the same from her. She touched her face, remembered, and gasped. "Where's the bathroom?"

"A few steps down that hallway. Door on the left." He resumed opening desk drawers.

She wanted to yell or throw something, but

she didn't. Impervious to her stare, he stayed turned away. She gave up and went to the bathroom.

Old and shabby, the floor and walls were patterned with tiny black and white tiles. The claw foot tub had an aluminum frame attached that draped the shower curtain around it. Rust stained the drain of the worn porcelain sink, but it was clean. The mirror over the sink showed her reflection.

The view in the dresser mirror upstairs had been tempered by the low, soft light. This light was bald and harsh. Sooty dirt, sweat, and tears streaked her face. She reached up to touch her cheek and saw the ragged fingernails again. A sob rose to choke her.

Rachel closed her eyes and her mind. She didn't want to keep this image in her head to be stuck forever.

Her sad state was fleeting. With soap and water it would pass. With the help of a good nail file and clipper, her nails could be repaired. Her clothing? The silk shell had been vanity, as had the suit. She should never have indulged herself. A waste of money. Live and learn. As punishment went, fate had been gentle.

Calmer, she turned on the hot water and started splashing her face and arms.

When she returned he was bent over the phone book. The lamplight framed him as he ran his finger down the listings. Dark curls, free of the pony tail, fell forward across his cheek.

"You found the phone book."

The finger stopped and he looked up. "Yes. I called a couple of local tow companies. But it's late. Mike's garage is nearest. He's also a mechanic and he's reliable, but he can't get out here until the morning."

"What else?"

"Pardon?" He frowned.

"What else can go wrong?" She rubbed her temples. At least, the grit was gone. "I need a taxi then. I can leave the car here overnight, right?"

He stared. The moment stretched out long and taut. Surely, he wouldn't refuse.

She prompted, "Which hotel is closest?"

"You're talking going all the way into Richmond. At least to Short Pump."

"Is it far?"

The moment stretched out again. This man didn't owe her anything and she didn't want to be in his debt, but she was fresh out of options. Rachel met his eyes and watched thoughts play across his face. She read reluctance in his tight jaw and resignation in his sigh.

"Don't mistake this for hospitality." He pushed up from the desk chair.

"What?"

"I could give you a ride into town, almost two hours of my time there and back, and then what will you do in the morning? The car will be here, but you won't. It's too late to hunt down another tow or a mechanic tonight. As for a cab…from out here…."

He uncrossed and re-crossed his arms. He

scratched his five o'clock shadow, already well-underway.

"I hope I won't regret this. Stay here tonight. You can have a room up near where you were trespassing. Lock yourself in and get some sleep."

His great sacrifice of allowing her to stay the night annoyed her. Rachel skipped the customary thank you.

"You've been trying to throw me off the premises since we met this afternoon. Now, you're inviting me to stay the night? Why the change of heart? Aren't you afraid I'm going to run off with the copper pipes?"

He frowned. "If you knew how hard it was to keep a hulk like this from getting ransacked, you wouldn't be so flip about it. Let's just say it's inconvenient for you to stay, but more inconvenient for me to drive you into town."

"Earlier you said you weren't the owner. That's not true, is it?"

"Is that what I said? Is it any of your business? No, it isn't, but let me tell you about a house like this." His face flushed to a deep red as his voice grew louder. "You don't own it. It owns you. It's a money pit. It's an anchor mired way down deep where you can't pull it out."

Choices. Did she have any? Yes. Did she really believe this man had stood outside the door while she tried to hook her jacket? No.

"Thank you. Before you withdraw your offer, yes, I appreciate the help." She clasped her hands together. "I watch the news, so I do know people vandalize old or empty houses. Sorry to have made light of it, but I didn't think of looting and theft in connection to me."

Instead of appreciating her conciliatory response, it seemed to frustrate him more. He snatched a large, old-fashioned ring of keys from a board on the wall near his door. They jangled as he stalked past her.

Fatigue hit like a solid mass that touched the top of her head in a heavy caress. It gathered weight and force as it rolled over her shoulders and down her body.

Missing brother. Juiceless cell phone. Dead car. Ruined clothes. This rude man's offer was the best thing to happen to her today, which kind of summed it all up in a really depressing way.

Her stomach gave a resounding grumble. He heard.

She shrugged. "I haven't eaten since breakfast."

"You'd like a meal, too." He didn't say it as a question.

"I need to get my suitcase from the car."

His eyebrows drew together. He touched his jaw as if it hurt. Rachel felt a perverse satisfaction lightly mixed with shame at her own ingratitude.

Jack led her back down the hall to the doorway where she'd smelled food. He reached in and slapped the light switch. The kitchen was painted a putrid shade of yellow, overlaid with years of grease. The stainless steel refrigerator and oven were modern and shiny, making the old, worn-out furnishings look all the sadder. He leaned into the fridge and emerged with a casserole.

"I hope you're not picky." He turned on the oven and slid the dish inside. "Wait here. I'll get your suitcase." He held out his hand for her keys.

When he left, Rachel collapsed onto a dinette chair at the chipped yellow Formica table, but as the minutes passed and the aroma of the baking casserole grew, she recovered. With one finger, she traced a crack in the Formica while eyeing the contrast of the dingy walls with the shiny Dresden china in the Welsh cupboard.

Porcelain. Blue and white. Blue Onion pattern. That was it. She'd seen a picture. Heaven knew where. Her imagination and iron-clad memory were assets and a curse, but, without doubt, her greatest weakness was curiosity, and the conflicting images around her stirred up intriguing questions.

The Welsh cupboard looked like it was attached to the wall. She shook it, but gently. Those pretty dishes rattled, but the cupboard didn't budge.

Rachel went to the kitchen sink. The pipes moaned as she ran water over the dishcloth and squirted dish detergent into the cloth. She sudsed it up and scrubbed, but the counter and table weren't dirty, merely worn and stained.

The casserole was browning nicely. Chicken, if her nose was correct. Half the dish was empty, and the scraped remains were baking onto the glass. It was going to be a bear to clean. She chose plates and utensils and set the table.

Her host returned and stopped short when he saw two place settings.

He grabbed an oven mitt and removed the dish from the oven, setting it directly on the old Formica table.

"I already ate." He tossed the mitt on the counter. "I left sheets and towels out for you. I hope you can make your own bed. Go ahead and eat. I'll be back."

He didn't wait for an answer. That was good because she didn't have a socially acceptable one handy.

She should've known he'd already eaten. By the hour, for one thing, and also due to the aroma she'd smelled earlier. Showed how exhausted she was. Steam rose as she spooned chicken pasta casserole onto her plate. He was doing her a favor. He wasn't obligated to be gracious about it.

What was there about her own behavior that would encourage courtesy? Nothing.

Rachel's lower lip trembled. She wouldn't cry no matter how tired she was. She blew on a hunk of chicken. After a few bites, there was no more trembling because she was busy eating.

What to call him? Jack?

Jeremy had said he worked for the Wynnes. Surely, this guy was Jack Wynne. Of Wynnedower. He was one heck of a cook. She could forgive him a lot for this. Perhaps she could dredge up some niceness for him.

She chewed, considering. The room he gave her would be similar to Jeremy's. A shiver seized her at the memory of the imprisonment, but it passed quickly. She was determined and resilient. No matter how saggy the mattress or unswept the floor, she'd make sure Jack Wynne knew how much she appreciated his efforts whether he liked it or not.

"Ready?"

Rachel swallowed the last bite. "Let me tidy this up."

He grabbed the casserole dish and put it in the sink.

"What about the leftovers?"

"This way," he said.

She added her plate and utensils to the items already in the sink. Jack led her back down the dim hall and around that dark corner. They passed within sight of the foyer and front door, but then ascended the stairs, the same stairs she'd climbed earlier.

He passed Jeremy's door and unlocked the next one, swung it open and placed the key in her palm. It was a skeleton key. She'd never actually been where they were still in use. She closed her hand around it like a lucky charm or talisman, capturing the feel of it.

"This is the sitting room. Go through the next

door—this key fits that lock, too—and that's the bedroom. The bathroom is the door on the left."

She started forward, but he stopped her.

He continued, "This is important. Lock the door and keep it locked. If you hear noises during the night, ignore them. Intruders do break in. That's why the doors are kept locked. It slows them down and reduces the opportunity for damage. Here's the number for the house phone." He handed her a slip of paper. "You have your cell phone?"

"Yes. It needs charging."

"Then charge it. Call me if anything alarms you. Stay in your room and keep it locked until morning."

He was gone before she could begin to register his sinister words. He hadn't even said goodnight.

His warning about intruders? Rachel wasn't fooled. He wanted her to stay out of his way.

The sitting room was shoebox-shaped and windowless. A lamp burned in the corner next to a sprung chaise lounge, but as with every bulb in this house, it was weak and the room was full of shadows. The door at the far end, to the bedroom, was open, and a lamp also lit that room. Rachel locked the sitting room door before moving on.

Her suitcase waited on a red satiny bench at the foot of an inviting bed.

Doors and doors. This was a house of doors. The bathroom door was to the left of the bed, but there were two other doors on the far side.

One opened into an empty closet. The other was locked. Rachel tried the key Jack had given her. It didn't work.

The bathroom was more than acceptable. Old-fashioned, but not neglected. She inspected the claw-footed tub and was delighted to find it clean. She opened one of the faucets. The water ran clear. No rust.

Rachel ran her hands along the tub's smooth porcelain curves and murmured in appreciation, "We have a date tonight."

There was a connecting door in the bathroom. To Jeremy's room, surely. The door was locked, but the location seemed right. The rooms were as anonymous as a hotel room.

The bathroom window pushed up easily. A nice breeze swirled through the stuffy air. Rachel opened the bedroom window, too. Delicious, refreshing night air. These rooms were better maintained than the one in which she'd been trapped. Even better than her host's from what she'd seen. She gave the mattress the sit-and-bounce test. Nice. Better quality and better maintenance in here, without doubt.

With the water filling the tub, Rachel stripped the ruined shell over her head. Suddenly, she felt exposed. She was in a stranger's house. Wasn't it a little late to worry about ulterior motives?

Rachel considered it and admitted she felt no distrust, but there was no harm in caution.

She stacked a chair and an end table in front of the bedroom door as a crude alarm, then plugged her phone and charger into the bathroom outlet within easy reach.

A hot, relaxing bath could do amazing things for a gal at the end of a dreadful day. Rachel stayed there, soaking her worn body and trimming her ragged fingernails, until the water grew cold. Finally, she dried off and pulled out a pink t-shirt and striped, lightweight cotton pajama pants. Her hair, coal black and straight, was cut in a bob that brushed her jawline. She had only to run a comb through it and let it dry.

Rachel did a quick job of making the bed, then curled up in the over-stuffed chair near the window. She enjoyed the fresh breeze while she dialed Daisy.

Daisy answered on the second ring. "Rachel? How was your drive? You made it okay?"

"It's been crazy here, but that's a long story. Too long for tonight. The end result is I'm stranded."

"Do you need help?"

In her head, Rachel saw Daisy already reaching for her keys. "No, I'm fine. My car wouldn't start. It might be the battery. Like I know anything about cars, right? All I know is it doesn't work."

She propped her feet up on the windowsill and rested her head back against the tapestry fabric of the chair.

"Could be the battery. Possibly the alternator. Where are you? I hope you're not standing on a roadside?"

"I'm at The Mansion."

Daisy breathed, "Wynnedower? What's it like? You found Jeremy?"

"No, not yet. He was here, but has gone somewhere.

"You don't sound worried. Might be he's with that girl he told you about."

"Jeremy wouldn't take off like that. He has too much going on in his life, too many plans. I'll talk to his employer tomorrow morning and if there's no good explanation I'll speak to the police."

"The police? So you *are* worried."

"I am, of course, but not as much. I've seen where he was living and met the owner. The man is rude, but I don't think he did anything to Jeremy."

"Isn't it nice that bad people wear signs and we don't have to guess?"

"Ha-ha." Rachel shifted in her chair. "What I mean is, most of Jeremy's stuff is gone. As if he left. But if someone was trying to make it look like he left when he didn't, they'd clear out everything, right? Plus, the owner is genuinely angry at Jeremy for taking off without notice…not that I believe Jeremy did, but the owner certainly does."

"So you met the owners? What are they like?"

"He. A guy named Jack Wynne. Honestly, I can't tell you what he's like. He's different, looks sort of eccentric. Bad-tempered. On the other hand, he's set me up here tonight very comfortably."

"Oh?"

That 'oh' was full of insinuation. "It's not like that, Daisy. In fact, all he wants is for me to stay out of his way. He told me to lock my door and not come out until morning."

"What is he? A werewolf or a vampire?" She growled in the background.

Rachel laughed. "If you saw him, you might lean toward werewolf. He has lots of hair. Long, dark hair that he keeps pulled into a ponytail."

"Lots of hair? Is he hairy like *Beauty and the Beast* hairy?"

"*Beauty and the Beast?* Oh, please. No, not beastly at all. He has good bone structure, nice cheek bones and a strong jaw and dark eyes that seem to swallow you up."

"You and bone structure. Please. So, he's good looking. How good looking?"

She hesitated. "In an aggressive sort of way. In fact, he seems familiar somehow. Not specifically familiar, but generically familiar. Do you know what I mean?"

"Flowing hair. Strong, aggressive good looks. Sounds like he stepped off the cover of a romance novel. One of those historical ones. Is he showing any bare chest?"

"No, definitely not."

"Not wearing a kilt, is he?"

"Not nice, Daisy. Stop teasing me."

"But it's so much fun, and I'm not entirely teasing. The whole situation sounds suspicious. If you need me, let me know. I'll be there right away."

"Daisy, you're the best. That's why I put up with your strange sense of humor. In reality, his reason for asking me to stay locked in the room is simple. He says looters break in."

"What? Wow. Well, then stay in the room."

"He just wants me out of the way."

"What are these people after? It's a big house, right? But lived in, so what's going on?"

"He mentioned copper pipes." She shrugged. "The man didn't say this, but Jeremy told he'd heard rumors about something valuable being hidden here at Wynnedower."

"Like what?"

"He said something about artwork. Paintings or something. He teased me, saying we could go on a treasure hunt."

Daisy laughed. "That sounds right up your alley, both the art and the treasure hunt."

"Well, that was before he got angry with me, and apparently, moved without telling me."

After a pause, Daisy changed the subject. "If you only made it as far as Wynnedower, should I ask about the museum reception?"

Rachel pulled her legs up into the chair and sighed. "No, didn't make the reception. It's okay. Tomorrow is another day, per Scarlett."

"Don't let it get you down. Always remember what's important. Anything else is nice-to-have. And Rachel, have some fun."

Daisy was always saying stuff like that. She and Daisy were very different personality types, but friends. Her best friend. Only real friend.

"I have fun. Often. And this is an interesting place. For a night, anyway. After I find Jeremy–"

"After. Always *after*. You're too much in your own head."

"I'm solitary, true, but in my own head? I'm interested in lots of things."

Daisy started laughing. At first, Rachel was annoyed, uncertain, but then couldn't help laughing with her. She didn't understand the joke, but she trusted Daisy's heart.

They said goodnight, and she laid her phone on the nightstand. Lying there in the dark, suddenly she felt lost in the near silence. Only cricket noises came through the window. Country life? It seemed almost too quiet to sleep. In the distance, a train rumbled past. A long train. As the sound faded away, so did she. She fell off to sleep without noticing.

She woke the same way, with the sudden realization that she was awake. The time on her phone read one a.m.

Lying still, listening, she heard a creak from somewhere outside the room. Creaks were to be expected in an old house.

Another sound, difficult to identify and location hard to pin down.

Could it be Jeremy? Suppose he'd returned? He wouldn't know she was here unless he recognized her car in the dark.

It would be fun to surprise him. He'd say, "Rachel, when did you get here?" and she could tell him about getting trapped in his room.

Cautioning herself not to be disappointed, she felt along the floor with her feet, searching for her slippers.

She moved the furniture, unlocked the bedroom door and peeked out into the empty sitting room. When she turned the key in the sitting room door, the sound of the mechanism unlocking sounded like a shot in the silent night. Breath held, she eased the door open. There was no light peeking from beneath the other doors, including Jeremy's.

He wasn't there. It was disappointing, but while she was up she'd retrieve her pantyhose.

The door was still unlocked. One quick moment and she had her hose. She shoved them into the pocket of her robe. As she stepped into the hallway, a faint scent tickled Rachel's nose—a tantalizing wisp of flowers that was quickly gone.

In the far alcove, a whitish shape moved and vanished. Instinctively, Rachel surged forward, and then stopped. Was she really going to chase after a blur? It was probably nothing more than lint on her eyelashes. She spun around to return to her room and bumped into a solid wall of warm body. Hands grabbed her arms.

"How hard was it to respect my one request? That you stay in your room? Believe it or not, it's for your own safety."

He released her arms. She rubbed them.

She asked, "How did you get over here behind me?"

"What are you talking about?"

"I saw you go into the alcove. I saw someone in white." Rachel pointed at his white t-shirt. He was wearing the same jeans as earlier.

"You saw someone?"

"Just a shape."

He shook his head. "You're lucky. It could've been an intruder."

"I was hoping my brother had returned."

"Go." He waved in the direction of her room.

A couple of steps along, she stopped and turned back. "Jack?"

She could tell by the shift of his shoulders and his sudden stillness otherwise, that she'd startled him. "You said to call you Jack."

"That's fine."

"Why is Jeremy's door unlocked? Every other door in this place is locked tight."

"Rachel. May I call you Rachel?" He stepped closer.

The hallway was small. Claustrophobia touched her. Her stomach did a little jump.

His voice dropped, low and tightly controlled, "Rachel, your brother left without notice and took the key with him. I won't bore you with the details of the key situation here, but until I find one that fits, it will remain unlocked. Any more questions?"

She scooted back to her room. She looked back. He was standing there watching.

"Goodnight," she said.

He barely acknowledged the 'goodnight' and headed down the stairs, apparently in pursuit of whomever or whatever she'd seen. Rachel closed her door and turned the key, this time reassured by the sound of the internal mechanism as it slid closed. She hoped it was enough to guarantee a safe night's sleep.

Rachel wondered...if Jack thought she'd nearly run into a looter, wouldn't he rush off to catch him instead of staying to lecture her?

The elusive scent. The blur of someone disappearing into the alcove...someone feminine?

Perhaps Jack had another guest at Wynnedower—one he hadn't chosen to mention.

One who was none of her business.

Chapter Three

Rachel stood at the bedroom window willing the tow truck to appear, hoping to spot the dusty plumes it would throw up as it traveled the dirt road to Wynnedower. Nine a.m. It should be here anytime now. While she waited, she rehearsed the call to Martin Ballew.

She visualized him at his desk. His day would just be getting started. He'd be doing interesting museum stuff, not thinking about their interview scheduled for eleven a.m.

The job was at a small museum, and didn't pay much, but it was in the Richmond museum district and connected to a much larger museum. This job could be a stepping stone to a better future.

It was important to strike the right blend of professionalism and courtesy. Rachel carried her phone as she went downstairs. With her newly short, but neatly groomed fingernails, she was as good as new. No red suit, but that wouldn't have been appropriate for the interview, anyway.

Today she wore a dark blue slacks and blazer outfit with a cute but elegant pleated dress shirt. The blazer was cut loose and gathered. It had large interior pockets especially nice for carrying stuff.

She saw no one on the way out and left via

the unlocked front door. She wandered down the steps and across the yard, speaking aloud as if Mr. Ballew strolled alongside.

The morning was beautiful; the grounds were dismal. The grass was peppered with tufts of tall weeds, and littered with sticks, pine cones and gum balls. As she walked, Rachel explained to Mr. Ballew that she arrived in town yesterday and was looking forward to the interview, but had some car trouble and was hoping they could meet later in the day. He was very receptive—in Rachel's head. She was successfully wrapping up the imaginary call, and Mr. Ballew was promising to keep his schedule open for her, when she found the terrace.

The brick and stone terrace was appended to the western end of the house. It was semi-circular and paved with large flat stones. Waist-high brick walls and brick columns with big, round concrete balls bordered it. Access to the house was through a room that was also curved and appeared to be constructed mostly of glass. Dirty glass, of course, and a few panes were cracked, but it snared her interest.

Rachel did a slow spin. The woods began many yards away to the east and west. Between the forested areas a broad expanse of green carpet sloped down, far down, to the river. The wide sweep to the river had been hidden by the angle of the house and woods, not to mention that she'd been staring at the ground and talking to an imaginary Mr. Ballew.

Here and there, a few colorful shrubs created islands of red and pink.

The ground sloped over a distance and appeared to drop off abruptly. Below the drop off, the James River flowed past.

The beauty drew her. Did she have time for a walk down to the river? Tingling began between her shoulder blades. That watched feeling. She shook it off along with the scenic distractions. Back to business. It was time for the live show.

The receptionist answered the phone. She said Mr. Ballew wasn't in.

Rachel sat on the top step. Not in. She hadn't anticipated that. "But I have an interview scheduled with him this morning."

"Yes, ma'am. I was about to contact you. Mr. Ballew was called out-of-state on an emergency late last night. I'm canceling and rescheduling his appointments for the next few days."

"Next few days?"

"Yes. He doesn't know how long he'll be gone. When he returns, shall I call you to reschedule?"

Rachel sagged, flat as a blow-up snowman with a bad leak on a cold morning.

What was she supposed to do? Stay in a hotel? Four years of college for Jeremy weren't cheap, plus she'd paid the deposit and fees for the upcoming graduate program.

No need to panic. Focus on the important part. The rest will become clear.

Rachel put on her professional voice. "Yes, that will be fine. May I call you in a day or so and see if there's an update on his schedule?"

"Certainly, Ms. Sevier. You're welcome to call me. My name is Carina."

"Thanks."

Disconnect.

She dropped her face to her knees.

Now what? Rachel wrapped her arms around her knees and head. If she could've curled up in a ball like a roly-poly bug, she would've. She emptied her mind and regulated her breathing. This would be okay. It would work out. An answer would come to her.

"Are you sick?"

Rachel peeked sideways and saw his paint-splattered, rundown loafers. The slacks looked better than yesterday's jeans. She raised her head and smoothed her hair.

"I slept well. Thank you. And thank you for your hospitality. I don't remember whether I expressed my appreciation to you yesterday."

"No problem. Mike's Towing called. They'll be here soon."

"Thanks." She looked away. She wanted him to leave, knowing she couldn't hide the despair in her face or voice.

After a pause, he nodded and walked away.
****

Mike's Repair and Towing arrived mid-morning. Rachel saw the big, flat-bed tow truck through the window. As it stopped next to her car, a youngish blond-haired man jumped out of the passenger seat and strode up the steps and into the house. Another man, a bit older, exited more slowly from the driver's side. Rachel went straight out to the porch.

"Hi. I'm Rachel Sevier. I guess you're Mike? Thanks for coming."

"Yes, ma'am. Mike Mills. Wynne told me the car won't start?" He popped the hood. "What happened?"

"I don't know. I know nothing about cars."

"Well." He looked around the open hood and said, "It's a good idea to keep the cables connected to the battery." His expression was curious.

"What are you talking about?" She rushed to his side. She couldn't recognize much in a car engine, but she knew those clips shouldn't be dangling. "How would that happen?"

He reattached them. "Not likely to unhook themselves. Likely someone was messing with it. Let's try starting the car now."

"Whatever you say." She stepped back. "Are you sure they couldn't have come loose on their own? That dirt road is very bumpy."

His expression bespoke pity. He let her question go and asked one of his own. "Wynne said you arrived yesterday afternoon?"

Wynne? Jack Wynne, of course.

Could Jack have unhooked her battery? Nonsense. Rachel pushed the thought away.

"I drove down from Baltimore yesterday. It was parked in this spot for several hours." She shook her head. "Who would do such a thing?"

Mike started the engine and it hummed sweetly.

"What's the cost?" Rachel asked. She pressed her fingers to her temples. If she'd looked under the hood herself maybe she could've–

"Hello."

Startled, she looked behind her. The young man smiled broadly. Both his jeans and his boots were well-worn. He looked at home in them.

He asked, "Are you just passing through? Or here for a visit? You're a friend of Jack's?"

"I'm Rachel Sevier. I came here looking for my brother, the most recent caretaker. Do you know him? Jeremy Sevier? A little over six foot and skinny with blond hair? About your age?"

He looked aside, crossing his arms.

"Nah, don't think so. Usually, I go in the opposite direction, toward town. I do odd jobs here from time to time." He looked at Mike. "You ever meet him?"

Mike wiped his hands on a towel, and then shoved it into his pocket. "No, don't think so."

Rachel turned to Mike and asked again, "How much do I owe you?"

He shook his head. "I drove out and I'll have to drive back."

"I understand. How much?"

"Wynne promised me one of May's casseroles so I think we're about even."

"May?" A calendar popped into her head showing casseroles of the month.

The younger man spoke. "May Sellers. She cooks for him, lucky guy."

Mike added. "Worth a drive out here any time."

"It sounds like an excellent deal for me."

"Wynne's a good friend. Known him all our lives. Happy to help a friend of his."

"Thank you." Now that she had transportation, she was in a hurry to visit Jeremy's employer and to get away before her car suffered some other vandalism.

She wondered briefly about the person who had stood in the hallway as she begged for help. If it truly wasn't Jack Wynne, then could it have been a vandal? Perhaps the same person who tampered with her car? Someone with a grudge against Wynnedower?

"I'll tell Jack the car's fixed," she said and headed to the porch to fetch her suitcase.

He was already there, coming down the front steps with her suitcase in his grip "So, Mike's got your car all fixed? Good deal."

"Especially for me. May Seller's casserole?"

He laughed. His face lit up, and the heavy brows now seemed to fit his face, his dark eyes and strong features. Rachel noticed his hair was smoother today and neatly controlled by the band. He'd shaved. He looked almost civilized.

She added, "The only thing wrong was that the battery cables were unhooked. Any idea how that happened?" She watched his face closely, but saw nothing more than mild surprise.

"Not a clue." Jack turned away He stowed the suitcase in the trunk and closed it with a firm slam.

"Good luck, Rachel. If I hear anything from your brother, I'll contact you. Probably nothing to worry about. He's a young man, and there's a lot more life in the city than in this old place." With a quick wave, he walked straight over to Mike and the younger man. They all went into the house together.

She was left holding her farewell 'thank you' like a wilting bouquet that nobody wanted.

Good riddance could work both ways.

She drove through the broken gates and down the old dirt road, looking in the rearview mirror one last time, almost disbelieving she'd spent the night in Wynnedower Mansion.

Thick woods lined either side of the dirt road. The road followed a ridgeline, and it was about a mile to the main road.

With a little luck, Jeremy would be at work when she arrived. He'd be sitting at his desk with a perfectly obvious reason for why he was no longer at Wynnedower Mansion and why he wasn't answering his phone or returning voicemails. She'd listen, and then she'd kill him for putting her through this worry.

The car jolted down and up again. She avoided a big rock and concentrated on navigating the ruts and potholes.

****

Strom and Sons was an accounting firm on

the west side of Richmond and probably only a thirty or forty minute drive if she hadn't gotten lost. The firm was the perfect employer for Jeremy, poised, as he was, between a Bachelor of Science and the master's program he was beginning in September. Then the CPA exam. Rachel enjoyed teasing him they were both making careers of counting things. He'd stopped laughing a while ago, so she needed to think up a new joke.

It was a building of steel and glass. Only two stories, but shiny and appearing transparent at the same time. Every angle was perfect.

Rachel walked into the lobby and stopped at the reception desk. "Hi." She nodded at the receptionist, a young man with perfectly mussed hair. "I'd like to see Jeremy Sevier."

He tilted his head as if considering her request, then looked down to punch a button on the phone. He listened, presumably to ringing. She found his manner dismissive.

"He doesn't answer. Would you like to leave a message?"

"I'd like to speak to his manager."

"Do you know his manager's name?"

"No, but surely, you can find out."

"Excuse me." He consulted a list, then punched a line and looked away. When he turned back, he said, "He doesn't answer. You're welcome to leave a message with me."

She leaned halfway across the counter and dropped her voice to a low, more serious key.

"My brother, Jeremy, doesn't answer his

personal phone, and I don't know where he is."

"We can't give out personal information."

"I understand, but if he's not showing up at work, then he's missing, so I need to know."

"I'm sorry, ma'am. I can't help you." He tapped his pen, one quick snap on the desktop.

Arrogant twerp. He'd said 'ma'am' like an indictment.

She leaned against the counter. "Understand this is a courtesy visit. A check with Strom and Sons before I go to the police. The authorities will be around asking questions. Hopefully, they'll be discreet. Police tend to make clients nervous."

Would the police take her concern seriously? She didn't know, but she read in the twerp's face that he wasn't willing to take a chance if it might boomerang back on him.

"Have a seat over there. I'll see what I can do."

Rachel sat. He spoke low into the phone, and she couldn't hear a word. A few minutes later, an older man entered the lobby and walked over to her.

"Miss Sevier? I'm John Brookes. Jeremy reports to me. May I see your ID? A driver's license, maybe?"

It was a commonsense request. "Here it is."

"Thank you, Miss Sevier." He handed it back.

"Please call me Rachel."

"Thank you. Rachel, Jeremy isn't here. I'm sure that's obvious; otherwise, he'd be out here speaking with you. You understand I can't give you specific information, but I'm also sure Jeremy wouldn't want you to worry. I can tell you he requested some time off."

Relief lightened her mood. "When will he be back? Do you know where he went?"

He leaned toward her. "That's all I can say. Privacy, you know."

"But I'm his sister. Surely, you can...."

"If he wanted you to know, or thought you needed to know, he would've told you. Likely it was an oversight on his part, but I have to respect his right to privacy. I will let him know of your concern when he returns or if he contacts me. Again, I'm sorry."

"Thank you. I appreciate your help. Do you mind if I keep in touch? Here's my number. If there's anything else you can tell me, please call."

Rachel pushed past the glass doors and walked to the car. She rested her head against the seat back and sat in silence. It felt like giving up.

So, Jeremy was on leave. A trip? For how long?

And with whom? Her heart sank.

He knew she was planning to visit, but not for another couple of weeks. If he hadn't gotten her voicemails, he couldn't know she'd moved her plans up.

How long could she hang around waiting? There was the interview with Mr. Ballew, but she could drive back for that. She'd taken two weeks of vacation time to spend with Jeremy, intending to stay at Jeremy's place— Wynnedower. He'd said the house was empty. Now, he wasn't there and it certainly wasn't empty.

She preferred to stay in the area.

A hotel would break the budget.

There was a room available at Wynnedower.

Ridiculous.

Well, she wasn't done in Richmond yet, anyway. She'd passed a hospital on her way in. Silly of her not to have thought to check the hospitals. After that, she'd visit the authorities, but she had to face facts, including the reality that Jack Wynne and John Brooks were probably right.

****

The police weren't very helpful, but at least the folks at the hospitals would talk to them. Not so with her. Turned out she couldn't just stop at the desk and get info about recent admissions, unknown or otherwise. The good news was there were no recent John Does.

She was driving the dusty road back to Wynnedower. Jack had been friendlier this morning. Probably because she was leaving, but still…hadn't he bribed the tow truck driver with a casserole to help her out?

In her head, she heard Daisy saying that life was about choices and options. Rachel might have only a few options, but it was still her choice to make.

Wynnedower's wrought iron gates were permanently propped open because otherwise they'd fall down. Here she was, back again. Like in those scary haunted house movies where the gates, once passed, never allowed an exit.

An iron-clad memory and vivid imagination could be a curse. In this case, she didn't worry. In fact, she laughed. Jack Wynne would tolerate no haunts and no vandals. He'd bring those thick, dark brows together and exorcise them instantly. She liked that—no distractions, no hemming and hawing.

A mystery, too. Both the man and the house.

The house and grounds looked as deserted as before. Rachel parked a short distance from the house, but not as close as yesterday. Even in daylight, she didn't want to be near the ground level floor and that dark area behind the bushes.

The front door was unlocked. She found him in the kitchen, leaning into the fridge, one hand clasping the top of the door. When he stepped back, a pickle jar in his hand, he saw her.

"You're back."

Not an encouraging welcome. "I need to speak with you. I hope this is a good time."

He went straight to the counter and unscrewed the lid. Tossing it aside amid the usual sandwich preparation litter, he used a knifepoint to skewer a pickle. "You went to his workplace?"

"How did you know?"

"Not hard to figure. Judging by your expression, I'd say you didn't find him, but you also don't look as worried as before, so they must have been able to give you some information."

She was stunned he'd read her face so easily.

"Have you had lunch? There's bologna." He picked up his sandwich and his cup of coffee and settled at the table.

"Help yourself if you want a sandwich or coffee. It's still hot."

"Thanks, no." She watched him turn away, regretting the 'no.' A companionable approach could be very helpful. "Coffee would be great."

"Mugs are in there." He nodded toward the cabinets next to the fridge. "Don't worry too much about him. I used to be that age. I remember, at least vaguely. Let him live his life."

Rachel was taken aback, but calmly took a mug from the shelf. "I don't interfere in his life. In fact, I've done everything I can to help him get a good, solid start in life. I want him to be independent."

"Sorry, not my business." He turned away, as if his interest had evaporated with the rebuff.

"No, I'm the one who's sorry. I've made it your business. Believe me, I don't want to live through my brother. I want to know he's well and happy and then I can get on with my own life." She poured the coffee, added milk, then wiped the counter with a paper towel, mopping up a few spilled drops as well as the stray crumbs from Jack's sandwich-making. She picked up the terrycloth towel to dry her hands.

"I raised him. Well, there was Aunt Eunice, but that's another story." She folded the towel and hung it neatly over the oven door handle, then faced him squarely. "I have a lot of nerve asking this, but I'd like to wait around a few days. Here."

He choked on his coffee. Dark droplets splashed from his mug onto his shirt. She grabbed the towel and rushed toward him, but he waved her back.

Towel still in hand, she continued, "His manager said Jeremy asked for leave, but he wouldn't tell me for how long. Plus, I'm hoping to get a chance at a job interview in Richmond." She refolded the towel as she finished, "I don't know anyone else in this area. I'll stay out of your way."

He didn't speak and she added, "I can pay. Not a lot, but something." She thought of the dingy walls and half-hearted patching and painting. "I noticed signs of restoration going on. I can help."

Jack leaned back in his chair. She was being measured. Casually, she took the chair opposite him and pulled her coffee cup closer.

"Restoration? That's a pretty grand name for a project that never gets off the ground. The lack of progress mirrors my ambivalence."

"Ambivalence?" She spooned some sugar into the coffee and stirred it, focusing on the aroma.

He crumpled the napkin as he finished his sandwich. "Time, money and will."

Encouraged because he hadn't said 'no,' she asked, "What are your options, then, if you're not sure about restoration? If you don't mind me asking." She sipped the coffee, then added another teaspoon of sugar.

"I was away for several years, only coming back now and then for short stays. Even when I'm here I usually keep a caretaker because I can't watch all four sides of the house."

He toyed with his mug, pushing it in a circle. "I have to sell or renovate. Wynnedower used to be in the middle of nowhere, but the city is coming out to meet us. Or suburbia is." He went silent and seemed to be thinking, then continued, "I had the house inspected. It's amazingly sound. Mostly needs cosmetic work, but even to re-shingle a roof this size—well, the cost is prohibitive."

"Last night you called it an anchor, but not in a good way. Anchors can mean stability."

"Anchors also hold you in place; they hold you back." His attention seemed to drift and he spoke as if to himself. "I'm tired of anchors. I'd like to get rid of them, not take on more."

Rachel seized the opening. "I could help while I'm here. Watch for vandals and looters and such. Plus, my car parked out front shows the house is occupied."

Jack shook his head. "Too dangerous. These folks operate in secrecy and usually in the dark. Even the not-so-dangerous ones can be if they're surprised."

"I could alert you to their presence."

He opened his mouth, and then shut it. He was staring in the direction of her coffee. She took another sip, trying not to grimace at the taste.

"I could do some painting and some lighter tasks. I can also make project plans and take inventory."

She paused. There was no response. She gave it another try. "I came here to interview for a new job thinking it would be fun to live in the same town as Jeremy. Not to interfere in his life, but because we're the only family we have. I was hoping for a better job, too. The thing is, I set up an appointment knowing I'd be here visiting Jeremy, but the man who was going to interview me went out of town on an emergency, so I can't even take care of that.

"I'd like to hang around a few days in case Jeremy returns. I want to make sure he's fine, and then, when I know he is, I'll...well, he'll be sorry."

"Of course." His mouth quirked up in a smile. "Why do you think he'll come back here?"

"I just know it. He knew I was coming to visit, so he'll expect to find me here."

Jack spoke in a soft tone, "He knew you were coming and he left."

"Oh," she shifted in the chair and tugged at her jacket to straighten it. "I arrived a few days early." No need to mention she'd arrived considerably early nor that Jeremy had met a girl. No point in giving the wrong impression. She shrugged and smiled. "I'm in limbo. I can stay or go back home. I'd rather stay. What about my offer?"

"To work for room and board?"

"That sounds about right."

He looked her up and down, conspicuously so. "Okay, so today you look more useful than you did yesterday in that red suit and the high heels, but…."

"Carnelian red."

"Carnelian. Is that significant?"

"No. I like the sound of it." Silly, yes, but she didn't care. She'd laid out her best arguments. Now, it was time to move forward as if a decision in her favor was a foregone conclusion. "I can get dirty with the best of them."

"Is that so?" He raised his eyebrows.

"I'm not afraid of hard work." She sat back. "I'd like to know about your vision."

"My vision?" He frowned.

"Not your eyesight. Your *vision*. For Wynnedower. You said you were gone for years. Why did you come back?" Nosy, but she sensed an opening and pressed the advantage.

"My family was rarely here. My parents preferred city life. My father did the minimum to keep it habitable. He expected eminent domain to claim it sooner or later, but most of the city and industry went in the other direction."

"Why didn't he sell it?"

"Good question, but a boring answer. It was 'in the family,' and he couldn't bring himself to dispose of it. Guilt. Now, it's mine. My problem."

"What do you want to do with it?"

"Sometimes I want to burn it down." He tapped his fingers against the table. "I'm not wealthy. I can't afford to restore it merely to live in it. It's huge and inconvenient. I've considered turning it into a bed and breakfast combo party rental facility. For things like weddings and such, but–"

Rachel ceased hearing Jack, but instead, in her head, she saw a bride poised on that grand stairway with the guests looking up in admiration. Her pulse quickened.

"Are you staying with historically correct renovations? Or a mixture? Maybe a combination? Or perhaps eclectic?"

His black eyes fixed on hers. She shivered.

"Tell me what you mean."

"Well, historically correct is lovely, but your house defies that. It's so ugly."

"You think Wynnedower is ugly?"

"Ugly beautiful, I mean. For instance, the exterior looks like it's straight out of the Cotswolds in England, except for the grand entrance which smacks of ante-bellum south. Those iron key plates on the doors…they're like something from an even earlier time, almost colonial.

"Make the combination an asset. Elegant distinctiveness." She had no idea what that meant. Where had those words come from? She wasn't really lying. A pretender, then? She'd read an article or two and maybe seen some photos, and it all came together in her head—with her acting like she knew what she was talking about.

"Elegant distinctiveness? I like the sound of it. What do you do for a living? Are you a decorator? An historian?"

"No, I'm not a decorator, but I've always enjoyed that kind of thing." How was that for vague? She touched her nose, half-convinced it was growing. "In real life, I'm an inventory specialist."

"Really?"

"It's as boring as it sounds."

"You said you're here for a job interview?"

"At a museum in town. As an assistant. But the man I was supposed to interview with was called out of town for a family emergency." She tapped her fingers on the table. "I'm overreaching anyway. Not really qualified, but it was tempting to think of doing something different. When they contacted me to schedule an interview, well, I never expected it, and I was so excited."

"If it's only for a few days, then maybe you could stay here. No need to work."

He didn't say it like an offer, but more as if he was thinking out loud. This time Rachel didn't interrupt his thoughts. Instead, she clasped her hands together and tried to be patient.

"As you say, you'll have a view of the front of the house. But, I'm firm about this—you aren't to confront anyone. If you see anyone outside or anywhere around here, you call me immediately and stay out of it."

"I want to be useful. I can't sit around doing nothing."

"But for only a few days…. There's no point."

She leaned forward, her elbows on the table.

"I can use my training to your benefit. I'm methodical, thorough and detailed. I can go through the house and make a list of tasks and suggestions. We can review it and sort out what you'll need to do if you proceed with the renovation."

Jack chewed on his lip and played with the coffee cup. "An inventory specialist, you said. Actually, that skill might be useful. There are some furnishings in a few of the rooms and in the attic. I don't have a list. Whether I stay or sell, an inventory would be good. It's a big task, though."

He frowned, but not in anger. His eyebrows almost touched. "I suppose you could get it started. Perhaps the next caretaker will come with inventory skills and can finish what you begin." He fixed his eyes on her face. "You'll be alone in the house with me. Will you be uncomfortable?"

She stared right back. "I'm the one who suggested this, remember?" She added a smile. "It's only for a few days while I wait to hear from Jeremy."

Jack rose, picked up his empty coffee cup and reached for her cup of squishy tan sugar. Rachel's stomach cramped at the sight of it.

"I think you're done with this?"

"I am."

He tilted the cup back and forth without change of expression, then placed both cups in the sink. "A trial basis, then. For both of us. One day at a time."

"It's a deal, and thank you."

****

He returned to the kitchen holding out a large ring of skeleton keys. "These aren't identified by room. Some open multiple doors, some only specific doors. There's no logic. Try each one until you find the door it fits."

The keys jangled and clunked when Rachel shook them. "How do you manage without knowing which doors they match up with?"

"I have others that are identified, but spares are important. As you identify which key works which door, tag it in some way. I'll get some tags at the store. I have a notebook you can use for the inventory."

"Do you have Internet?"

"No Internet. I'll show you around the main floor. Upstairs you can find your own way around."

She walked with him into the open area near the stairs.

"Skip the rooms at that end, upstairs and down." He pointed eastward. "Leave them alone. You'll have your hands full with the other rooms."

"What's downstairs?"

"A basement. Coal used to be stored there, and half of it was finished off for servant rooms and storage. There's nothing down there, so ignore it, too."

She nodded. "This is the largest living room I've ever seen. It's more like a ballroom."

"It's called a central hall. Don't know why, it just is. It was used like a living room."

He pointed toward the alcove that had been so pitch black the night before. In the more helpful light of day, she could see the closed double doors inside that short, dogleg hallway.

"Straight back, through those two doors, is the dining room. It's a huge room with amazing light. I'm using it right now for my own purposes, so ignore that room. You already know what's to the right of that, the hallway with the windows, the kitchen and my quarters."

Ignore the east end of the house. Ignore the basement and the dining room, too. She tried to tamp down her exasperation.

"What you said about the mix of historical periods in Wynnedower, is right on target. You're perceptive for an inventory clerk."

"An inventory *specialist*. We're paid to notice things."

"No offense intended." He cleared his throat. "Much of the stone and exterior features, like the windows, were shipped from England. Other parts were cannibalized from derelict mansions in the general area around Richmond."

She stopped short, not quite believing him. "Stone shipped? Across the Atlantic? The cost must have been exorbitant."

"New wealth. The industrial age. It was a time of easy money and excesses—for the wealthy. Think of the houses in Newport, Rhode Island. Wynnedower's stone came from an abandoned estate in England. That house had become unstable due to coal mines that undermined the foundation. The stone used in Wynnedower is only a fraction of that estate."

Rachel turned in a slow circle. "So that explains it."

"Explains what?"

"Why the layout is more suggestive of the houses built by the robber barons. Like Astor and Fisk and Mellon." She laughed. "But with the veneer, literally, of history and lineage. A very mixed pedigree."

He nodded. She thought she caught surprise in his eyes and felt encouraged.

Jack pointed to the west. "The library and the conservatory are in that direction."

"Conservatory? It's the round glass room, right? I saw it this morning from the terrace."

"It is."

"Lots of windows. More amazing light." She echoed his sentence about the light in the dining room.

He smiled. Was it the first time? No, but it touched her as if it was the first time. He smiled, and her heart jumped.

Why? Was she that lonely? The man wasn't handsome, not in the usual sense, and had no manners. Her concern was all about Jeremy, right? She turned away to hide her face. Heaven knew what was written there.

Chapter Four

Jack Wynne said, "My great-grandfather, Griffin Wynne, loved light. He was an artist and an eccentric."

He looked down at the woman. His houseguest.

He couldn't believe he'd agreed to let her stay. Not only that, but he was showing her around Wynnedower and sharing family history.

Rachel prompted, "An artist?"

She sounded interested in Griffin, but then again, she expressed interest in whatever topic came up. She had a knack of focusing in like a laser and those eyes—topaz eyes—were unsettling. But it was hard to tell what was sincere and what was manipulative. She was a puzzle and he didn't need a puzzle of any kind in his life. Yet he couldn't help having some curiosity. She was as unlikely a woman to walk uninvited into Wynnedower as he could've imagined.

Deliberately, he let her go ahead. She was short, but with a very nice figure. Her hair was black and straight. It hung perfectly even, as did the seams and pleats in her suit, which, he noticed, she kept checking and twitching back into place. He took the perfectly put-together-yet-constantly-tweaking manner as a warning. But a warning of what?

It'd be a lot smarter to send her on her way. Instead, he pushed his doubt away and continued, "An artist for his own enjoyment. He couldn't make a career of it. Lucky for him, he didn't need to, but his eccentricities drained the family fortune."

"There are lots of blank spaces on the walls." She pointed to a row of light-colored rectangles framed by darker areas. "Paintings? Family portraits? Are they in storage, too?"

"Not much. Any paintings, sculptures or bric-a-brac worth anything was sold years ago or moved to New York with my mother. None of the artwork was really valuable in a commercial sense, anyway. The valuable paintings are long gone—before my time. Only a local legend. I doubt they ever existed, but every so often the rumor resurfaces, and we get an uptick in trespassers. That's one reason I insist that no one is allowed in this house without my approval."

In the library, Jack stared at a spot near the front windows. Mahogany paneling, deep and rich, covered the walls.

"I remember my father at his desk, right there, trying to make the finances work and fighting the illogic of pouring money into this place when it cost a lot less to provide a more comfortable home for us elsewhere."

Wasn't he doing the same thing? The weight of being tied to the past, and to the present, had gotten worse with each year that passed, and still showed no signs of letting up.

"Down by the conservatory you'll find the stairs to the attic. This time of year the attic is hot by noon, so I suggest leaving it 'til early morning. Now, let's go back this way."

He stopped mid-step. She hadn't heard him. She was admiring the paneling, trailing her fingers along the grain.

She said, "This wood is exquisite."

That's how she talked. Exquisite wood. Carnelian red.

He'd first seen her upstairs on the landing with her face pressed to a keyhole. She'd looked like a teenager dressed in some kind of getup, and he'd yelled out of habit. But when she jumped back, he realized his error. Not a kid. Definitely not. But short and with the sleekest black hair...in that redder than red suit and waving those heels at him like she was going to shoot a few rounds out of them. He'd felt bad about yelling and then remembered that whatever else she was, she was still a trespasser.

He felt a tug on his sleeve.

"Are you listening?" she asked.

"Who or what did you think was attacking your car?"

"What? Oh, last night." She blushed and smiled. She shook her head. "My nerves got the better of me, and maybe my imagination did, too."

They'd made it back to the central hall.

She added, speaking softly, "You know, the bedroom door truly was jammed shut. I'd like to know how it came to be open and how my jacket got moved to the bedpost."

If she hadn't imagined that—and considering the torn sleeve, he was inclined to believe her—then he had an idea of how it had happened. He kept his mouth shut. Intriguing or not, he wouldn't be talking about it, certainly not with this temporary guest.

"Can we take a look at the dining room?"

Jack said firmly, "No, I keep it locked."

"To slow down looters and trespassers?"

A scoffing noise had slipped past her lips along with the words. It irritated him.

"Don't laugh. I've chased off quite a few myself. The worst are the ones we don't discover until after they've done damage. Come through here."

They bypassed the closed dining room doors and entered a small room. He gestured toward an exterior door on the far side.

"This is called the flower room because the door goes out to the garden—or where a garden used to be." He turned back toward the hallway. "There's the kitchen and through there, in the pantry, is a washer and dryer. You're welcome to use them, though I doubt you'll be here that long. My quarters are that way. I live in the old hunting room and butler's quarters."

"I'll start with the keys and make an informal list of tasks as I go through the rooms."

She smiled and her eyes laughed.

How stupid did that sound? Eyes couldn't laugh. He blinked against the strong light in the corridor. Clearly, it was playing tricks with his vision.

"It is bright in here, isn't it?" She waved at the long wall of windows lining the hallway. "Your great-grandfather really did love light. When did your family leave Wynnedower?"

"When I was ten. We came back for visits, but after my father died, my mother refused to return. Still won't. She lives in New York."

"And yet, you're here now."

"I am. Time to move forward with restoring the property or get rid of it."

"Thanks, Jack. I hope I'll be able to give value in exchange for you allowing me to stay."

That was the dilemma, wasn't it? Value? No one ever gave more value than they consumed in time and obligations. He was well into his thirties, closing in on forty, and here he was, still trying to find a way to shake free of those obligations.

But it was more than obligation. There was also love. That's how they got their hooks in so tight.

Rachel walked away, moving with determination, heading toward the central hall and to who knew where? She didn't look back, as if she'd read his second doubts and knew exactly when to exit the stage.

Well, this wouldn't be a new obligation. This was simply about doing a favor for a woman who'd been ditched by her brother. It was a day to day arrangement. They'd agreed on it and an inventory of the attic would be good to have.

She'd get tired of the whole thing in a few days and decide to wait for her irresponsible baby brother back home in Baltimore where air conditioning and modern conveniences were easy to come by. In the meantime, he needed to explain this arrangement to some people, especially to May.

He twisted the knobs on the dining room doors. Locked. Good. As he walked away, it hit him that her eyes weren't topaz-colored at all, but more like golden amber.

Chapter Five

Rachel was so blissfully far from being trapped in warehouses and businesses with electronic inventory equipment that it didn't take long for her to prefer the smell of 'old' to that of concrete and steel. On the other hand, Wynnedower wasn't air conditioned and could get hot, especially upstairs.

If only Jeremy were here...if only she knew he was okay, knew where he was and with whom.

She changed into shorts and a loose cotton shirt to work her way through the house. It was inevitable that she passed the closed dining room doors many times. The doorknobs were like glowing, blinking beacons shouting, 'try me,' and she did. The doors were locked.

There were many other doors and most of them were locked, too. She had about thirty keys on the ring and no doubt many were duplicates. She'd number the doors and write the number on the tags, but she needed the tags and a marker, so trying the keys was a half-hearted effort. She did identify the keys to the doors around her rooms and she kept them with her, close to hand.

She spent time on the list. She worked it room by room, beginning with the library, making notes about restoration tasks. The furnishings were few and pitiful.

After a while, when she grew hungry, she realized they hadn't discussed meals and Jack was nowhere to be seen.

In the kitchen, Rachel went through the cupboards and found some food supplies. In the fridge, there were a couple of covered casseroles, presumably May's.

Rachel spooned pasta casserole into a smaller pan and slid it in the oven to heat. While it was warming and the smell of baking tuna was filling the air, she went through the cupboards in the adjoining pantry. It was spacious. No food, but lots of cookware and implements, all wrapped up in paper and plastic, were stored in the upper cabinets. She was going to need a stool or step ladder to go through them properly. The lower cabinets were largely empty.

A soft clatter, as if distant and imagined, echoed in her head. The movement of pots of pans. A remembered sound. *Gosford Park*— that was it. Or maybe *Downton Abbey*. Rachel closed her eyes. She could see them in their white uniforms and caps, professional servants with their own class systems and their own cares. It had probably been almost that long since this house was filled with life and laughter and purpose.

And now, she was here.

****

Jack was pouring coffee when she entered

the kitchen the next morning. He asked, "I got caught up in my work last night. I'm glad you went ahead and ate supper."

"No problem. What kind of work do you do?"

His pause was barely perceptible before he said, "May comes in to cook. She prepares the meals in advance so I can reheat them. You'll run into her. She's my…she's like a member of the family."

"May? Of course. Mike accepted her casserole as payment. He also called you Wynne, your last name." Rachel opened the fridge and decided not to repeat her question about his work. She'd try again another time. "I'm going to scramble an egg for breakfast. Can I fix one for you?"

"No, just coffee for me this morning. I'm guessing you don't want any coffee. Unless you'd like some with your sugar?"

She looked down at the floor, surprised, but not really embarrassed. "It always smells so good. Seems like it should taste good, too."

"No law against using it for air freshener, I guess. Or that dried stuff that smells? What's that called?"

"Potpourri?"

"Yes, that. Java potpourri." Jack paused near the door, his cup of coffee in hand. "Wynne? Some of the guys I grew up with around here call me that. I won't be back for a few hours. Are you set? Do you need anything?"

She pulled a folded square of paper from her

pocket. "Here's a very short list. Colored tags and a marker and a couple of other things."

"I'll take care of it. Remember, if anyone suspicious comes around, call the police. I taped the sheriff's number to the fridge."

He was gone. Definitely not a guy who wasted time on goodbyes.

She melted the butter in the pan as she whisked the eggs, then popped bread into the toaster. She had a full day planned. She intended to focus on the keys, identify all of the rooms where items remained to be inventoried and make lists. She liked lists. Neat lists, colorful lists with big checkmarks to show progress.

****

Day three with no Jeremy. She kept her cell phone in her pocket and carried it with her everywhere. It was irritating to know he might be anywhere, even close by. Or he might have taken a trip, but the world was a very big place.

After a morning of testing keys and affixing orange, red, blues and green tags, she took her notebook and pencil up to the second floor and entered the stairwell area at the far end. The heat hit her. She returned downstairs, happy to change her mind. She wasn't in the mood to work up a sweat while she was still reasonably well-groomed. Where was Jack? Not returned yet?

As she passed the dining room doors, Rachel slowed. The hallway with its wall of windows, blind and void at night, changed with the daylight to bright and shining, a stunning interplay of the sparkling glass panes and shadowed patterns cast by the window inserts. The dark shadow lines ran from the ceiling, down the wall, and spread across the floor. Like some crazy kind of art work. Like an invitation. She exited into the garden.

The dining room extension was to her left. The dining room windows faced this way, but their elevation was well above the level of the garden and a lot of scraggly bushes and weeds occupied the area between the dining room and where she stood. It impossible to make out what was inside.

Never mind. She turned to stare at the wasted garden.

Standing there, seeing without really focusing and letting the garden speak to her, she understood how the bricked paths had run, how the dry fountain, now overwhelmed by grasping vines, had anchored the layout, and how the spindly, neglected vegetation had bloomed in decades past.

Eyes half-closed, Rachel let the garden form in her mind. It came together in vivid colors and charming scents of Jasmine and sweet roses. After a few minutes, she had a pretty good idea of how this had looked once upon a time. Her fingers itched to dig in the earth.

Virtual earth? What did she know about gardening? She'd never owned a square foot of ground.

Okay, so she knew nothing in practical

terms, but she'd thumbed through enough landscaping and horticultural books over the years to give herself a jumpstart.

The smells changed. The energy thickened. Her eyes popped open. She saw blonde hair and faded blue eyes framed by crow's feet.

She stammered, "Who are you? What are you doing here?"

The man said, "I'm sorry I disturbed your concentration? I wanted to speak with you about your brother."

He had her attention. "My brother?"

"You're Jeremy's sister, right?"

"You know Jeremy?" Curiosity warred with caution. Where had this man come from? He was older than Jeremy. A little older than she. Maybe Jack's age. Rachel glanced back at the house and the dining room.

"Don't worry. He drove away a while ago."

That was creepy. She took a long look at his crisply ironed shirt and highly polished shoes, and was reassured.

"Did he? What do you know about my brother?"

"We were, are, friends. Not close friends, but we spoke often. I haven't seen him in a while. I was concerned."

When she looked at this odd man, she couldn't see him as a friend of Jeremy's. "I haven't heard from Jeremy. I'm worried."

"I was, too. I spoke to one of his co-workers, away from the office, you know? Jeremy was seeing a young lady. His co-worker suggested they might have eloped."

"What? A young...eloped?" She shook her head. "That's nonsense."

He placed one hand on his chest. "An affair of the heart, you know? I was afraid his disappearance might have been the result of a favor I'd asked him to do for me, so I was relieved."

Annoyance wrapped itself around her. "What did you ask him to do? Did you introduce him to the girl?"

His eyes opened wide and he took a step back. "No, sorry, I wasn't clear. I meant that I was worried he'd gotten into hot water over a favor I asked of him. When dealing with Jack Wynne, you never know what will touch off his temper."

Temper? Yes, Jack had a hot one. Was this man suggesting it was a dangerous temper? "Go ahead."

"Have you ever been in love? The heart and soul kind?" He stared down at the bricks. "Do I sound corny?"

"Yes." Rachel frowned. "What does that have to do with Jack? Or are you talking now about Jeremy and what his co-worker said?"

"No, this is about me and a big mistake I made a long time ago."

His hair was disordered from where he'd dragged his fingers through it. He did it again. Almost engaging. Boyish and sympathetic, except for the crow's feet.

She crossed her arms. "That's how

everyone sounds when they describe falling in love. Really, how many different ways are there? Boy meets girl. Girl meets boy. And so on."

"You make love sound optional. It wasn't. It isn't, even years later. I'm David Kilmer."

He extended his hand and, after a pause, she accepted.

"Rachel Sevier."

"I'm very pleased to meet you."

He walked alongside as they passed the old rose bushes and approached the wild arbor until he stopped suddenly, moving in front of her and blocking the path. His voice sounded hungry. His words were spoken in breathless rhythm.

"Let me tell you how I fell for the love of my life, Helene. Fell hard. I saw her on a street in London. Early spring, damp and misty, and it suited her. Mermaid-like. As delicate as the dew on a rose. As if the very tears of heaven couldn't resist touching her, sharing some space, or a moment of time with her."

Who was this guy? A stranger baring his heart? A lunatic? She looked around again thinking this would be a good time for someone sane and boring to come along.

A rangy Abelia snagged the hem of her shorts. She detached the thin branch. "Overgrown. I wonder how much of this can be salvaged?" She paused, wanting not to ask but unable to stop herself. "Did you speak with her that day? Was it the same for her? Love at first sight?" She ran her hands lightly through the long, twiggy branches.

He moved away, pausing near a chipped and stained concrete bench. He sank down upon it and leaned forward, both hands clasping his knees. "I thought I'd gone to heaven. At the very least, that I was dreaming. I approached her and she spoke. Oh, it was innocent. But it was also fate."

He held out one hand to her. He was a stranger, but a friend of Jeremy's. Almost mesmerized by his strange behavior and poetic tale, Rachel accepted his hand, and he tugged her down beside him onto the bench. His breath was rough, excited.

"She was timid with everyone else, but together we were special. She warned me about Jack, but I already knew. She said, 'he won't like this.' I was prepared to take on anything, anyone, for her." He pressed his hands to his eyes. "I failed her. I failed us both. I'll never forgive myself, but if I could know she was well and happy, not under the thumb of that monster, then I could move on."

Stunned, she repeated, "A monster?"

"Jack Wynne."

Rude, yes. But a monster? "What business was it of Jack's?"

He whispered, "He's her brother."

"He hasn't mentioned a sister."

"I asked Jeremy to help me find Helene. Or, rather, not find her, but to find out where she is and how she is, so that I'll know she's okay. Up until a few months ago, she was in a safe place.

The man stared toward the sky at an overarching branch whose leaves rustled in the breeze. "Helene is different. Very delicate. But then one day I discovered she'd left where she was living with no forwarding address. She wouldn't have done that on her own. Jack would have been involved. Why didn't she surface anywhere? Jack showed up here, but where's Helene? You see why I'm worried."

"No, I don't see. How could Jeremy help you with that anyway?"

"By looking around. Listening. Asking a few questions. Whether Jack was here or off traveling, Jeremy was my best chance of finding out what Jack was up to."

"Jeremy spied for you? How can that be? He wasn't here while Jack was."

"Don't you see? It was perfect. Jack was out of town, but when he returned, Jeremy would still have access whenever Jack left the house. He could enter Jack's quarters without fear. Could have, if he hadn't gone away."

Rachel cringed. Would Jeremy have agreed to do that? No, she didn't believe it.

"No, I still don't see. You, Jack, his sister, wherever she is, you're all adults. Why can't you manage your business without involving my brother?"

His words came out on separate breaths, ragged. "Would you help me?"

As if he was deaf to her words.

This was too much emotionalism and illogic.

She reclaimed her hand and turned away. The dining room and Jack's quarters flanked both sides of the garden. Before them was the window arcade. Windows, windows, everywhere, and Rachel didn't want to be seen sitting here on the concrete bench consoling David Kilmer.

"I don't blame you for despising me, and I don't deserve another chance at love. I took money and abandoned her. And left my heart behind, too. I'm a loser and I always will be without Helene. I'm not someone to depend on, not even for someone I love."

He took money. But it wasn't her business and it was long ago, anyway. "Don't be so dramatic." She tried to soften her tone. "Everyone makes mistakes. You were young and foolish." No longer so young, but foolish was a hazard for all ages.

"And afraid. Jack would have never let us find happiness. It seemed the best choice all around—get out of her life and give her a chance at a new love and life."

First he was a bum, and now he was selfless? She was repulsed. "I should get back inside." She stood and he grabbed the hem of her shorts.

"But you'll try, please? Don't do anything that could put you in danger, but if you can find any evidence…no, I don't mean you should spy. But if you hear or see anything I promise I'll go away quietly as soon as I know she's safe and well."

Discomfort at his groveling, guilt because she was more concerned with her discomfort than with his pain, embarrassment because she knew she wasn't above giving into curiosity and snooping. It was a lose-lose situation for her. Guilt won out.

"If something comes up, perhaps I can help."

"Promise you'll tell me?"

"You should go now." Not a promise. She clasped her hands, her fingers entwined.

He nodded, his color heightened and his eyes wet. "I'm not sorry I told you. I don't mind humiliating myself if that's what it takes to make sure she's safe."

He walked past the arbor and directly across the back lawn, roughly parallel to the house, and toward the woods.

Going where?

Rachel was touched and appalled at the same time. Disturbed, too, because she couldn't embrace his open emotion. Maybe if she'd ever been in love she would understand better.

Wait. This guy was a stranger and she was concerned that she hadn't been sympathetic enough?

She wished she'd asked the name of the co-worker.

Jeremy in love? More likely a crush. Could it be an elopement?

She put her face in her hands. This was worry all over again, but of a different kind. He might be okay, but he might also be about to ruin his life. Might have already done so.

Where was he?

Gloomy, she wandered back into the house and tried to work up enthusiasm for trying keys and making notes about renovation. She ended up leaving by way of the French doors that opened into the conservatory, and from there, onto the terrace. She sat on the steps and watched the narrow band of river visible beyond the slope flow by.

The sound of a car brought her to her feet. Was Jack back? Her mood lightened. Not for Jack, of course, but merely for the distraction from her troubles.

With a light step, she passed through the house until she reached the central hall. She stopped at the window when she realized Jack wasn't alone.

He and a woman were standing by a shiny SUV. On the side was a magnetic sign, but the angle was wrong to read it from where she stood. She trotted to the library window. The woman was getting into the car. The sign read, Hartwell Realty, with a logo and a phone number. Beyond the SUV, nearer the corner of the house, was Jack's sedan.

Well, hadn't Jack said it was time to decide whether to stay or sell?

Distracted by the signage, she didn't notice Jack leave. She assumed he'd stepped up to the porch and she went to the foyer and opened the door to greet him.

No Jack.

He must have gone around by the side. She heard the distant sound of a door closing somewhere within the house. She did the same with the front door. She waited a few minutes, but when it became apparent that he didn't plan to be social, she dug a book out of her suitcase and went out to the terrace to read.

Rachel dined by herself again. After supper, she washed up the dishes and then strolled outdoors, leaving by way of the flower room. She walked a wide arc around Jack's quarters heading toward the eastern end of the house.

She directed her attention to the house and grounds and tried to take in everything from the state of the gutters above her head to threats posed by unpruned trees.

Jack's car was there, parked on the eastern side near an exterior side door. He'd said it was a loaner while he was in town. She stopped and casually scanned the area, not really expecting to see Jack because he seemed to have made an art of hiding.

Rachel decided not to mention David Kilmer's visit. The more she replayed it in her head, the stranger it sounded. It seemed unnecessary to go through that mess of a conversation.

She turned back, traveling beyond the outskirts of the garden. The dining room windows were dark as she rounded that wing. On the far side of the house the only things worth noting were the wide double-doors in the back wall. They were ground-level and padlocked. Snug up against the base of the doors the grass grew close and thick. They hadn't been opened in a long time.

After a solitary evening, she headed upstairs. Near the top, she heard a creak in the shadowy alcove, then a swish, as with fabric. It was barely more than the whisper of sound like that caused by cat fur brushing against silk.

Goosebumps prickled her flesh. She held her breath. The switch that controlled the sconces in the upper hall was inside the alcove.

The shyness of whatever she'd seen, and the hint of fragrance, encouraged her to lean into the alcove opening and flip on the switch. Nothing and no one.

The hallway beyond was dark. Rachel knew from her touring that it went to the far end of the house, Jack's end, past those rooms he'd told her to ignore. It ended in a stair, the twin of the stairs at her end of the house, and as dark and steep.

Wispy figures? Perfume? Her imagination. That's what Jack would say. Probably right, too. Except the trace of scent still lingered and sooner or later she knew she'd follow it.

Chapter Six

In the early morning, about dawn, Rachel heard the rise and fall of distant voices, probably male. The tone of the voices sounded conversational.

Jeremy?

She sat up, excited. She bypassed her slippers, shoved her suitcase away from the door and swore at the locks she had to undo before she could race down the stairs. By the time she reached the central hall, sanity had returned. Her feet were bare; her hair was crazy from sleep. If Jeremy was here, he wasn't alone, and she was a sight.

The voices had stopped. She strained to hear. A board squeaked, then a huge ripping scream of forced wood razored through her head, a noise terrifying in its violence.

Jack? Was it Jack?

She raced into the library.

Two scrawny men, strangers in dirty jeans and t-shirts, were prying the wood paneling from the library wall with the claw end of a crowbar. Rachel patted her robe pocket, forgetting she hadn't put it on. She had no robe, no pocket and no phone.

"Jack," she shrieked. "Jack!"

The men turned and stared. They were unshaven and grimy.

Rachel continued yelling, "Who are you? What are you doing? Stop it now!" Her voice resounded throughout Wynnedower's empty halls and rooms.

One grabbed the other's arm saying, "Let's get out of here."

Jack pushed her aside.

A gun. He was holding a handgun. She reached out to grab his arm, then stopped herself and moved a few steps away.

He said, "Don't move. I'll shoot."

"We'll leave, man. We thought the place was empty."

She shouted, "It's private property."

"Stand back, Rachel." He moved closer to the men. "Call 9-1-1."

Reluctantly, she left, moving swiftly, slipping on the wood floor as she turned the corner. Quickly, she retrieved her cell phone and made the call as she was running back to where the action continued.

"...Wynnedower. Do you know it? On the river." She broke into the woman's reply, saying, "I have to go. I have to help Jack."

The skinny guy with the shaggy hair tugged at the belt loops on his jeans and shifted from foot to foot. "Mister, you can't shoot us if we're not threatening you. We're gonna leave. That's all we want to do."

"I'll shoot if you move. You could be armed. If you move a step in my direction, I'll shoot in self-defense."

Jack's tone was calm and deadly serious.

Rachel didn't think he understood the law correctly, but this wasn't the time for a debate.

The dark-haired man spoke in a stronger, deeper voice. "You're blocking the door. We thought the place was abandoned. We're leaving now."

"There's a car parked out front," she said.

"We didn't see it. We came in from the side."

Jack nodded his head toward the front door. "Rachel, please go wait outside on the porch."

She was struck by the rage in his eyes, so at odds with the icy, controlled voice. She went, but listened. She heard 'bolt' in their voices. Jack might not be cautious enough—or too hesitant and they'd get the jump on him. Or he'd shoot them and get in trouble himself. Primed with adrenaline, she was all but tap dancing in the open doorway.

"No need for this, man. We're gone and won't be back."

"This is one of the few times I've had the chance to catch you lowlifes and I'm not letting you go. Think real good before you try me."

The deputy arrived first, then the deputy's sergeant and a State Trooper, all with lights flashing and sirens blaring.

Anxiety over anyone getting injured, or maybe even killed, whooshed away and she let pure excitement take over. This was like stepping onto the set of COPS or CSI, but without the bodies or gore. She bit her lower lip and tried to keep mum as she watched the officers and the action.

"Ma'am?"

She turned abruptly. She was the only ma'am here.

"Could I get some information from you?"

"Me?"

"Yes, ma'am. You discovered them, correct?"

The officer was young, but official looking in his uniform and with a confident, low-key attitude. His manner appealed to her, reminded her that this wasn't a game.

"I did." She tucked a lock of hair behind her ear, smoothed her clothing and realized she was still in her pajamas. From the corner of her eye, she saw Jack cast a glance their way and his eyes lingered. "Everything okay?" she asked him.

Jack shook his head, his expression serious, but a vague smile played across his lips. "Yes, everything's okay. Now." He nodded toward the library and his dark look returned. "I'll be back." He left with another officer.

They took her statement, Jack's statement, and photographed the damage in the library and in the conservatory where a glass pane had been broken to unlatch the door. The pickup was parked out by the terrace. The police took the men aside to speak with them separately. Her energy was draining and by the time they drove away with the men in the back seats of the cruisers, she was glad to see them go. Jack came back up the stairs to the porch where she was standing.

He looked at her pajamas and bare feet. The storm cleared from his face, and he laughed.

Annoyed, she said, "You're rather disheveled yourself."

He'd managed to drag on his jeans and shirt, but was also shoeless.

"Disheveled. I haven't heard that word for a while. And I *am* disheveled. I'm also hungry. Are you up for some breakfast? I need a cup of coffee."

"Breakfast, yes. No to the coffee."

He paused at the door. "After you."

It took her back—a whole three days ago? It seemed like she'd been here forever, but in a good way.

"They're sending a tow truck for the pickup," he said.

Rachel pulled out plates as he grabbed the frying pan.

"I told you not to confront intruders. You agreed."

"It was pure chance, Jack. Their voices woke me. The sound must've come up through the heating vents. I thought it was Jeremy."

"Proves I can't be everywhere. Not so long ago some of the copper downspouts were torn down. They busted into the basement to pull out the copper pipes, but didn't get far with that before something ran them off. Maybe our resident haunts." He laughed, but with disgust.

"They're getting bolder." He poured his coffee while the pan heated.

"The economy, maybe?"

He glanced around at her. "None of them knocked on the door asking for work."

"I hope the paneling can be repaired."

"Does it matter? A year from now...."

"A year from now, what?" She stopped and waited.

He focused on the pan heating on the stove, "A year from now it may be gone. I'm told it's a prime location for some expensive new houses."

Still not moving, she asked, "Then why do you care? Why not let the thieves take the paneling and downspouts?"

Jack stared at the wall behind the stove and spoke, perhaps to her, perhaps to the house. "Because it's mine."

Rachel let his words settle while she poured herself a glass of orange juice. Finally, she said, "You need an alarm system."

"I had one, but the phone lines are old and unreliable. It caused more problems than it solved."

Jack broke the eggs in the pan and she popped the bread into the toaster.

"Is that why you got rid of the furniture? Oh, goodness. Don't tell me it was stolen."

"No, there's plenty of furniture. Haven't you made it to the attic yet? It's locked away to keep it safe until I sell or renovate. Frankly, I don't have time for either and, sooner or later, some vagrant is going to set this place on fire, and it'll all go up in flames."

An alarming picture. Her mind filled in the

horrible details. Flames climbing high, searing the night, *a la Jane Eyre*, a raging conflagration that consumed everything it touched—fabric, wood, and flesh. And poor Mr. Rochester, blinded and scarred for life. Her skin burned at the thought.

Passion drove her voice. "You have to do something. You can't wait until it's too late. Get motion detectors, the kind with lights. Install a siren or two. Bring an expert in. There's bound to be effective ways to get it done."

"No time. Same with carpenters and painters. Cost aside, it's a full time job setting up appointments, getting estimates, setting schedules, all that. Besides—"

"I can be useful to you," she interrupted. "Let me work on that list. First, though, we have to do something about people breaking in and damaging the premises."

He went quiet. She felt a 'no' coming on, but then he nodded. "I'll give you the number of the security company I used before, and you make the appointment. Don't agree to anything. I want to review and make the decision. And that's all. Don't bring anyone else in. I don't like strangers in Wynnedower."

"You bet." Rachel smiled, and glowed on the inside. If this place had air conditioning and Jeremy was here, safe and sound, and single, Wynnedower would suit her fine.

****

As Jack had said, some keys opened more than one door, but others seemed to fit no doors at all, and he said there were more keys.

She tried them one by one, finding the key and door matchups.

In the narrow stairwell at her end of the house, she stood on the second floor landing at the base of the stairs to the attic. The door squeaked as she opened it. The stairway was very wide and very steep, and disappeared into darkness.

There was no handrail here. Rachel touched the unfinished walls, the boards, to steady herself as she ascended. Sunlight filtered in weakly, but it was sufficient to get her to the top of the stairs.

The attic, of course. She scanned the vast area as her eyes adjusted to the dim light. The ladder back of a chair seemed to rise from a hulk of no particular dimension. The nearest mound was covered by a sheet, and she touched it gently, tracing the rounded back of a chair.

Inventory this? Rachel was flabbergasted.

This was a Himalaya of settees, dressers, tables—unimagined treasures for antique collectors. But in an attic?

It was dry up here, but got very hot and very cold. This was not an acceptable environment for preserving antiques. She could inventory this, but Jack had to bring this stuff downstairs or sell it. Soon, if it wasn't already too late.

Beyond a few yards, the dark hung like a wall, and she couldn't see the far end of the attic. Within the fringe of the natural light, the shapes seemed to shift ever so slightly—a trick of the lighting and uncertain footing. Gingerly, she stepped back, avoiding the rounded, covered corner of something big, and turned directly into Jack.

She fell back, too stunned to scream. He grabbed her arms.

"I see you found the attic. Sorry I startled you. Are you okay?"

"I'm fine." Exasperated, she asked, "Why do you keep turning up like this?"

He released her arms. "I heard a noise and wanted to make sure it wasn't… I'm not used to outsiders roaming the house."

"Looters, right?" She waved her hands at the furniture. "I need light up here."

He pointed toward the ceiling. "There it is."

She pulled the string. It wasn't exactly a flood of light, but it cast a general glow.

"I presume we can get a stronger bulb?"

"Of course. I'll take care of it tomorrow."

"I'll wait until then to get started." Fact was, it was a bit overwhelming. She wanted to plan out the approach.

"Are you ready to go back down?" Jack reached up to kill the light.

She preceded him down the stairs. "How was all of this furniture moved up here?"

"One piece at a time?"

"Funny. How long has it been up in the attic? Don't you worry the elements will spoil it?"

At the base of the steps, Jack closed the door firmly and waited while she locked it.

"If not up here, it would have been vandalized or stolen. I hope not too much damage has been done, but it can't be helped. You've already had a first-hand look at the challenge of keeping this place secure."

Rachel said, "Most of these rooms only need cosmetic work. Why don't you spruce them up and move some of the furniture down? You can store it in a few rooms and keep them locked as you already do. Minimal heat in the winter and a few window air conditioning units for the summer to cut humidity should do the trick. I'm not an expert, but if there are valuable furnishings upstairs…."

"It costs and it's a lot of unnecessary effort when I can sell it right from the attic. Beyond that, it's one more chain."

"You can still sell the furniture, and you'll get more for it if you can see exactly what you're selling, and if the buyer can see what's for sale."

The shadows had pooled around his face. It wasn't a physical shading, but more of an intuitive feeling, like shadows seen by the mind's eye. Though ready to argue her point, she let it go.

"Jack, would you walk in the garden with me?"

He ran his hands over his face and shook his head.

Trying to dispel whatever was troubling him? She almost reached out to touch him. Why? This man didn't need her pity or her kindness.

"What garden?"

"Walk with me. Please."

They passed the closed dining room doors and walked through the flower room to the garden door.

"This must have been beautiful at one time. What are your plans for the garden?"

"Plans? No plans."

As they traversed the broken remains of the brick path, she persisted, "This is the time, Jack. The time to clean it out, prepare planting beds, all that sort of stuff. Enrich the soil now, plant in the spring. Of course, certain bulbs should be planted now, but I don't think we're…you're ready for that."

"But–"

"It's a small commitment and can't hurt whether you stay or sell."

He walked forward. He was thinking, and she stayed back to give him space. He looked to his right, then to his left, and then turned all the way around. She thought how different he appeared from that first time they met—that bad-tempered stranger with the crazy hair and ragbag clothes.

She'd only been here a handful of days, and he hadn't really changed, had he? So what was different?

A trill pulsed through her. A shot of fear. She didn't know this man. This stranger. She saw the character traits she wanted to see, but someone who'd known him much longer, David Kilmer, saw him differently.

Jack was staring at her as she stared at him. His fists were on his hips, and a lock of hair had fallen forward across his temple.

She should leave now, but she didn't want to.

Was she using Jeremy as an excuse to stay? Was it Wynnedower? The restoration? Maybe to help Jack? She almost opened her mouth to tell him what David had said about Jeremy possibly eloping, then closed it back tight. There was no point in bringing it up.

"What do you know about gardening?"

Her mouth was dry from fear or something else. She swallowed. "I read a lot."

"You've never had a garden or tended a garden, have you?"

"No."

"But now you're an expert."

No, not an expert. Merely a gal who'd spent too many years in warehouses and shipping facilities and anywhere else somebody needed something counted. At least, when it had been books, there'd been something to feed her brain. But never creating. Never doing. Only dreaming. Her fingers itched. This was a canvas—her canvas.

Rachel spread her arms to encompass the garden area. "How hard or expensive can it be to weed and amend the soil with manure?"

Jack glanced in the direction of the dining room again. He massaged his hands, working the knuckles. When he stopped, he said, "You'll have your hands full with the attic inventory.

Never mind the garden." He walked up to her and spoke gently. "I appreciate the interest, but I don't understand it. Regardless, forget the garden. This...I'll be gone from here long before spring."

He left. She watched him go. Frustrated, she set off in the opposite direction almost at a run, going deeper into the garden. She needed a long, brisk, head-clearing walk, not merely due to her annoyance with Jack, but for her own foolishness. She passed the bench and brushed the Abelia as she exited through the arbor gate, going to wherever her mood might take her.

****

"I've given it a lot of thought, and you're wrong." She set two plates on the kitchen table.

Jack was leaning into the oven checking the casserole. He stood and let the oven door slam shut. "Wouldn't be the first time. What am I wrong about?"

"The empty house and the furniture crammed into the attic."

Jack grabbed an oven mitt, pulled out the casserole dish and turned the oven off. "You've given it a lot of thought...for what? A whole hour? Two?"

"Don't mock me." She folded paper napkins and set them next to the plates then added a knife and fork. "You should appreciate an objective opinion. It's up to you to decide what to do with my suggestions."

He smirked. "An hour or two and you think

you know what's best. I've been living here on and off for all of my life."

"Exactly."

Jack removed the knife from his place and returned it to the drawer. "I don't need this. No reason to dirty it." He turned back. "Exactly? Why do you say that?"

"Here and there. Back and forth. All of your life." Rachel pulled her chair out and sat while Jack put the steaming casserole on the table. "This poor house was never a home to you or to your parents, at least in later years. No wonder people think it's vacant. They don't worry about intruding in someone's home because it looks...well, it doesn't look like a home. Just a big, empty, forgotten pile of stone and sticks."

Jack was busy eating. She let the banter die down and took a bite herself. Tonight, the casserole was ground beef, rotini and Alfredo sauce. It was wonderful. Eating made sense. Jack had the right idea about that.

He stopped to sip his tea. "The furniture stays in the attic."

She held the fork with one hand and tapped the fingers of her other hand on the table. She took her time chewing. Jack expected her to jump right back into the conversation, but if he didn't appreciate her efforts, why bother? Plus, if she annoyed him too much, would he call off the deal? She wasn't ready to leave yet.

She tried to pull back the emotion. Shrugging, she said, "It's your house and your furniture. Do what you want."

"Honestly, you've been here three days."

"Four."

"First day doesn't count. In fact, I'm surprised you haven't blocked it from your memory."

"Yeah. Wasn't at my best, was I?"

"Nor was I. I apologize for not realizing how seriously concerned you were for your brother."

His apology caught her by surprise. His attitude was usually hard and high-handed. Where had that tender tone come from?

She cleared her throat and sipped her tea. "I won't be here long, Jack. Let me help you as much as I can while I'm able. He'll call or show up any day now. I'm sure of it."

"Maybe."

"Although I don't understand why he hasn't called. He has a phone."

"Phones get lost. I remember in the men's room at the airport, some poor guy's cell phone fell in the toilet. He started yelling like he'd lost a kid."

"Lost. They also get forgotten." She sighed. "Why don't you have one? You're the first person I've met in a long time who doesn't have a cell phone."

They'd finished their simple meal. Jack leaned back in his chair as if in no rush. Rachel wasn't in a hurry either.

"I had a cell phone several years ago. Not my thing. I'm better with—well, non-technical tools. I don't like to be that reachable. I don't like interruptions."

She waited. What didn't he want interrupted? What non-technical tools did he prefer? If he'd give her some clues, she could figure out how he spent his time. She was clever that way. But Jack didn't take her silence as bait. He ignored it.

"I'd better get moving. Sorry, I know you're bored in the evening."

"Not so far. I enjoy the quiet."

Jack scraped his plate into the trash and left it in the sink. She lingered over her tea. He went toward his quarters, not to the dining room.

She put her own plate into the sink. She ran the water until it was hot and sudsy. It was an unusual pleasure to wash up the few dishes. The smell of it, the tickle of the bubbles on her wrists took her back into the distant past.

To momma? Back before Aunt Eunice. Before Jeremy was born. She hardly remembered so long ago. Maybe standing on a chair? A shrimpy kid with a dish towel pinned to the front of her shirt like an apron? The dish cloth swirled the suds around the plate as she laughed at the bubbles and momma, standing close beside her, reached out–

"You don't need to do that."

She jumped and sloshed water up onto the counter. "You startled me."

Jack came over and pulled a clean dish towel from the drawer. He picked up a plate. "May will wash these when she comes over."

Rachel tried to shake off the long-ago

memory and return to the present. "No need to leave them for her."

He set the dry plate on the counter and took another. "Leave them?" He laughed. "She has her way of doing things. It doesn't pay to upset her."

"Then why do you keep her around?"

"May's been here longer than forever. She's allowed to be dictatorial anytime she wants. She's—well, like family. She's earned it. Wynnedower means more to her than to anyone."

Rachel put the last of the utensils in the drainer. Jack picked them up all in one big handful and gave them a quick wipe. He dumped them into the drawer and slammed it shut.

"Good enough?"

The damp towel dangled from his fingers. She lifted it from them and folded the towel to hang it over the oven door handle.

"Yes, good enough. If any dishes are in the wrong place, I'll put the blame on you." She said it with a smile.

His hand almost touched her arm, and then abruptly he pushed away from the counter. "Remember, don't wander at night. No telling what, or who, you might run into." He finished with his own smile before he ducked out of the door.

****

Wandering implied a lack of destination. Rachel knew where she wanted to go.

Jack's little smile had stayed with her well into the evening. Her restless mood took her from her room to the end stairwell and down the steps to the first floor which ended near the entrance to the conservatory. On cats paws, she walked, imagining herself weightless, determined not to creak so much as a splinter.

The moon was up, and the glass walls and ceiling of the conservatory were dirty. The light filtered through the grime all the more delicately.

She held her breath. Moonbeams surrounded her disguising the cracked panes and bathing them in surreal glamour. Even the cardboard patch over the glass broken by the vandals took on a mystical appearance. The moonlight was kind to the dry fountain and dead vegetation, casting it as stone—colorless and frozen. A work of art. Sculpture.

A romantic place. Rachel twirled in a solitary dance, and her robe swirled out around her.

Romantic only in her mind.

She came to a standstill at the door and considered going down the long slope to see the river dappled by the moonlight.

This was a night for serendipity. Or an opportunity for it. For foolishness, too, because this was definitely not the kind of silliness in which an inventory specialist would indulge.

The robe was white and would shine like a neon sign. She left it on a chair.

Crickets or cicadas, whichever insects were scratching their legs together, created a roar of vibrating sound that decreased as she walked in their midst, but then grew louder again as the night absorbed her. The closer she got to the river, the more rustles she heard in the nearby woods despite the cacophony of the crickets. They were little noises though, the kind that belonged to bunnies and does.

Rachel sat on the banks of the James River and watched the surface patterns change as it flowed by. It was beautiful. Orion reigned above, and the water rushed below—through countless centuries. She was only one more being passing through time. Its time. Her own presence on earth counted in mere seconds by comparison.

It should've been romantic. It felt lonely. She hugged her knees.

The grass was damp, and the novelty was brief. She stood and brushed off the seat of her pajama pants. Chill was setting in, and her bed was calling.

She'd almost crested the hill when she saw a figure moving up near the house.

Not so lonely, after all? Her heart quickened, then skipped a beat.

Chapter Seven

The figure moving between her car and the porch light was slighter than Jack. He moved differently. Precisely what that meant she didn't know. It was a visceral reaction that tightened her muscles and slowed her breathing.

She dropped to her knees and sat back on her heels, hoping her profile was low enough to be hidden.

He vanished into the darker than dark area amid the bushes at the base of the house. She waited, straining her eyes to see, but in that pitch-black area he could be dancing a jig and she'd never know.

A vandal? A thief?

David Kilmer? Maybe.

But sneaking in the dark? Kilmer was sneaky, but he didn't strike her as a night stalker. That took a special sort of sneakiness. Someone a little less blubbery.

A burglar?

She stared, trying to see into the darkness, to distinguish a human figure from the deep of night.

"Rachel?"

She uttered a soft scream and in her haste to rise she toppled over backward.

"Jack?" She scanned the area. "I saw

someone near the house. Was that you?" She reached up to accept his outstretched hand. As she rose to her feet the chill hit her bottom. Her pants were seriously damp now, and clammy. Annoyed, she felt like the butt of a joke.

He released her hand, but didn't move away. "I saw someone, too." He pointed at her. "I thought I was finally going to catch a ghost."

"Very funny."

The light tone dropped from his voice. "What were you doing out here?"

"The moonlight. The river. I felt like a walk."

"Not exactly locked in your room, are you?" He scratched his neck. "I don't entirely blame you, though. When the moon is this bright, watching the river is almost...sort of like being a part of...."

"The continuum."

His smile was clear in the moonlight. "Not quite where I was going. I think I had something more like 'being part of nature' in mind, but membership in the continuum works. Tell me, Rachel, do you do one of those vocabulary-word-a-day things?"

"You're making fun of me." Her own enjoyment felt spoiled. Stupid of her to think she could recognize or not recognize Jack in the dark.

"You're lucky you didn't get locked out for the night. I was checking the doors and saw your robe."

Checking the doors, really? It hadn't looked like that to her. "Lucky me."

Her disgruntlement communicated itself to Jack. She was annoyed with Jack and herself as they walked back to the house in silence.

****

When she arrived in the attic the next morning, Jack was already there, standing on a step stool as he worked on the overhead light.

She set her notebook and pen on a nearby table and approached him. He was rigging a large spotlight type of lamp, like a photographer's lamp stand. The juice to run it came by way of a large orange cord that snaked down the stairs.

She asked, "Isn't there an outlet in the overhead fixture?"

"There is, but I thought you might like to be able to plug in your computer."

"Thoughtful. Thanks."

"No problem."

"I mentioned this last night, but I don't think I was clear. Before you joined me, I saw someone crossing the yard, going toward the house and the conservatory area. Was that you?"

"Not likely."

She heard doubt in his voice.

"What'd he look like?"

"Just a shadow."

He stepped down from the stool. "If someone was out there, I think I would've seen them. I saw you, didn't I? Speaking of which— don't take any more late night strolls, okay? At least, not alone. Next time you're overcome by the moonlight continuum, let me know. I'll go with you."

His words surprised her, unsteadied her. She hurried to cover the gap, "Will do." She turned away to hide her smile. "Now, about the furniture up here…we should take photos, but these aren't the right conditions. Too crowded and the lighting isn't right."

He didn't answer. She looked from the corner of her eye and saw he was moving the electric cord out of the walkway.

She turned her eyes back to the furniture and to the pencil she was flipping around her fingers like a mini-baton. "Jack–"

Still, no answer. She turned and saw he was gone.

Suit yourself, Jack Wynne.

So his offer of a moonlight stroll had been an admonition, not an invitation. Just business.

The furniture and other items were stored in groupings that left pathways every ten feet or so. She walked up and down, pulling aside white dust covers to reveal brocaded chairs and fine wood surfaces with the most beautiful burls she'd ever seen. Not that she'd seen much in the way of fine furniture—not personally, but she'd read about it.

With the protective sheets back in place, she mapped each group and numbered it by region. The far reaches of the attic were deeply shadowed, and it wasn't until she was near the end of a row that she realized she was seeing only a portion of the attic. The far end appeared to be a solid wall, painted black. One half of the attic was somewhere beyond that blank wall. Was the other half of the attic accessed from the east-end stairway? Resolving to explore that possibility later, she returned to her task of cataloging the contents of this half.

Before the attic heated up, she gathered her workman's tools, her pencil and paper, then clicked off the overhead bulb, snapped off the spotlight and descended the steps to settle in the conservatory. She'd copy the inventory list with a neater hand and then enter it into her computer. Jack didn't have a computer, much less a printer, but they'd figure it out.

The conservatory had high ceilings rising to a point in the center almost like a carnival tent, with segments shaped like slices of pie. Decorative fretwork trimmed the ceiling and the windows. The room had a unique essence, a distinctive lightness, even in the daylight when the deterioration was obvious.

Rachel flipped the page over to the next blank sheet and lined it to suit herself. It was fun doing an inventory the old-fashioned way. No company processes and methodologies. She felt a bit like a maverick and laughed out loud, thinking it took very little for her to feel wild and out of control. And that included her silliness over Jack.

Her attraction to him was embarrassingly like a teenage crush, but she could laugh at herself about it. This was merely a moment in time with no real meaning. No harm was being done to anyone and she'd keep it that way.

The back of her neck prickled. She turned to face the house. No one. She resumed copying her list. There was no sound except her own breathing and the faint scratch of pencil on paper—until imagined fingers tickled the back of her neck and the sensation traveled down her spine.

She jumped up and spun toward the door to the house. Still no one. She placed her notebooks and pencils on the seat of the chair and went inside to see what was up.

There was no one in the library. The central hall was empty. She entered the foyer and peeked into the small rooms on either side. She stopped at the wide doorway leading back to the dining room. The locked dining room doors gnawed at her. She touched one of the knobs, but before she could test it, she heard pans rattling and her nose caught the aroma of cooking. Good cooking.

She tiptoed through the flower room. The kitchen door was closed, which probably explained why she hadn't smelled the heavenly scents sooner. She eased the door open and peeked around it. No ghosts here. A solid woman in a purple paisley dress and a full apron was stirring a pot on the stove. Her black hair was short with tight curls and liberally mixed with gray.

"You must be May Sellers."

The woman turned, half-raising the spoon, but not losing a drip of sauce. "Hah! You surprised me." She wiped her hands on her apron and extended a hand. "You are Miss Sevier."

Her hand was plump and the skin soft, but her grip was iron. When Mrs. Sellers released her hand Rachel couldn't help a quick finger flex.

"Call me Rachel, please. When did you get here? I didn't hear anyone arrive."

Mrs. Sellers opened the oven door as she bent. "Browning nicely. You liked my chicken noodle casserole, I think?" The door closed with a slight slam. She took a colander from the sink.

"It was wonderful."

"I've known the Wynnes all my life. They come, they go, but they're always a part of my life. Family, in fact. I watch the house when they're gone and visit when they're in residence. Do some cooking. A bit of laundry. Lend a helping hand."

Rachel swallowed a cynical remark about the family being 'in residence'. She cleared her throat, then said, "Jack told me how dedicated you are."

"Some things are worth being dedicated to." She dumped a pot of something dark green and weedy into the colander. "But it's not work to me. It's a pleasure."

"How long does Mr. Wynne stay when he visits? Does he come often?"

"Depends."

"Depends on what?"

She glared at Rachel, but her tone was mild.

"On whatever he decides to do. You're full of questions, aren't you?"

"I was wondering if you might have been here while my brother was caretaker. Did you meet him?"

"The young man who was most recently here? I suppose Mr. Wynne could've told you that himself."

"His name is Jeremy. Tall and blond, do you know anything about him?"

"I might've seen him. All those young men blur together. I don't bother to learn their names. Mr. Wynne told me about him taking off without notice and you asking about him. His big sister, that right?"

Her dismissive tone rankled.

"Yes. His big sister. He's usually a very reliable young man. That's why I'm concerned."

"I'm sure, Miss Sevier, but when it comes to a house such as Wynnedower, extra special care is required. If you don't mind me saying, you and your brother don't favor each other at all."

"No, you're right. I take after our mother; he takes after our father. Except the eyes, of course."

May gave her a long look. "Yes, same eyes. Unusual eye color."

She made it sound irresponsible, as if their eye color had been a choice, and an ill-advised one. The silence drew out and finally, Rachel fumbled for something to say. "If you need help, let me know."

"I'm best on my own and happy to be cooking for the Wynnes, and I don't imagine you'll be around that long."

Rachel hesitated. Something was off. It had nothing to do with Jeremy, but only with May Sellers. She called Jack Mr. Wynne and yet she was speaking of a man many years her junior whom she'd known since his childhood. It was that professional servant class feeling again, but in real life and present day.

Wynnes, plural, hadn't she said?

Rachel, like a fisherman, cast her line back into the water. "With the family gone so much, your devotion is remarkable."

"We have strong ties."

"These days most people are looking out only for themselves. You must have been very fond of the children."

She fussed with the dirty dishes in the sink, rinsing and stacking. She spoke to the dishes. "Yes, indeed."

Her back had turned more squarely toward Rachel, purple paisley and all. Rachel understood the body language. Yet she persisted, squaring her shoulders as she spoke, feeling the inappropriateness of such a question to the old woman who cooked for the family. "Does she ever come back to visit?"

No sound except that of water rinsing over dishes for a few moments, then Mrs. Sellers spoke in a muffled voice. "I'm busy now, Miss Sevier. I suggest you take your questions to Mr. Wynne."

Word-slapped, and well-deserved, too.

"I'll get out of your way. Nice to meet you." She left, closing the kitchen door behind her.

It would've been easy to blame David Kilmer for stirring up her curiosity, but this lapse of manners was all on her.

Propelled by guilt, Rachel moved swiftly, passing the dining room as one of the doors opened. She side-stepped to miss it and bounced off Jack as he exited. He caught her with one muscled arm and slammed the door shut with the other. The movement mimicked a half-turn in a waltz and left her nearly breathless as she struggled to regain her footing.

Jack tightened his hold and laughed. He kept his arms around her for a moment after they'd stopped moving.

"Steady now?"

"Yes." She was breathless. "I'm fine."

He released her and stepped back with a slight bow. "Thanks for the dance."

A brief blankness hit her, then impulsively she tugged at the hem of her shorts and curtsied. "Delighted, sir."

"The pleasure was all mine."

Timing is everything, they say, and hers was usually clumsy in social situations, but it felt perfect in that moment, here with Jack as their smiles met. Then his eyes shifted away. She followed his gaze and saw May Sellers in the doorway, her expression prunish.

Apparently, Mrs. Sellers disapproved.

Jack extended his hands. "May, would you care to dance?"

"Hmmph."

May walked back into the kitchen, but before she'd fully turned away, Rachel saw her expression soften.

****

"Hey, Sharon."

"Rachel? How's your vacation?"

"Not much of one."

"What?"

"Well, I made it to Richmond. Or rather, outside of Richmond. Far outside. Practically to the mountains, it feels like with all the hills. But my brother's not here."

"What? Why?"

"He's not here. His employer said he asked for time off. I presume he's okay, but he's not answering his phone, so–"

"You're worried, and it's no wonder, but if he asked for time off, then he's gone on a trip or something. Probably forgot his phone or lost it in those turquoise Caribbean waters I hear about but never get to see."

"I'm sure you're right, still I'm anxious to hear from him. While I wait, I'm hanging out at his place. I mean, the place where he was living. I was wondering if we ever get clients down this way? I've been thinking about checking out possibilities down here. He's my only family, you know."

"Are you seriously considering relocating?"

"I've been thinking about it for a while now,

especially sitting here, twiddling my thumbs and waiting for Jeremy to either come back or call me. A change might be good." And that possible change of career she'd hoped for was still in limbo and feeling less hopeful every day.

"If you're serious, let me make some calls, but honestly, I've never heard the boss talk about expanding, certainly not out-of-state."

"I'll be down here a while longer, waiting for Jeremy, but if you come up with something interesting here or back home, keep me in mind."

****

The alarm system had to be very limited due to the condition of the wiring and the sheer size of Wynnedower.

"It's not perfect," the installer said, "but it will deter intruders and provide some warning."

He smiled at Rachel, his eyes earnest. She referred back to their earlier discussion.

"As you said, without significant infrastructure work, wiring and all that...."

"The motion lights will help. Let me know when you want to discuss more extensive options."

Would Jack ever be willing to discuss more? She shook her head. "We're talking about protecting paneling and copper pipes. Mostly, we want to discourage people who might think the house is abandoned."

"Sometimes simple things can count for a lot. For instance, make the premises looked lived-in. Trim the bushes and so on." He lowered his voice. "It's a fascinating place, but it's the kind of place you either commit to or not. It was a pleasure meeting you, Rachel. Call me anytime."

That evening, she and Jack tested the motion lights. They were more a psychological deterrent than a physical one, but it was a start, and Jack was pleased. They began at the east end and the lights popped on. They walked along the front of the house and past the front steps where the lights blazed on cue. As they neared the conservatory, another bank of lights came alive.

"Effective, I think," she said, pleased with the glow. They stepped back out of the bright half-circle. "They burn for about ten minutes." Down towards the far end of the house, those lights were already extinguishing.

She turned away and caught sight of the river far down the slope, dim reflections of moon and starlight danced on the surface of the water, and the space between was a vast dark gulf.

"Thanks for taking care of this. The results look good."

Rachel faced him. Jack was highlighted in the thinnest fringe of the security light.

"We can do more," she said.

Jack stayed silent. She'd said the wrong thing or maybe he'd misinterpreted her words. She continued, "I mean there's more that can be done to make Wynnedower secure."

He smiled. "I understood."

Speechless for a moment—what did he mean? He sounded almost insinuating. She pulled her hand back, shocked to realize it had been resting in the crook of his arm.

"We'd better get back inside."

No longer smiling, Jack asked, "Are you okay?"

So the insinuation had only been in her mind. She relaxed, but only a bit, and slapped at a fictitious insect.

"We'd better get back inside before these mosquitoes get serious."

****

In the eastern wing of the house, Jack's end, at the top of the stairs, she tried the attic door and found it locked.

Key after key, none worked. Jack had said to leave the rooms at this end of the house alone, but he'd said nothing about the attic. When he'd spoken of the furniture in the attic, he hadn't mentioned this half at all.

Giving up, she walked the length of the second floor, back to her end of the house and her stairway and on up to her side of the attic.

She worked her way down the first row, lifting the dust covers, getting a look at the furniture and then making notes on the pad. Climbing into the outer rows of furniture near the back, she tripped over the leg of something, bounced off a cushioned chaise, and rolled under a table.

Unhurt, she laughed in relief. She pulled herself out by way of the same route and from that angle on the floor she saw a break in the wall. A narrow break running up, across and down, in the shape of a door. No trim, no hinges, no knob. Only a slide bolt near the top.

Barely breathing, she bit her lower lip. Carefully and deliberately, she released the bolt, placed her hands flat upon the wood and pushed. Nothing.

Not giving up so easily, she followed the narrow gap in the wood. Down near the floor, she felt around and found another bolt.

This time when she pushed the door, it moved, but then she grabbed the pin on the slide bolt like a handle and pulled the door closed again quickly. It was too dark on the far side.

She'd never feared the dark and wasn't going to start now, but it wasn't reasonable to walk into a strange, dark place unnecessarily.

It couldn't be the other half of the attic or there would have been some kind of light filtering in. Some sort of hallway between the two attics? A flashlight would do the trick.

It was the unknown, the mystery of it—her personal Pied Piper—that attracted her. She knew it, but couldn't help, even though it sometimes led her into trouble.

****

"Daisy?"

"Can you hold a sec?"

Through the receiver, Rachel heard muffled kitchen sounds. Something loud clattered near Daisy's end of the phone. In the distance, on

Rachel's end, she heard a car drive up to the house. The decreasing volume indicated it had continued on around to the side.

Jack had returned.

A squirrel ran along the terrace wall. A bird landed atop the cement ball and chirped. The breeze skittered some dry leaves across the stone floor near her bare toes. Beyond, on the way to the horizon, the swathe of green lawn gave way to a narrow view of the water. She'd never experienced such a feeling of patience and satisfaction.

"You there, Rachel?"

"Oh, yes."

"Sorry. The new guy was…well, never mind. How are you doing? Any update on Jeremy?"

"I'm fine. Nothing new about Jeremy."

"So, how much longer are you going to wait?"

"I don't know. I might as well wait here as in Baltimore. I don't know what else to do." She leaned against the low wall. The bricks were warm from soaking up the sun.

"Maybe you should file a report to be sure."

"I spoke with the police, but other than checking the hospitals, they haven't done anything that I know of. I don't know if they even should. His employer said he requested time off, plus a co-worker said he was in love."

"Really? So maybe he *is* with that girl. You don't think they el–" Daisy broke off and coughed. "You said you spoke with a co-worker?"

"No, a guy who knows Jeremy. He said the co-worker told him."

"And he also knows you?"

"No. We met down here."

"How'd you find him? Or did he find you?"

"The guy who told me is named David Kilmer. He knows the family who owns Wynnedower, and he also knows Jeremy. I met him in the garden."

"Is he the gardener?"

"No, he showed up while I was out there."

Daisy sounded frustrated. "I'm confused."

"No wonder." Rachel laughed and strolled down the slope towards the river. "Wait while I move away from the house. I don't want anyone to overhear. He and my host don't get along, or so he tells me."

"Who tells you?"

"Kilmer."

The sweep of the lawn as it stretched down to the river, though neglected, was breathtaking beneath the blue sky and the green trees. It was hard to focus on the conversation.

Daisy asked, "You still there?"

"I am. It's beautiful here."

"What's that sound in your voice? Wistfulness?"

"Might as well enjoy it at while I can. And I am. I have so many ideas for renovating this place, Daisy. Even if no one else, including Jack, decides to use what I'm developing here, I've discovered where my talents lie, and it's more than inventory."

"What? Sorry, my cook is having some kind of breakdown."

"Never mind." She shaded her eyes as she looked up the hill. "I have to go."

"What?"

"Here he comes."

"Who?"

"Jack."

He was striding down the hill, arms swinging, then he broke into a half-jog. Not angry, but excited. Rachel moved toward him. As he came closer, she saw joy on his face. It transformed him. She picked up her pace.

"Rachel!"

"What is it?"

His arms moved toward her, and she caught her breath. The force of his personality surrounded her, and for one crazy moment she thought he intended to hug her.

Without thinking, she reached forward. Jack caught her hands.

"The phone, Rachel. Jeremy called the house. He couldn't get through on your cell number." He held out a small piece of paper. "Here's the number he gave me. He's waiting for your call."

"You're kidding. He called the house?" But she wasn't listening for a response. She was already dialing the numbers.

Two long scratchy rings, then his hello.

Jeremy. She wrapped her fingers tightly around the phone. "Jeremy? Is that you?"

"Yes, Rachel. I'm–are you–"

"The connection is bad."

"I know. Not many–here."

She raised her voice. "Where are you?"

"Rock...."

"What did you say?"

"Remember...girl I told you.... We–"

"What? You what?"

"–went and she had this–"

"Jeremy, this connection is awful. Tell me you're okay?"

"Great. I'm great."

Despite the static and clunking sounds, she heard 'great' loud and clear.

"Don't wor–try–call again soon."

"Jeremy? Wait–"

But he was gone.

"So?" Jack asked.

She stared at the phone. "Rock something. He said he was in Rock something, and he said something about a girl. I don't know. It was a terrible connection." She looked at Jack. "He said he was great. He said he'll try to call again soon."

"You're disappointed. Your questions didn't get answered, and you didn't get your chance to rend and tear."

"Rend and tear?"

"Sure. Big sister stuff."

"Ridiculous. You are ridiculous."

"Hit a nerve?"

"No. I'm glad he's okay, and he'll call again as soon as he can. I'll get more information then, but it didn't sound like he was on his way back." Deep breath. "I should go home now."

They walked back up the slope together.

He answered, "I guess you can."

"That's that, then. I'll print out the inventory when I get home and mail it to you. Maybe you'll find a new caretaker who can continue the work, as you said." She smiled. "I appreciate you giving me a place to stay. We got off to a rather rough start."

"An unusual start." He rubbed his hands together. "I wonder…well, I was thinking. This timing isn't good for me…not to say it's all about me, but I'm wondering if I might impose on you. Ask a favor."

"What's that?"

"If you could stay another week or so. Even a few days would be a help."

She bit the inside of her cheek to slow her response. Her good excuses for staying were gone. But if she was doing him a favor…. After all, he'd helped her, hadn't he?

"If you need me…and, of course, I'm still hoping for that interview with Martin Ballew."

"I have a trip coming up. I was hoping the progress could continue. We have the alarm system now, and I'll ask someone to stay over to watch the back, so you'd be safe. How would you feel about that?"

"Maybe I could hang around a little longer."

"Excellent."

He looked like a cat who'd found a bowl of melted ice cream. Satisfied. She felt a purr coming on, too.

Jack said, "I'll get the oven heating. Supper at six o'clock?"

"Sounds good. Thanks, Jack." She let him go ahead of her, hoping to contain herself until he was out of sight. No hopping, skipping or jumping in delight, not while in public view, anyway.

Jeremy, wherever he was, seemed to be okay, and she could hang around Wynnedower a while longer. She dialed Daisy who answered at the first ring.

"Hi, Rachel. Everything okay? You hung up so abruptly."

"It's fine. It's all good. I heard from Jeremy. Our connection was bad, but I think he's somewhere with a girl. *That* girl, I guess." She sighed. "Like Kilmer said." Jack had suggested something similar.

"Somewhere's a big place."

"He sounds good, Daisy, despite the poor connection. I was all set to pack up and leave for home, but Jack has asked me to stay for another week or so. To continue with the inventory."

No response.

"To keep the progress going in the house, you know. He has to take a short trip."

Still no response.

"Am I talking to myself?"

"I've been shaking my head and waggling my finger at you. Guess you couldn't hear it, huh? So, he wants you to stay."

"To keep on with—"

"Yeah. What you said. Funny how, now that you're all ready to leave, he's got reasons for you to stay. Reasons that have nothing to do with him, only with his house. Watch out, Rachel."

"You're reading too much into it."

"Far be it from me to interfere." She broke off, choking.

"Are you laughing at me?"

"Only a little bit. Listen to my question, Rachel. Are you safe at Wynnedower?"

She paused before answering. "Yes."

"Here's my advice. Take it for what it's worth. This is a pretty sorry vacation, but it may be the only one you get, so if you're having any kind of fun and you're safe, then make the most of it. Who knows, if you hang around, maybe that museum guy will come back. You should give his office a call. Stay on their radar."

"Good idea. I'll do that."

"Rachel, you think too much. It gets very crowded in that brain of yours. Listen to your heart occasionally."

"Bye." Rachel disconnected. She'd been asked to stay, and he'd mentioned supper so they were officially dining together. She looked down at her shorts. Her shirt was wrinkled. Wouldn't hurt her a bit to freshen up.

****

She reminded herself it was no more than a business dinner. Rachel set the table while Jack checked the casserole baking in the oven.

"A few more minutes," he said.

"No rush." She fixed a tall glass of ice water and parked herself at the table.

He half-turned. "Will you be okay here when I'm out of town?"

"You said you'd get someone to watch the back of the house, right?"

"Mike's younger brother. He's reliable. If you get uneasy, call the police. Don't do anything on your own. I want you here for your good judgment, not for physical security."

Her good judgment? Funny. "When are you going?"

"Thursday." His eyes were bright, and his complexion was flushed.

Jack put the casserole dish on the table. "These are delicious, but I'm getting tired of casseroles. Maybe salads would help. Do you cook, by any chance?"

"No. I usually eat in restaurants. It's not much fun to cook for one, and after working all day it's easier to grab a meal on the way home. I'm sure May can cook other things. Have you asked her?"

He laughed. "Sure. Ask her yourself if you're in the mood for a thirty minute lecture on why casseroles make more sense with her not living on the premises."

"I guess she'd rather live right here."

Jack paused with his fork suspended mid-air. "You're probably right about that."

"Where does May come from? How does she get here?"

"She walks. She lives in a house down the

back path."

"Really?"

"There's an old service road that leads to Wynnedower from the back. The house is on that road. It's part of the estate. It's small and definitely inconvenient to the rest of the world, but she likes it."

The idea of May in the retainer's cottage disturbed Rachel. A little picture bloomed in her head of May sitting in her small house waiting for her next appearance at Wynnedower. Waiting and planning between visits to Wynnedower. Everything for Wynnedower and the Wynne family.

"You look troubled."

"Just thinking about May."

"Don't worry about her. She's content with ruling this house. What about you? Feeling better about your brother?"

"Yes, but I have questions." She spooned the casserole onto her plate. "What's this?"

"It's the sausage, linguini and marinara sauce combo."

"Why didn't Jeremy tell me he was going somewhere so remote that he couldn't get a decent cell signal? How could he take off without notice, leaving this house and his responsibility here?"

"It's worked out, and it's not your worry. You aren't responsible for an adult sibling." He added, "It's the curse of the firstborn."

"I guess you know about that. It's probably not much different with a sister." It sounded sharp, and Rachel regretted saying it, thinking about that instead of the fact that she'd mentioned his sister. The silence fell around them. That got her attention.

"Where did you hear about my sister?"

His conversational, chummy tone had dropped off like an ill-fitting costume. She was reminded of quicksand.

"I believe May mentioned you had a sister."

He didn't speak. She saw disbelief in his eyes. She couldn't say 'Kilmer told me.' How could she bring him up now without seeming deceitful?

"I'm sorry if I wasn't supposed to mention her. I didn't know…that I shouldn't. Please don't be angry with May. The subject came up naturally when we were talking about my brother. It flowed from there. She said something about enjoying cooking for you when you were children. Plural. I should've let it go and minded my own business." She'd figure out a way to tell Jack about Kilmer later, if she had to. If Kilmer came back, she was going to tell him to go away, stay away and leave her alone.

Jack resumed eating, and she thought the awkward moment had passed. In the midst of the silence, he suddenly nodded and said, "She's very special, and I'm protective of her."

"Protective? I guess I know how that feels." She laughed softly. "Does she ever come here? I mean, if you don't mind me asking."

He gave her an odd look and shook his

head. "Sometimes."

"I'm sorry I won't get the chance to meet her."

Jack nodded, then suddenly his mood lightened. "Never mind. I have something to show you."

Chapter Eight

Jack wanted her to ask, expected her to be curious, but she said nothing. He watched as she scraped the casserole remains from her plate into the trash, and then set the plate and utensils on the counter while she ran the water, holding her fingers in the stream, waiting for it to get hot. She was taking her time on purpose. He knew it.

"It's obvious you're the firstborn."

She looked back over her shoulder. "You said that a few minutes ago. The curse of the firstborn? I don't feel cursed."

"Not exactly how I meant it."

"Bring your plate over. We'll get this done in a jiffy." She held out her wet, sudsy hand. "So, why is it obvious?"

"Because you give orders, not take them."

She fixed those amazing eyes on him. "And you don't?"

"Proves my point. Just rinse and stack the dishes." He understood the need to respond on one's own terms. He could respect that even if it annoyed him. He saw the potential in her. She was different from the people who depended on him. She could be irritating; she could also help him, but to do that she needed to know the truth. At least, part of the truth.

She squirted the dish detergent into the sink, then slid the plates into the suds.

"Okay, that's enough." He reached across and turned off the faucet.

"Enough for what?"

He tried to soften his impatience with a smile. "Come with me. This way."

At the dining room doors, he paused. He pulled the keys from his pocket. The skeleton key contrasted oddly with the modern keys. When he opened the doors, he reached in and hit the light switch. The chandelier sprang to life. Light from the dining room spilled out. This was the moment that gripped him each time. It was a feeling he couldn't put into words. He motioned for Rachel to enter.

The room stretched out long, and the end was rounded. The windows showcased a lavender sky with a setting sun. He waited as her eyes caught on the easel and a table, no more than a small island in the middle of an almost empty room.

A canvas tarp covered the floor beneath the easel and painting cart. Stacks of stretched canvases leaned against the side wall, turned to face the wall. A large cardboard box sat beside them filled with junky stuff.

"You're an artist? Like your great-grandfather?"

"Like my great-grandfather? I hope not."

As she approached the easel, he said, "Be honest."

He was apprehensive. Foolishly so. It didn't

matter if she appreciated art, or in particular, his art. That wasn't the point at all.

It was a landscape, a garden view as seen through the window. The viewpoint included the back half of the wing where his quarters were located on the opposite side. Far from finished, dabs of green and brown peppered the garden expanse, but large areas were unformed and untouched.

"Why did you keep this a secret? As if your art must be hidden?"

"It was a secret for a long time. Painting, anything connected to art, was frowned upon in my family, thanks to Griffin. It impacted all of us and our choices." He added, "Do you know much about art?"

"I hope so. I'm trying to get a job in a museum." She looked at the floor and her hair fell forward like a black, silky curtain. "But enough? I don't know." She pushed her hair back behind her ear.

"Museums and galleries are special places. I've picked up a few things from going there, and from reading, of course." She turned toward him. ""Now I understand why you vanish for long periods of time. How long have you been painting?"

"On and off for years."

"But you said you moved around a lot."

"Crate it up and ship it." He shrugged. "Not hard."

"Do you sell them?"

"I've sold a few. Had some small showings."

She walked over to the stacked canvases, and he was there ahead of her in a flash.

"No, these aren't for viewing. I'm just not ready to trash them yet."

She pulled her hand back. "The trip you're taking…is it connected to the painting?"

He smiled broadly. "I'm going to be very busy for the next few weeks getting ready for the showing and before that, I have to make this quick trip up to New York. If you could stay at least until I return, it would be very helpful. In fact, I have a list of contractors, painters and such. Could you meet with them and get estimates?"

"But you said not to."

"I've changed my mind. Since you'll be here anyway, it makes sense. Just stay with them. Don't let them go anywhere in the house alone. Or anywhere they don't need to be."

"Jack, how do you expect to have a career as an artist, oversee a renovation, and run a bed and breakfast or party facility?"

"I won't. I've painted in lots of places, but nowhere do I paint as well as when I'm here at Wynnedower. I guess that's why I keep returning. In the end, I might sell anyway." He felt slightly dishonest. Selling was more likely than any other outcome.

"Might? I saw that realtor's car, you know."

"I thought I had made up my mind, or close to it, but now I'm not sure. Those estimates will help me decide." And it would give her something to do, something that would keep her here a little longer.

"I'm glad you're staying open to possibilities." She refocused her attention on the painting. "This is wonderful."

She smoothed her hair back, that dark hair that instantly fell back into its perfect lines.

"It gives me so many ideas for Wynnedower. Your art. Old Griffin's art. I'm feeling a theme here. Those rumors of hidden paintings…surely we could use that in some way."

She was staring off into the distance again and he realized she was seeing a world somewhere inside her head. When she returned her eyes glittered. "I'm happy to help in any way that I can. Thanks for sharing this with me, Jack."

It was a new experience—someone who was helpful instead of needy. He liked that and he also liked her enthusiasm. It was contagious. Maybe selling Wynnedower wasn't a foregone conclusion, after all.

****

They shared a late night snack of pound cake and lemonade as they reviewed the list of contractors. Sudden light lit the hallway and drew them like two people-sized moths into the window arcade hallway.

She paused at the flower room door. "What do you think, Jack?"

They stood together in the open doorway and watched and listened, but heard nothing except the usual night noises.

She followed him out into the garden. "A deer maybe? Not necessarily a person."

"No way to know, but these lights might have done a good job tonight. If someone was warned off, then it's worthwhile."

"Now no one can stumble upon the house in the dark and mistake it for empty."

"True." He stared into the deeper shadows. "Who or whatever it was, they're gone now. Let's get back to work."

"Speaking of light, Jack, do you have a flashlight I can borrow?"

Chapter Nine

Rachel returned to the attic. The flashlight pierced the pitch black area beyond the small door and revealed a wide hallway that ran from the front to the back of the house. She found an overhead light midway along, but nothing happened when she pulled the string.

She ran her free hand lightly along the wall while training the flashlight on it. Roughly opposite to the door on her side of the attic, she found its twin. She searched the door's surface with the flashlight and found a tiny doorknob and almost flat hinges. If it had locks or slide bolts, they weren't on this side.

Rachel pulled the knob. The door opened.

She listened and heard nothing. Feeling braver, she opened the door wider and sneaked the beam of the flashlight inside.

There were no formal, sheeted rows of furniture. A jumble of stuff was grouped here and there and scattered across the floor. Rachel entered, located the overhead bulb and yanked the string.

Stacks of folded fabric filled a doll cradle. The cradle was pushed up against an old vanity with a cracked mirror. Around and between were odd and ends. These items had been left here with no thought to their preservation. The wood finish of the vanity was black and crackled like alligator skin. The mirror was discolored and peppered with dark spots.

Rachel laid the flashlight on the vanity and knelt to pick up a dried out leather shoe far too narrow for her foot. A lopsided bag of cast-off clothing spilled over onto a broken shoe shine box. A small glittery box sat atop a dark trunk with leather strappings and tarnished metal fittings. She lifted the lid carefully. Jewelry was tangled inside. None of it appeared to be more than costume quality, but vintage, of course. Still valuable. She touched a strand of beads, and when she tried to lift it out of the box, the beads scattered with a light, clicking cascade across the bare floor boards.

She scrambled to gather them up from the shadows into which they'd rolled, and poured them back into the box. She put the jewelry box aside hoping she hadn't upset any ghosts.

The trunk wasn't locked. She popped the two latches reminding herself these things were fragile and she could break them, witness the beads, and while they appeared to be forgotten and discarded, yet they didn't belong to her.

She intended only to peek beneath the lid. As she did, the fragrance of cloves embraced her. There were layers of garments in here. It was too shadowy to see more than that.

The feel of eyes upon her back stopped her. She closed the lid, looked around and called out softly, "Is anyone here?"

No response. Not a creak from the settling

house. Nothing more than her guilty conscience at being a snoop.

She lifted the lid again. She reached into the trunk and, from the top, as she touched it, a shawl all but floated out toward her. With the least encouragement, it spread about her shoulders as if intended especially and only for her. The long black fringe spilled across her forearm, and the silk draped across her hands. It was richly embroidered in a hypnotic pattern of green peacock feathers.

How could she resist touching it to her cheek? She stood, feeling the weight of it. Almost like a living thing, it seemed to move around her shoulders. The fabric felt delicate, not dry-rotted. She caught sight of herself in the vanity mirror. She raised one end of the shawl and draped it across her chest from shoulder to shoulder. She fancied her amber eyes had assumed an exotic tilt, and her lips looked full with a secret smile. The girl in the mirror was intriguing. Mysterious. Not like anyone she knew, but maybe someone she wouldn't mind being.

Rachel swirled the shawl dramatically, and it re-settled gracefully across her back and shoulders.

"The peacock shawl."

Her heart faltered. She froze, wondering if it would ever beat again. She saw his face reflected in the mirror, staring at her. She opened her mouth, but couldn't speak. She slid the garment from her shoulders and tried to fold it. The silk and fringe kept slipping and defied precise folds...crazy because it had spent so many decades neatly tucked away in that trunk.

Jack stepped closer and touched the fabric, his fingers to hers, stilling her attempts. "This was my grandmother's or maybe her mother's. Roaring Twenties, I think." He took it into his own hands and laid it back on top of the other clothing in the trunk.

He didn't yell or complain, but his manner was cool.

She changed the subject. "Why is it so different in here? The other side is neat, but this has no order at all. Everything seems older and more...used."

"Some of this stuff is older. Certainly, it's more used. Family things."

Changing the subject hadn't lessened her guilt. Best to say it out loud and be done with it.

"I apologize for handling the shawl."

Jack nodded. He picked up the flashlight. "This is why you wanted the light?" He shook his head and looked disappointed. "How did you get over here?"

"There was a door from the other side of the attic."

He reached up and scratched his head. "You came through the hall between the two?"

"Yes."

"Wasn't the door bolted?"

He spoke, but his gaze was focused beyond her, and she didn't think he actually expected her to confirm the obvious.

They walked back the way she'd come, not the direction from which Jack had entered the attic. He paused to kneel and check the slide bolts, then ushered her into the neat side of the—her side of the attic.

"Stay over here, please. No need for you to be over there."

"Of course." Chastised. She gave him credit for style.

"Thanks." He held out the flashlight. "Take it just in case." He walked back through the little door and pulled it closed behind him.

She was pretty sure the next time she tried to open the door to the other side, it would be locked.

Chapter Ten

Rachel scheduled appointments with craftsmen for estimates and continued working on the inventory. Jack didn't mention her trip to the far side of the attic, but there was reserve in his manner that reminded her of her inappropriate behavior, so it was a relief when he drove off for a day in town.

He showed up for supper with his hair trimmed, still longish, but the pony tail was gone. The ends curled around his ears and the nape of his neck. The bearded stubble had vanished, and his cheekbones and jaw line delivered all that the strong bone structure had promised.

"Nice haircut," she said. "What time are you leaving tomorrow?"

"Early. Brendan will be here by afternoon, and May will stay over, too. It's only for two nights. This trip is to meet with my agent and the gallery and work out some details."

With both May and Mike's brother here, why did Jack need her to stay, really?

She asked, "Are you nervous?"

"Nervous?" He sipped his coffee. "This is only a meeting. The real test comes in a couple of weeks."

****

When she came downstairs in the morning,

his suitcase was by the door. She hadn't planned to see him off, but the aroma of coffee had lured her back to the kitchen. Too bad it never lived up to its promise.

Jack was wearing a real shirt, one that fit properly and had buttons. And with a sports coat.

He waved as he walked up the hallway from his quarters, but then his phone rang. He dashed back to answer it, leaving his door open.

"Amanda, hi. Yes, leaving shortly." He listened, and then continued. "You have the flight info? Okay, I'll watch for the driver by the security gates."

She had no place in that conversation. She went into the kitchen and opened the fridge.

"Anywhere you like is fine," echoed up the hallway.

Were the new haircut and the presentable clothing intended for more than a business meeting? Maybe for Amanda?

He shouted, "Rachel? Where'd you go?" He appeared in the doorway. "Why'd you leave?"

"You were on the phone."

He gave her a slip of paper. "This is Amanda's number. May has it, too. If anything happens, call her, and she'll get word to me."

Rachel walked with him through the central hall into the foyer. "You should get a cell phone. I can't believe you don't have one."

"I've gotten along fine without it."

A moment of sentimentality pinched her,

and she picked a piece of lint from his sleeve.

"There. Now you're perfect."

The distracted look left his gaze. He met her eyes. She had his full attention, and it almost scared her.

"I'm leaving now."

She stepped back and nodded. "Have a safe trip."

"Don't lose Amanda's number. Call her if there's a problem and she'll get me. Don't take any chances, and don't hesitate to call the police. I don't want anyone to be at risk."

****

So, where did this leave her? Was she now the de facto caretaker? She had to laugh. He'd said, "Call the police if you think it's needed." He wanted her here for her good judgment? He was delusional.

The dust raised by the tires of Jack's car hung in the air as he drove through the gates and down the dirt road.

The responsibility was now hers. And her new housemates who'd yet to arrive. She made sure the front door was locked, likewise the conservatory door, then went up to the attic.

After a couple of hours amid the furniture, Rachel snagged the old bedspread from Jeremy's room and arranged it in a shady area of the garden. Having Wynnedower as her playground was the most fun she'd had in a long time. Maybe ever. It was her canvas on which to dabble. Unfortunately, when she left she wouldn't be able to take her project with her, so she'd make the most of it now.

She sat cross-legged with the notebook on her knees and considered the view.

Rachel sketched in the two wings—the dining room and Jack's wing—then filled in the garden area between, roughly drawing in the walkways, the planting beds, and the arbor and cement bench. She closed her eyes. In her head she could clearly see how the garden filled the area then fanned out with a slight curving slope. The bench and the arbor were like a demarcation line. The view through the arbor was open and rolling until it hit the forest.

Eyes open again, she stared at the reality. The original layout was still suggested by the remaining bricks and a few scraggly bits of surviving nature. The flower beds along the center path led directly to the arbor. The side paths should be re-shaped into semi-circles wrapping around to meet at the arbor, and along those the plants should be graduated to mid-size then larger plantings. Rachel chewed on the pencil. Those plantings couldn't be too large because the windows shouldn't be blocked.

What had she read on that pamphlet while working an inventory at a home improvement store? Mix texture, color and seasonality? Yes, that was it. The cover had had an eye-catching picture of chrysanthemums and snapdragons.

To her list, she added: Check with nursery about plantings to stagger blooms and color.

"Hey."

She jumped. Her pencil scored a deep line across the page. She released the notebook to save her tipping iced tea glass. Other, larger hands joined hers to save it.

A tall young man. Fresh-faced. The young man who'd come with Mike to fix her car.

"Got it. Sorry I startled you. I wasn't all that quiet, but you were concentrating. Meditating or something. Is that what you were doing?"

"You're Brendan."

"That's me." He gestured at the blanket. "Mind?"

"Please have a seat." If eyes were a good indication of personality, then Brendan was laid back and good-natured. His hair was a dishwater blond color, but in a kind of shaggy cut that gave it life. He wore a t-shirt and jeans, both of which appeared to be clean. She liked the way he kept his dusty boots off the blanket as he dropped his backpack onto the bricks and joined her.

He stared up at the leaves overhead and then around at the brown, neglected garden. "Nice way to pass a hot morning."

"Not morning. It's nearly noon." She waved the notebook slowly sending a bit of cooling breeze across her face. "How'd you end up house-sitting for Jack?"

"Need money."

"Unemployed?"

"I work for my brother. There's not much out here."

"Including *my* brother. Not out here, I mean."

"Is he still missing?"

"Not really missing now. He called. I have questions, but he sounds okay."

"A big relief for you."

She nodded. "Some relief, more worries. I raised him. A kid taking care of a kid."

He leaned back on the blanket, propped up on his elbow. "Parents?"

"Dead. We lived with an aunt, but she was a little eccentric. The real life stuff fell to me."

"Not much fun for you."

Not much fun was right and no need to relive it. She channeled the conversation in a different direction. "Do you have a good relationship with your brother?"

"Brothers. Plural." He'd picked up her pencil and was flipping it in his fingers. "Yeah, once we got past the beat-down phase, they were okay."

Rachel laughed. The way he said 'beat-down phase' made it sound almost nostalgic. "You seem well-adjusted, so maybe it was also a productive phase."

He pointed at the paper with its rough diagram of the garden. "So, what's this? Mike said you were doing inventory for Wynne. Are you a gardener, too?"

"Oh, I'm interested in lots of things. I'm having fun putting some of my interests into practice." A side-step answer, but not untrue.

He tilted his head and squinted at her. "Are you looking for a job? Here, maybe?"

"Here? Do you mean here as 'in town' or

'here' here?"

"Either."

"Not at Wynnedower. My stay here is temporary. Maybe in Richmond. I'm an inventory specialist. Most of my jobs are short-term."

"An inventory specialist. Like the people with those little machines you see in stores taking readings shelf by shelf?"

"No. Well, yes, but that's not me. My assignments are usually more complicated. I'm good at what I do, but I'm always open to other possibilities. You should keep that in mind when you find a job. Always be flexible and have a strong work ethic."

Brendan saluted. "Yes, ma'am." He dropped his hand and shook his head. "I know one thing, if I was taking time off, I'd find a better spot to spend it in than this place."

In one fluid motion, he came up off the blanket and onto his feet. "Well, I'll go in and see what's what."

"I don't know where Jack left the keys to his rooms. I didn't think to ask him."

"No problem. I'll get them from May."

"She isn't here yet."

"Sure she is. She looked out at us a while ago."

"Really?" She stared back at the house.

Brendan waved as he left.

She labeled the sketched-in boxes with ideas for plantings. She was always surprised to discover how much she recalled from her reading. For good or ill, she was no better than a sponge, absorbing everything around her.

A few leaves fluttered past on a slight breath of wind. It was a welcome breeze. Extra movement caught her attention. She turned toward the arbor gate. From behind the thicker vegetation, a hand waved. A face followed. He signaled for her to come to him.

Kilmer. David. Pest. Seeing him put the galling taste of guilt in her mouth.

She would've preferred that he simply never came back. She set her notebook aside, discreetly eyeing the house, hoping no one was watching.

A bush tugged at her shirt, and leaves brushed her face as she walked through the gate. When she reached him, she said rudely, "What now?"

"I'm sorry to bother you. I didn't realize it would be such an imposition."

She shook her head. "I can't help you."

"I asked you to tell me if you heard or saw anything that might relate to Helene, that's all. Now you're resenting me." His hands were half in his pockets, his shoulders slumped.

"I resent the position you've put me in. I'm his guest."

"You aren't doing anything wrong."

"You're right, I'm not. And I'm not going to."

"You came here because of your brother. This opportunity for me came up because you're here and you're a caring person. If Jack's not hiding anything, then he has nothing to worry about. He doesn't know we've spoken or that I'm in the area. What he doesn't know won't hurt him and could mean everything to Helene."

"Then why does my conscience feel so jagged?"

"I don't know. Rachel," he sighed deeply. "I don't want to put you or anyone else in an uncomfortable position for my happiness. It's only Helene's safety and wellbeing that drives me to ask." He faced her. "Never mind me. If you hear anything that indicates Helene is in danger, let the authorities know. Please."

No matter which way she struggled, doubt held her fast. Kilmer was a pest, but he might not be a nut. What if a woman's safety was at risk?

In frustration, she said, "What do you think has happened to her? How could he imprison her without someone noticing? That's what you're suggesting, right?"

Bright red brushed his cheeks. "I love Helene. Our families were so different; we were so different. It would've been a miracle if we'd made a success of being together, but the heart wants what the heart wants." He stared at his clenched hands.

"You already told me that, and you told me that Jack paid you to leave her."

His chest rose and fell rapidly. Rachel wanted to avoid another emotional scene. She felt no sympathy for him. Maybe there was more wrong with her than with him, but she didn't like him.

"I couldn't give her the life she deserved. I told you she is ethereal. Vulnerable. For the last few years, Helene has been living in a sort of home, like assisted living for well-to-do adults. Like a condo with privacy, security and servants. People kept me informed. I was content knowing she was safe and happy. But then, shortly before Jack returned here, she left that place or was removed. No one knows. The home would only say that she'd left."

"Did you ask Jack?"

"Jack doesn't like anyone to interfere in his relationship with Helene."

"Maybe he's following her wishes. Maybe she wants seclusion."

He slapped his hands together. "You're under his spell."

"Nonsense."

"You've seen it, haven't you? The mood swings? From menacing to jubilant, then down again?"

Rachel drew back. "Menacing? No. Taciturn and rude? Yes."

"He has charisma. You're not the first woman drawn to him, drawn to danger."

"Danger?" She nearly laughed in his face.

"Remember this when you see Jack coming and going and planning big events and wondering why he doesn't sell this place and move to the city—remember their father left Wynnedower and the family fortune to them, together. She and Jack are joint owners of

Wynnedower. Since he hasn't sold it yet, that tells me Helene is resisting him. If something happens to Helene, then it's all Jack's."

"Fortune? What a joke. The place is falling apart."

"Wouldn't surprise me if he torches it for the insurance, then he's free to sell the land to a developer." He lowered his voice. "When it comes to his financial state, you only know what he tells you."

Suddenly, David was close, his face so close she could feel his breath on her cheek. He added, "I don't want Helene trapped in that house at his mercy."

"You said that before. You said he might burn the house down. If you truly believe it, then go to the authorities. If not—if this is some sort of self-serving drama you're indulging in—then you'd better stop now."

She left him abruptly, but could she ignore the possibility of someone in danger?

All her life, she'd been the responsible person. For everyone and everything, and both a beneficiary and a victim of her imagination and curiosity. Why didn't those things come with an off-switch?

She entered the house through the flower room door as May turned the corner with a covered tray. May had turned right, heading toward the stairs at the eastern end.

If she chose to dine alone and in the privacy of her room, it was none of Rachel's business. In fact, she would welcome not sharing a table with Madame Sellers.

The aroma of chicken cacciatore unwound through the corridor like a ribbon of flavor. Rachel could have followed with her eyes closed, although she kept them open, of course, as she walked, and found herself standing in front of the old nursery and governess suite—one of the areas Jack had instructed her to ignore.

She stood quietly outside the closed door.

It was a puzzle.

May cooked for Jack when he was in residence. Now, Jack was gone for a few days, and May had moved in. Why? For Rachel's comfort? No.

Exactly what sort of protection did May's presence offer? A chaperone for her and Brendan? Not likely.

So May moves in and brings up food to the suite of locked rooms. The mystery suite. Rooms for which Rachel had no keys and at the east end of the house—the wing she'd been told to leave alone.

Her fingers touched her lips as if to silence them, as if she were in danger of blurting out the answer to this tricky equation.

She wasn't snooping on behalf of David Kilmer. This had nothing to do with him. This was for her peace of mind and her conscience in case there was a grain of truth in Kilmer's ravings.

Stealthily, Rachel stepped away from the door. May had entered; May would exit. Rachel would still be locked out and she had no intention of confronting May.

Her face burned. Once again, she'd inserted herself into business that didn't concern her. Daisy was right. She needed a more interesting life of her own. Then she could leave others to their own affairs.

An engine roared outside. Rachel went to her bedroom and stood at the window.

She saw a broad shirtless back, presumably Brendan's, riding a green mower across the grassy areas of the yard.

The ordinariness of a half-naked young man, sweating in the summer sun while cutting the grass, put David, siblings, and even May, out of Rachel's mind. She loved the homey sound and feel of it. It was almost an image from the brush of Norman Rockwell.

****

Brendan tapped the hilt of his knife on the table. He leaned forward, waving it in the air as he told a story from his childhood and of his misspent youth.

"Dad grounded me for a month. I can't say I didn't deserve it, but I learned all my evil ways from my older brothers and then built on the knowledge, so it was really their fault."

May said, "You took it too far. You always did. You're lucky you weren't killed."

"No luck to it. Hey, it worked in *Smokey and the Bandit*, one of my dad's favorite movies. I'm telling you, if I'd had a little more slope to the ramp, that Chevy would've made it over the creek."

May patted her lips with her napkin, then folded it neatly and laid it beside her plate.

"Your brothers should have been more mindful of the example they set. Aside from nearly breaking your neck, you made a mess down by the creek. I remember. By the time they'd dragged that car back up to the road, what had been a lovely path was a disaster. With erosion, over time areas of the creek silted up, and mosquitoes started breeding."

Rachel stood, and the chair screeched across the linoleum floor. May gave her a hard glare, but said nothing. Supper with Brendan was hilarious. May was a wet towel.

Why had May joined them anyway? Hadn't she already eaten? Her disapproval of their levity settled around their little group like a ponderous bank of dark clouds. Rachel was tempted to ask her why she needed two suppers, but kept her annoyance to herself.

Brendan stood, gathering his utensils, and crossed the kitchen to where Rachel was running soapy water. "I'll dry," he said. "May, thanks for cooking. We'll handle the cleanup." He gave her a bow.

May's cheeks pinked up. "You'll put things away in the wrong spots."

"We can't go but so wrong, now can we? The kitchen's not that big."

"Make sure the dishes are dry before they go into the cabinet."

Rachel tossed a clean dish towel at him and

jumped into the washing. May left, saying she had a book she was reading.

"Mosquitoes, huh?" Rachel asked quietly, in case May hadn't gone far. "So that's how they came to flourish in Virginia. Should've known it was your fault."

Brendan leaned close as he accepted a dish. "Don't mind May. That's her job."

"What's her job?" She watched him run the dish towel around and around the plate as if polishing it.

"Keeping us all on the straight and narrow."

"You've known her a long time?"

"All of my life, on and off." He added the dried plate to the clean dishes he was stacking on the counter. "She's lit into me more than once—before I learned how to charm the ladies." He turned around. "Isn't that right, Miss May?"

She was standing in the doorway, her face pink. "I forgot to take my tea. You deserved every lecture you ever received." She paused on her way back out. "And it must've done you some good because I haven't caught you playing pirate in a few years."

Rachel couldn't help herself. "Pirate? Did you wear an eyepiece? Yo-ho-ho and a bottle of rum and all that?"

He eyed her through half-dropped eyelids and a stern frown. "That was long ago."

"I'm sure."

"Gimme a break. I was a kid. Besides, it was the older kids that put me up to it."

"Up to playing pirate?"

"Up to the treasure hunt." His pained expression changed to a crooked smile. "In fact, I'm still a pirate at heart and willing to admit it. Yo-ho-ho, yourself."

May admonished, "You listened to every tall tale you heard and took every dare. It's a wonder you lived to grow up. Every time I see you down in the basement or roaming the house, I think of it." With that parting shot, she left.

"Treasure hunt? What were you hunting?" She looked down as she washed the last of the dishes.

"When I was a kid it seemed like whenever someone spoke of Wynnedower they got into the treasure story, about how there's supposed to be something valuable stashed here."

She looked up. "Jeremy mentioned rumors of treasure to me. Is there anything to it?"

"How do these stories get started anyway? Nah, no treasure, but I've yet to meet the kid who could resist the temptation."

They took a walk before full nightfall. They went out by way of the east end vestibule, and he tripped the motion sensors like it was a game.

"I hear this has made a difference."

"It has. Right after we had them installed, they came on a few times, but then it stopped. The system is far from foolproof, and we probably scare the occasional deer, but our uninvited visitors aren't exactly James Bond. I think word has gotten around that we're in residence and armed. Trespassing isn't tolerated."

"Armed?" Brendan gave her a quizzical look. "Are you?"

"Not me. Jack is, and I'd be willing to pull the trigger if I had to." Big talk. He couldn't know she'd never actually touched a firearm.

He held the door for her, and they came back inside. As they walked up the hallway, Brendan put his hand on the small of her back.

Perhaps only gallant or intended as polite, but it was a personal sort of gesture. She walked faster leaving Brendan and his hand behind.

"Goodnight, Brendan. Sleep well."

****

Late in the night, Rachel awoke to a distant tapping sound. Or knocking?

She listened and heard nothing more. She rolled over and buried her face back in the pillow, but had trouble dismissing the noises. Not likely to be someone knocking on a door and too well-defined to be house-settling. Rodents, maybe? Bats?

She sat up, checking her ceiling, then settled back down again, but now she was wide awake.

Intruders, maybe? Quiet ones?

She groaned and pushed the covers aside. She donned her robe and slipped her phone in the pocket. This was what Jack paid her the big bucks for, right? Right. Big bucks. Funny. In fact, he'd told her NOT to confront intruders, but was she really going to call the police only to find out the house had rodents?

Leaving the sitting room door unlocked behind her, just in case, she stood in the hallway and strained her ears, listening, waiting.

Silence. Satisfied, she turned to go back to bed and was stopped by a soft thud, thud, thud. But where? She couldn't tell the location. Not above, not below. Rachel walked quietly down the hall, pausing every few yards to listen. She felt her way through the alcove and emerged in the hallway that led to the old nursery suite.

Another tap. A thud. Equally hard to place.

Should she wake Brendan?

Rachel went to the stairs. As she descended in the dark, she sensed no intruders and heard nothing more. By the time she reached the window arcade hallway, she realized none of the exterior motion lights were glowing. The nighttime world seemed peaceful.

If she heard one more sound, she'd do...something. But there was nothing more.

She didn't want to wake Brendan because the memory of his hand on the small of her back was too fresh. Instead, she dragged herself back up to bed, slept uneasily and woke with the dawn, wondering if she'd made a mistake this time by *not* following her intuition.

Chapter Eleven

"Did you hear anything last night?" She watched May and Brendan for reaction. They were seated at the kitchen table sharing breakfast.

"No," May answered.

Brendan said, "It's an old house."

"A noise that sounded like knocking or tapping?"

He laughed and rapped his knuckles under the table. "Ghosts, maybe?"

She ignored him. With no sign of damage or intrusion and a clear lack of concern on the part of everyone else, Rachel let the subject drop.

May said, "There's bacon on that plate for you. Would you like an egg and toast?"

"Thanks. I'll fix it." She pulled the egg carton from the fridge.

"I'll see you ladies later. I have to run." Brendan's pushed his chair back and stood.

May nodded and Rachel waved. Unfortunately, with his departure the atmosphere in the kitchen soured. As Rachel fried the egg, May excused herself, too, and left the room.

Rachel ate her breakfast alone. She was glad not to make small talk with May, but still, it was an odd feeling to have been left alone so summarily. She dropped her plate and utensils into the sink suddenly in a hurry to get up to the attic.

She'd intended to resume the inventory, but it was inevitable she would open the attic door again, cross that dark hallway and attempt to visit the other side.

The jumbled, disorderly side of the attic drew her. Jack didn't care about the attic. Why would he? No, he only cared because it was located at this end of house. His end. The end he kept warning her away from. Maybe because it was the end that was located over the old nursery suite?

If he'd slid those bolts closed, then she was out of luck. If not, she'd take it as a sign.

Not locked. Practically an engraved invitation.

Was there a slight nibble in the back of her mind about Brendan and treasure?

In the attic? Only if dust was suddenly going to become a hot commodity.

She stepped as lightly as possible across the attic, pulling the string to the overhead bulb as she passed. The flash echoed in the stained vanity mirror and caught her eye.

The trunk drew her like Pandora's Box.

She knelt and popped the locks again. Who would know? Jack was gone, May was two floors below, and Brendan was somewhere else and wouldn't care, anyway.

Rachel removed the shawl from the trunk and set it aside carefully. She touched the layers below, looking and feeling around, until she touched lace. It felt different from the rest. Gently, she eased it out.

Off-white lace cascaded across her arms and pooled in her lap. Tiny pearl buttons reflected the weak overhead light. Peach-colored silk, lace and pearls. The scent of cloves and ancient fabric enfolded her. She stood and held the dress to her chest. The hem swirled down to her feet. A few wisps of tissue paper fell nearby. Someone had taken the trouble to pack the gown carefully.

In this iffy light, she couldn't tell if the lace was yellowed with age or originally off-white. As with the shawl, she stared into the mirror and saw someone else. An image from an unremembered magazine, or a picture from a book? Her haircut could have been a sleek twenties bob, but this dress wasn't from that decade. This was Edwardian. It was vintage and perfect. She held her breath.

Madness.

This was rude and wrong. She was prey to her own curiosity and imagination, so much so that she was violating the most basic rules of respect for others. But what was the harm? She'd be gone soon, and this trunk—indeed, all of Wynnedower's secrets—would be beyond her reach.

With distance, the temptation would fade and she'd be wondering why this had seemed so intriguing.

In the mirror, her face was now downcast. Her hair was only straight and short, the dress was a wilted relic from a time long past.

She folded it and laid it atop the garments in the trunk, along with the shawl. With a sigh, she refastened the catches and returned to her side of the attic, hoping she was leaving foolishness behind.

****

Rachel stood at the front windows watching as Jack's sedan flew along the dirt road.

He was back from New York. She was sad to be leaving, but also relieved to be free of the temptation that surrounded her at Wynnedower, including this juvenile attraction she felt.

Her work papers were stacked on the dresser. She hadn't completed the inventory, but had a representative sampling of the furniture. It was time for Jack to bring in an appraiser to provide specific, expert advice.

The contact list was the topmost sheet. Two appraisers with excellent references were first on the list. Further down were carpenters, painters, etc., all of whom could provide proof of insurance. She laid the pen neatly on top.

Her clothing was half-packed. Her phone was fully charged for the trip home.

Jack's voice boomed, echoing up the stairs. "Rachel? Rachel?"

She picked up the papers and the pen and came out through the sitting room. He was already standing at the top of the stairs.

"Ah, there you are. I thought you might be in the attic."

"I could've heard you shouting if I'd been all the way up on the roof."

His face was lit with excitement. "Everything went okay here while I was gone?"

"No problems," she said. "Your trip went well?"

"Good. Great. Better than great. I want to celebrate."

She pushed the stack of papers in his direction. He reached out and took them.

"What's this?"

"Your lists. A partial inventory. You need to bring in an appraiser now to help sort the wheat from the chaff. There's also a list of artisans and workers. I spoke with them, but didn't set up actual appointments for estimates because I didn't know when you would be available."

"For me." He looked at the list as if it were written in code. "For me?"

"You asked me to stay until you returned from New York. You're back and, frankly, I should be moving on."

"What about your brother?"

"What about him? He hasn't called back yet, but he has my cell number. If he calls again, it will be to that number. He isn't in danger, at least not until he returns, and then we'll have to see how that chat goes." She smiled. "So, you've been wonderful and I appreciate all that you've done for me."

"No, no. I don't have time to meet with these people. You'll do that for me won't you? Stay a little while longer—through the showing? Will it cause a problem with your job?"

"I don't have to take another assignment yet, but when I planned my vacation time, I thought I'd be spending it with my brother. That's not going to happen. I've been here more than a week, and it's time for me to get back to real life."

"What about the museum job?"

"I doubt it's a possibility any longer. I suspect it isn't. It was a pipe dream anyway." She hadn't expected to hear a defeatist whine in her voice. She cringed.

He frowned. "No, this isn't right." He shook his head and tried to hand the papers back.

"No, keep them, Jack."

"I'll hire you."

"Hire me?"

"As a part-time caretaker, plus pay for inventory and supervision and estimate gathering and stuff."

"Jack, I appreciate the sentiment, but I need a real job."

"That's what this is, but I understand what you're saying, so let's call this a temporary assignment. Until after the gallery showing. A month."

"A month? You mean in addition to the time I've already spent here?" This man who'd been so arrogant was begging her to stay a bit longer. Her will softened. "Your showing is in less than two weeks."

He shook his head. "I'm not sure how long I'll be in New York."

"Oh, Jack, I don't know…."

"Stay until you get a better offer?"

"Stay until Sharon calls with an assignment I want?" Was she really considering this?

"Yes. Why not? It's only a few hours' drive back to Baltimore."

She felt like he'd stolen her oxygen. Swept her off her feet. She felt wanted, if only for her skills, but maybe also a little for herself.

"You want me to stay here, meet with the appraiser and renovators and get estimates, plus complete the inventory. For that, you'll pay me and if a better job comes along I can leave without notice for the new job."

"Yes. Take these back?" He held out the papers.

"Let me call Sharon first. If the schedule is open, then we have a deal."

He was suddenly serious. "Thank you."

"Don't thank me yet."

His hands seemed to hover near her arms. She thought—what did she think? Nothing.

"I'll put the papers back in my room unless you want to review them now?"

"No. I want you to make your phone call, and then I want you to tell me you'll stay."

With each 'you' the force of his personality, as strong as his eyes were dark, touched her. She warned herself not to read more into it than there was.

He continued, "Finish your call, then come downstairs. Tell me who to contact to make the arrangements so you'll officially work for me.

Then we'll have supper while I tell you about the plans for the showing."

When Jack left, she took her phone and went down the end stairwell and out to the conservatory and the terrace to call Sharon. It was nearly five, but Sharon never left early. She leaned against the brick wall and dialed.

"Stillman's Consulting, Accounting and Inventory Group."

"Sharon? Hi, it's Rachel."

"Hi, there. Great timing. I have an assignment you'll like."

"Oh." She wasn't expecting that. She needed to drum up a little enthusiasm. "What and where?"

"It's an estate. An old woman, practically a hoarder, but of good stuff, has passed. Her executor needs an inventory. I thought of you. You know something about everything. I understand that's about what she left— something of everything. They need you right away, though. I'll assign some assistants to go with you."

Not so different from what she'd been doing here. New place, some interesting stuff.

"What's wrong, Rachel? Was that a sigh? Are you back in town?"

"No, that's just it. I'm still down in Virginia."

"This is a nice assignment. You won't want to miss it."

"It sounds great. Thing is.:..." She made her decision. "I'm hoping Jeremy is on his way back...and I want to be here." Not entirely a lie.

"I can't postpone this job. It's an estate. They're anxious to get it settled. Listen, I'm pretty sure Stillman would give a nice bonus for this one."

"I totally understand. Thanks for thinking of me."

Sharon's voice slowed in hesitation. "If you're sure. Stillman suggested we ask you. He thought you might want to come back to work early. It's a good one, Rachel."

There were others who could do the job, but if she let Sharon down, then next time she might not think of Rachel first when she had a choice assignment. Alan Stillman signed the checks. She didn't want to sour that relationship.

She pushed the words out. "I'm sure. Sorry to put you to the trouble. Thanks for thinking of me, but I have a bit of news of my own. I have a potential client who'll be contacting you."

"Who?"

"Jack Wynne. A short gig, but it's here. Handy while I wait for Jeremy."

She waited out the long pause before Sharon answered, "Okay, keep me posted and good luck with your brother."

"Thanks again." She hung up. Had she really turned down a job? Guilt stung her. *Your brother*, Sharon had said. But she hadn't turned it down because she was waiting for Jeremy. Had she done it for Jack? Oh, crap.

Not Jack. No, she just wasn't finished here. Not with the work and not emotionally. When she left, she didn't want to take regret with her.

Her hands trembled as she closed the phone. She'd crossed a second threshold. The first, when she'd arrived at Wynnedower. This second was a minute ago when she turned down an assignment and chose to stay.

But only for a little while longer—until Jack's New York show was done.

Jack thanked her when she told him she'd stay. He thanked her, took Sharon's name and number, said he had to finish some brush strokes while the paint consistency was right, and then disappeared into the dining room, closing the doors behind him.

Rachel slapped the papers on the table in frustration. Was this important or not?

Several times during the course of the afternoon, she passed those doors. Other than an occasional, muffled noise, she heard nothing. She didn't like the quality of those sounds and caught herself tiptoeing. When suppertime hit, she didn't disturb him. Rare faint noises, a horizontal line of light shining below the doors in the dark hallway, well into the night, was far from inviting. Now she hoped the doors would stay closed.

She sneaked down for a glass of water and a snack to take back upstairs. She was barely through the hallway when the dining room doors flew open, then slammed shut. He moved so quickly she only caught a glimpse of his back. The heavy footsteps ended down the hall near his quarters, and another door slammed.

Did Kilmer have a point when he'd warned her about Jack's temperament?

Tonight she wasn't tempted to linger but scooted right on up the stairs to her room, seriously reconsidering her decision to stay.

****

Bright sun lit the room and bird song trilled right through the window glass. Rachel awoke and immediately began worrying over her decision to stay. She kept at it as she washed and dressed. Becoming a paid employee, instead of a gal helping out, put them on a whole new footing. She wasn't sure she wanted to be on that new footing with Jack.

Rachel dusted the top of the dresser and arranged her brush and comb neatly on a doily she'd found in the attic. How big a mistake had she made by agreeing to Jack's plan? Could she get out of it?

Did she want to get out of it?

She picked up the key ring. Considering how preoccupied he'd been the afternoon and evening before, maybe he hadn't made the call after all. Might not be anything to get out of.

She went from worried to depressed.

By now, locking doors behind her was routine. Before she was halfway down the stairs, she heard the clatter of pans coming from the kitchen. Something fell, and the bang and cursing told her it was Jack, not May.

As Rachel reached the kitchen door, she blurted out, "We have to get some things straight."

He faced her with twenty-four hours of dark stubble and red-rimmed eyes.

She asked, "Are you sick?"

Jack lifted his coffee mug. "I got caught up in the painting last night. I need coffee before my shower."

"Oh." How could they have a frank discussion when he was in this state?

He paused in the doorway. "I apologize for leaving you on your own for supper last night. I'll make it up to you."

****

Rachel spent the early morning hours in the attic writing descriptions of furniture. Her efforts were half-hearted, but she wasn't on the payroll yet, so her time was still her own. She returned to her room and saw the garment on the bed.

In the strong light from the windows, the lace, pearls and silk gown was more obviously yellowed than it had appeared in the attic, but the shade gave the original beige more of a soft ecru tone. Shoes were placed neatly on the floor below where the hem of the dress fell over the coverlet.

Ice and fire alternately raged through her body. She couldn't think. Guilt—smack in the face, you're-a-nosy-person-with-no-life embarrassment—made her lightheaded. The door lintel kept her upright.

She closed her eyes and placed one hand over her diaphragm. *Breathe deep. Breathe slow. Once again, deep and slow.*

When she opened her eyes, the dress was

still there.

Who? Someone who'd seen her in the attic digging in the trunk where she didn't belong? Who wanted to humiliate her?

She checked the room. First, the bathroom, and then the closet. Under the bed. The other doors were locked.

Slowly, Rachel sank down on the bed. The movement of the mattress dislodged the dress, and it began to slide in rippled waves over the edge. She grabbed it before it hit the floor.

Her breath caught in awe of the tiny, delicately embroidered roses on the bodice and running down the skirt, at the pink-tinged pearls and at the filmy lace covering the flesh-colored silk that would rest so lightly against the wearer's skin.

She re-laid the dress on the bed and picked up the shoes. Slippers? Their color matched the underdress, and the fabric felt satiny. The bottom was soft leather, darkened with wear and age, but smooth to the touch. Rachel kicked off her sandals and held one shoe alongside her foot. The shoe was way too narrow.

How? Who? Why?

Jack? No. May and Brendan might have been in the house when she found the dress, but how would they know she'd been digging in the trunk in the attic? She touched the garment. It had survived the heat and cold of the attic for how long? A long time.

The dress needed to go back to the trunk

now.

She folded the dress lengthwise and draped it over her forearm. She picked up the slippers and stepped cautiously out into the hallway. She could only reach the far side of the attic by going through her own side, so she headed toward the western stairwell.

"Rachel?"

She froze, not wanting to turn around. But she did. What choice did she have?

"Jack?"

His gaze fastened upon the gown as if interested, but not recognizing what she held.

"It's a dress from the trunk upstairs."

"Upstairs?" Understanding spread across his face.

"I found it on my bed."

He continued staring at the dress, and she stared at him. His jaw tightened.

"On your bed. Any idea how it got there?"

Rachel searched for sarcasm in his words, in the tone of his voice, and found none.

"No, I don't, but they're fragile. I'll return them to the trunk immediately."

He moved closer. He slid his hands between the dress and her arm. His touch tingled clear down to her toes. Stunned, she released the dress and stepped back.

The garment draped across his large hands and his forearms. He looked up abruptly and said, "This is the answer. This is exactly what I need."

She shook her head. "It won't fit you."

He ignored her wit.

She shrugged. "I don't know what you're talking about."

His eyes burned dark, almost possessed. Deftly, he found her hand and pulled her along at top speed, along the hallway and down the stairs. His excitement unnerved her.

"Hurry. Come along." He strode through the open dining room doorway. "Come in, please."

She entered the hallowed space. She'd been invited in only once before, only a handful of days ago. He acted now as though no prohibition had ever existed—as if she'd never been locked out. She found this annoying and charming. She'd been accepted by him. She glowed. She didn't need to see her face to know it.

"Sit, here." He placed a stool near one of the windows. "Please?"

She did as instructed. He placed his fingertips along her jawline and gently tilted her face toward the light.

She was accepted—as a mannequin.

"That's it. Perfect. I need your help."

"If you're asking me to pose for you, forget it."

"No, please listen." He tugged at her hand. "Come, see."

The same garden painting stood on the easel, but the painting had changed.

He had added a woman, brushed in roughly, seated on a concrete bench. Rachel moved closer for a better look. Jack had painted life and color into the dead garden. Now it was in bloom, and he'd added the woman, but she was unformed. She didn't fit and the lighting was off.

"You can see there's a problem. But that dress. On you. You'll sit for me? Not long sittings, just here and there."

"Impressionistic? Is that the style?"

"In that vein, but with more form."

He waited while she stared at the colorful canvas.

"It reminds me of *Flowering Garden at Sainte-Adresse,* but with a female figure added, of course."

He crossed his arms. "Monet."

"The Father of French Impressionism." She laughed at his puzzlement. "I read a lot, remember?"

"Are you, I mean, do you have a photographic memory?"

"No. I have a strong visual memory. Photographic or eidetic? Not sure I really understand what that is. I don't have it." She shook her head. "I have to think about this, Jack. I'm not sure why, but the idea of putting on the dress and posing makes me feel uncomfortable." Was it posing? Or posing for Jack?

When he spoke, his voice dropped to a soft low tone. "Think about it until tomorrow morning. The light is strong in here by mid-morning. Please consider it. I'll be waiting here for you at ten a.m."

Chapter Twelve

"Daisy? You're not going to believe this. I'm standing in front of a mirror. I'm wearing a dress from the turn of the century. The previous century, not the millennium."

"Hang on, Rachel. Let me mark my place. I'm entering expenses. Mid-morning is the only time I have this much quiet here." Rustling noises came through the receiver. "Okay. Say it again."

"I'm wearing an Edwardian dress. A tea dress, it's called. It's lacy, embroidered and so very fragile. I'm decked out in it. There are slippers, too, but they don't fit."

"Don't fit? Can you return them?" Loud hoots of laughter came through.

"Very funny. Seriously, you should see me. It's unbelievable. I'm in front of the mirror, and, if I may say so, I look amazing. The way the dress is made…well, the outer part is lace and it's sheer, and the lining is silky and flesh-colored. It's almost like I'm naked beneath the lace. I don't think I can leave the room like this."

"You lost me. Why are you wearing the dress if you don't like it? Why do you need to leave the room?" Her tone changed. "Oh, this is about Jack, isn't it?"

"No. Yes. It's complicated. He's waiting for me downstairs. He needs me to model for a painting."

"A portrait? Are you kidding me? He's painting a portrait of you?"

"No, no. Not like that. It's a small figure in a big painting. He needs someone to pose while he works out that part of the painting."

"Sure."

"Really."

"Then what's the big deal? Go sit for him. If you don't like it, don't do it again."

Her friend had the knack of reducing gnarly problems to the basic issue.

"Thanks, Daisy."

"Not a problem. Everything's really pretty simple if you break it down and toss out the crap and the emotionalism."

"Diner owner and philosopher extraordinaire, I salute you."

"As well you should. Change of subject here. I was going to call you later today. I'm heading in your direction in a few days, on my way to Myrtle Beach. I thought I'd stop in and check on you."

"I can give you a tour of Wynnedower."

"Oh, you betcha'. I want a tour and to meet the master of the house."

"You aren't making kissing noises, are you? Because if that's what I'm hearing, you can forget the tour."

Daisy laughed. "I'll give you a call when I'm on my way. If you decide to finish out your vacation days elsewhere, come along with me to the beach."

"I'm serious. Don't get silly about it. I expect

good behavior."

"Gotta go. Bye."

She could count on Daisy. Daisy wouldn't do anything to embarrass her.

Rachel ran her hands down the front and sides of the gown, then snatched them away. Natural oils were destructive. Same with stalactites, right? So she held her hands away from the fabric and admired her reflection yet again.

Such elegance. On her.

The question remained: how had the dress gotten to her room? Didn't she already know the answer?

The shoes dangled from her fingers as she stepped down the stairs. She paused at the landing, her free hand resting on the banister. Her fingers rested on the silky smooth wood like on that first day. And shortly thereafter she was being called a trespasser and getting kicked off the property.

Enjoy it while it's good. That had never been her motto, but she was feeling reckless. Perhaps some bit of attitude caught from Daisy? Maybe from the boldness of wearing this dress.

The dining room doors were open. Jack stood in front of his easel, brush in hand. The mid-morning light touched him, stripping the wild man look from his hair, something the barber hadn't managed to do. The angular face, bent toward the canvas, was somber. His face was surprisingly, unexpectedly beautiful.

No, not beautiful. That was silly.

Daisy might embarrass them all if she saw him like this—in his element. It was as if an angel had cloaked him with an aura of power and mystique.

He turned to face her. He laid the paintbrush across the palette and extended his hand.

Her lungs seized and her knees locked. She couldn't breathe and didn't need to. She wanted to suspend this moment in time. Forever. But Jack awaited.

She held up the shoes. "They don't fit."

"Your feet are perfect without them."

Her unpainted toes tried to curl under.

Jack pointed toward a stool near the side windows. "Sit there."

He put his hands on her arms and positioned her, deftly touching her shoulders, then her thigh. "Pretend you're sitting on the bench."

He stood back and stared, then moved forward and knelt. "Your feet, just so."

His fingers on her calf, her ankles, caused her to shiver. He lifted her hands in his. "Your hands, like this." He stepped back again, then nodded. "Hold that pose."

The pose felt natural for about thirty seconds.

"Sit straight." He looked around the canvas. "Please."

Instinctively, she turned toward him.

"No, no. Please don't move your head." He crossed back to where she sat and, with his fingers on her chin, repositioned her head.

187

"Gaze into the distance."

She didn't know about straighter, but her back got stiffer. This was not her cup of tea—posing in an antique tea gown. Rachel almost laughed at her silent joke, then remembered she wasn't supposed to move. This was not only uncomfortable but incredibly boring.

"Jack, I don't think this is working out." She spoke, barely moving her lips, not changing her pose at all. "I want to help, but I don't have what it takes to sit silently staring into nothing."

"I know what you are."

It sounded alarming. "What? What I am?"

"I knew the word but couldn't pull it out of my brain yesterday."

"What are you talking about?" she asked, barely managing to hold the pose.

"Autodidactic. Someone who teaches themselves—an autodidact."

"Is that like being one's own doctor? Foolish is as foolish does?"

"Don't deflect."

She didn't answer, but stared into the distance as instructed.

"You see how well I'm getting to know you?"

He sounded smug. She ignored him.

He moved away from the canvas and came over. "I need to arrange your legs." Jack touched her calf and gently moved her leg back nearer the other foot. An infinitesimal movement, yet it seemed to please him. He slid his hand under one of hers and lifted her fingers.

"Take these shoes and dangle them from your fingertips like you did when you walked in."

She tried to hide her reaction. Was her face flushed? She felt hot and trembly. Any words he spoke during the interaction tumbled in her brain, their meaning lost in the sensations evoked by his touch.

"Rachel, give me your hand." He shaped her fingers, slipping the toe of one slipper over them.

"Now, hold it like that."

For one tremulous moment, he lingered, his eyes meeting hers, then he went to his canvas.

It was ridiculous for her to respond this way to a man's attention. Especially a man who usually forgot she was even around. It wasn't as though she'd never dated, even if the dates weren't exactly memorable, at least not in a good way. In fact, they were marginally better than a visit to the dentist. Ed with his ceramic dog collection. Jimmy with the restored car. He insisted on driving it everywhere and never exceeded thirty miles per hour. The car was more interesting than Jimmy. It was just as well. She didn't have time for a boyfriend. Her life was busy. She worked hard to take care of Jeremy.

Was he supposed to stop being her concern now? Because he now belonged to some other woman? As simple as that?

Well, not so fast. Jeremy would stop being her concern after she'd had it out with him about his trip to Rock-somewhere. Once she was sure he was okay, then she'd have only herself to worry about, to live for. Just her.

Jack's voice brought her back to the dining room combo studio. "You can get up now."

"Oh? Okay."

"I don't want to use up all of your goodwill in one sitting. Can we do this again tomorrow morning at ten?"

"Shorter than I expected. Not so bad, after all."

"You sat for an hour."

"No way."

"You were lost in your thoughts. Not all of them looked pleasant."

"I'd better go change." But she stood there, shoes still dangling from her fingers.

"Is something wrong?"

"I'd like to know how this dress ended up in my room."

It was a long moment that stretched across the six feet separating them, a moment that drifted on the sunlight streaming in through the many tall windows in this room. It floated and hung there. She fancied Jack saw it, too, and knew it was time to be honest with her.

"My sister saw you liked it." He watched her face.

"Helene."

"Yes. You aren't surprised?"

"No. Does she live in the old nursery quarters?"

"Yes, the governess/nursery suite. Don't disturb her, please. She's very fragile."

"Okay." Rachel turned away and headed toward the door, her bare feet cool against the wood floor.

"Wait." He frowned. "You're curious about everything. Aren't you curious about her?"

"Yes, but you'll tell me about her when you're ready. Now I'm going to change." She walked away, sashayed, in fact, swinging her hips. Suddenly those watched moments, the wispy figure disappearing around the corner, and that first night when she'd awakened, the floral scent she sometimes encountered in the halls—it all made sense now. Watched, but not threatened. Helene satisfied her curiosity in her own way. Rachel could respect that.

****

She went to her room, carefully unfastened the pearl buttons and slipped the gown down to the floor so that she could step out of it. She laid it on the settee in the sitting room, arranging the fabric and lace so it wouldn't wrinkle. She pulled on her shorts and blouse, and made her way to the nursery suite.

Rachel knocked softly. She put her face close to the wooden door and spoke, "Helene?"

After a full minute with no response, she backed off. After all, she didn't know how extreme Helene's emotional problems might be. The gift had been like an invitation—one that didn't involve her brother, Jack. But perhaps not. Maybe it was less an invitation and more an acknowledgement.

Helene confined herself, except for

nighttime excursions around the house, to her suite. And the attic? Jack had told her to stay away from that side of the attic. The facts were falling into place. If she wanted to meet Helene maybe it would be there.

Jack had asked her not to approach Helene. She had no trust in what David had told her, and Jack's tone when he spoke of Helene was gentle. Yet if there was any chance of Helene being in trouble and needing help, then she had to do something about it. She couldn't count on David's unreliability or Jack's seemingly caring manner to put the question to rest. She needed Helene to do that.

Chapter Thirteen

A few Sweet Gums were tinged with brownish-red. Not yet autumn, but it had been hot and very dry.

Rachel held her phone tightly, much the same as she would've held Jeremy if he were here in person. "I can't tell you how relieved I am to hear from you. We have a better connection this time, thank goodness. When are you coming back?"

"In two weeks. It's been an unbelievable trip. We've been mostly backpacking."

"We? Is that male or female?"

"Most definitely female. Her name's Lia, and I can't wait for you two to meet. You're going to adore her."

"Was this trip her idea?" She tried to keep the edge from her voice, but didn't succeed. Jeremy was silent. She envisioned some dark-eyed, dark-haired femme fatale seducing her relatively innocent brother into taking an exotic trip—camping and hiking in the Rocky Mountains. Or maybe not a femme fatale and not exotic. Maybe a tall blonde Viking type who could lug a pack with the best of them.

"You knew I was coming to visit. Why didn't you tell me you weren't going to be here?"

"I was going to be there, but you arrived

early. You're not even due in Richmond yet."

"I got worried when you didn't call me back, so I moved my trip up. I expected to find you here. You never mentioned going off anywhere."

"My phone died on the way out of town. It took a hard fall going through airport security. I'll replace it when I get back."

He'd avoided responding to her charge that he hadn't mentioned a trip. She sighed and let him get away with it. "How did you know then? That I was already here? When you called before, you called Wynnedower."

"I called Wynnedower after I tried your cell phone. I tried your cell phone because I called John Brookes, my former…my boss. He told me you'd been there looking for me."

She'd run out of words. She didn't feel like number one any longer, that was for sure.

"Sis, I want to talk to you about it, but not until I return. We should speak face to face. How much longer will you be at Wynnedower? Which, by the way, I find it unbelievable that you're still there."

"I don't know. If you have something to tell me and you don't think I'm going to like it, then I'd much rather you told me now."

"When I get back. If you've already returned to Baltimore, I'll come there to see you."

"I think you need to spend some time worrying about your job and grad school."

"That's part of what I want to speak with you about."

She bit her lip.

"I love you, sis. We'll talk in two weeks. Please don't worry about me."

The call ended abruptly. She waited to see if he'd call back, knowing he wouldn't.

So, what didn't he want to tell her? That he was in love and getting married? That he was throwing away his opportunity to be a CPA? She'd worked so hard to get him what he wanted. Her heart felt bitter.

Dried leaves, their edges brown and brittle, were caught here and there along the brick wall, leftover, discarded, unwanted—futile. She shook herself. She'd done her best. That's all she could've done.

Jack's big show was just over a week away. She hadn't promised for certain sure that she'd stay all the way through. She stared out at the woods, glad to be alone. She felt bereft and knew it showed on her face, but it didn't matter because there was no one here to see or care.

Slowly, she returned her attention to her list. She'd met with an appraiser and wanted to make the notes while it was fresh in her memory, but she couldn't stop herself from glancing down at her phone every few minutes.

Jeremy, oh, Jeremy.

The appraiser had given her pointers about differentiating the less valuable from the valuable. He also seemed excited, and she knew Jack would be pleased. She was a little sorry about that because he might be tempted to sell it all off, and having done that, he might find it easier to make the decision to abandon Wynnedower. Jack was in town for the day, tied up with something. There was still no sign of Helene. May had already cooked some casseroles, and left.

Rachel was heartily sick of casseroles. Too much of a good thing.

The phone rang. Startled, she dropped the clipboard. Loose papers took flight on a breeze. She grabbed the phone and scrambled for the papers at the same time.

"Hello?"

"Rachel, hi. I'm on my way. I'll be there in a couple of hours."

"Daisy? Great. It'll be good to see you."

"Is something wrong? You sound odd."

She set the clipboard like a paperweight on top of the papers. "I'm fine. I just got off the phone with Jeremy."

"He's okay, right? He's not hurt or anything?"

"No, he sounded fine. Maybe too fine."

"The girl?"

"We can chat when you get here. How long can you stay?"

"An hour or so, that's all. It's a long drive to South Carolina. Is the master of Wynnedower in today?"

"He's not here now. Could be back any time. Maybe not." She cleared her throat. "Daisy, sometimes your sense of humor takes you a little too far. Don't embarrass me, okay?"

"Well, that's real nice. After all the trouble

I've gone to?" She laughed. "No, now I really am teasing. I won't embarrass you, but tell me how it stands between you so I can watch where I put my big feet. You've been down there forever. Are you two friendly? How friendly?"

"He has these moods and tempers. Not dangerous, but disconcerting. He's been much better lately. He asked me to stay for the inventory and to help watch the house and now for modeling. So, I think that means we're getting along well."

"Unpaid labor is what that means. And did you say, 'not dangerous'?"

Rachel ignored the last question. "He contacted my employer and arranged a part-time assignment, so I'm officially on the books, but only part-time so I can do what suits me. Part-time caretaker, part-time inventory specialist, part-time model."

"Sounds interesting. I'll see you when I get there."

"You know the way?"

"I have GPS."

"Drive carefully."

She hung up, then gathered up and clipped the errant pages back with the others. What would Daisy think of this place? Of her host?

She had a visitor. He strolled out of the woods and to the terrace as if he owned the place.

"Where do you come from? Aren't you afraid Jack will spot you?"

He laughed softly. "There's lots of old tracks and paths in these woods. You probably don't know that I live near the main road. A nice walk. I don't mind going to a little extra effort."

"You've gone to that effort for nothing. I told you I wouldn't spy for you."

His smile never faltered. "I understand and respect that. You look well. Wonderful, in fact. I'm going out of town and wanted to make sure you were doing okay here before I left."

"Don't concern yourself. I'm fine."

He leaned back against the brick wall, half-sitting on it with his arms crossed. "No word about Helene, I guess."

He mentioned it casually. Did her expression slip? Did she see a hardening of his expression? Along with a trace of smugness?

"I told you I wouldn't spy or pry."

"But you know something. I can tell."

"No."

"Don't protect him."

"There's nothing to protect. He hasn't done anything wrong that I know of."

"If he hasn't done anything wrong, then tell me what you know. I told you, I want to be sure she's safe."

"There's nothing to tell." Rachel slapped the concrete ball with the flat of her hand. "I've said this before, but let me be clear and unmistakable. Leave and stay gone. You've been trying to manipulate me. I don't appreciate it."

"Yet you haven't told Jack." He paused. "No

answer, so you haven't. Maybe because you're not so sure about him after all?"

"What I think is none of your business. I've tried being nice, I've been rude, but you won't accept it. I didn't say anything to Jack because I didn't think it mattered. You've forced me to change my mind."

As she spoke, she watched the muscles in his jaw tighten. His crossed arms tightened and ceased being a place to hang his hands. She knew he was trying to hide his anger, but his color gave him away as his complexion reddened.

"Go now. I'm not bluffing."

Without further argument, he said, "I apologize. I'll leave."

He walked off, leaving her fuming.

A quandary. Should she tell Jack? Yes. Not yet, though. He wasn't here and Daisy was on her way. Rachel grabbed her clipboard and went inside to get ready for Daisy.

****

Daisy arrived in her shiny red Audi and parked it next to Rachel's not-shiny older sedan. She slid from behind the steering wheel and stood, never taking her eyes from the house. Rachel ran down from the porch.

"It's big," Daisy breathed.

"It is. But more than that, it has twisty-turny hallways and doors, door, doors."

They climbed the steps. Daisy's head turned this way and that, taking it in.

Rachel smiled. "What are you thinking?"

"*Dark Shadows*, that's it. Do you remember that show…well, the reruns. I can loan you the DVD set."

She ignored her friend's joke. "Come on in. Would you like a soda or something? Maybe a cup of coffee?"

"Nope."

They stopped in the central hall. Daisy continued looking here, there and all around.

Rachel asked, "Have you eaten? It's a little early for supper, but there's nothing to stop us from popping one of May's casseroles into the oven."

"May?"

"May Sellers. She does some cooking and general upkeep for Jack and whoever else happens to be here."

Daisy said, "Nice."

"Nice? I guess so."

"Show me around."

Rachel wondered if Helene could hear their chatter and laughter while hiding in her rooms. Did it make her feel lonely?

Daisy 'oohed' and 'ahed' as Rachel led her through the mansion. Rachel noticed her friend's fingers moving and asked, "The doors, right?"

"Have you counted them?"

"No. I've had enough fun sorting out the keys."

"The keys?"

"Skeleton keys. Believe me, everything I thought I knew about skeleton keys—well, I didn't think there was a lot to know and that's true, but they aren't interchangeable. There are master keys that open multiple locks, but your average skeleton key opens one or two locks, and it takes forever to figure out which when there are this many doors."

Rachel escorted her through the first floor, and when they passed the closed dining room doors, Daisy pointed.

"What's that room?"

"The dining room, but Jack uses it for his painting. We don't go in there. He demands privacy."

"Maybe a peek? I'd love to see."

Rachel shooed her along. "He's my host and this is his house. It's important to respect his wishes."

****

Daisy continued exclaiming over the rows of furniture in the attic as they negotiated the stairs back down to the first floor. Instead of turning toward the main house, they went out into the conservatory.

"You know what this makes me think of?"

"*Dark Shadows*, you said."

"No. Robert Redford. *The Great Gatsby* and all that. His lover's name was Daisy, you know. That's why I paid attention when we read it in high school."

"You mean you read the book?"

Her laugh was short and sharp. "No, I watched the movie. It was quicker and far more entertaining. I never liked my name until I saw

201

that movie." She walked the wide circle of the room, gazing up at the ceiling, the window walls, and seeming to draw the feel of it into herself. "I imagined myself as Daisy, that Daisy, the Mia Farrow version, of course. I dieted until I got sick. I was determined to get that hollow-cheeked, deep-set eyes look."

Daisy was tall and slim, and the vision of health and energy.

They settled on the terrace.

"You're headed for the beach?"

"That I am. I haven't had a vacation in two years. A cousin offered me a timeshare right on the ocean."

"You left Bonnie in charge?"

"She assured me she could manage it. I know she can. She'll feel more empowered, in fact, without me there. If anything goes wrong, I'm only a day's drive away, plus she's got good backup on site." She laughed. "Hey, if it works out, maybe next year I can take a cruise or something."

"It's well-deserved, Daisy. I'm glad you have this chance."

"I need to head off soon. I was hoping to meet your host. Or employer. Which is it?"

"Mostly host. He pays me a fee for the hours I spend on the inventory, but I've only been working on that in the mornings because it's too hot up there in the afternoon, as you've experienced."

"Why are you here, then? Not because of Jeremy. It'd serve him right to have to chase after you for a while. Come to the beach with me. It's a big condo. Lots of room."

"I want to finish the inventory. It's close to done. At least, as done as I'm going to get it. I've already engaged an appraiser, and I've been working with him. I'm no expert when it comes to antiques."

The breeze rustled the leaves overhead.

"Jeremy said he had something important to tell me when he returns. I want to be here. I don't need to, but I want to."

"Let him come to where you are. He's a big boy."

"He didn't ask me to wait here. It's my choice. In a way, this is almost a vacation for me. I know that sounds silly, but I've never had so much leisure. I sleep well, I feel useful, but only when I want to. I'm also serving a purpose. In fact, Jack asked me to stay a while longer."

"Oh, I see."

"No, you don't, and I know you're joking anyway. Jack's preparing for an art show. Something big and fancy in New York. By staying, I can continue the inventory and help keep an eye on the house."

"Well, where is he?"

"He went into town this morning. I don't know when he'll be back."

"Let's go grab a bite. What's nearby?"

"A towing service."

"Seriously? Well, we'll drive back toward the interstate. I saw a new shopping center."

"Eat here. I'll put one of the casseroles in the

oven. It'll be ready in thirty minutes. We'll share a meal, and you'll be on your way."

"This May is a good cook? I own a restaurant, and the food's not too shabby."

"How could I not know? I live right above. The food is definitely excellent, both at your restaurant and May's cooking, too."

"Lead the way."

When they reached the central hall, Daisy asked, "Left?"

"Correct."

Daisy turned, then stopped so abruptly, Rachel crashed into her and almost knocked them both over.

Jack had returned. He'd left the dining room doors wide open.

The late afternoon light had a golden quality, as if picking up the hue from the broad leaves of the tulip poplars and spilling it softly onto the scene, tinting it with the quality of an Old Master's Painting after centuries of aging, the gentle yellowing of the oils, the blurring of contrast. There stood Jack, his dark, curling hair falling forward to obscure his face but not hiding the strong jaw. The full shirt he wore as a painting smock gave his already broad shoulders an insanely broad appearance.

His entire being was focused on the painting propped on the easel in front of him. He moved the brush forward, placing the paint with sure and delicate strokes.

Daisy quivered.

It hit Rachel that, for centuries, women had

reached up to touch their hair, to check it for tidiness or whatever, when confronted with a male newcomer who might be welcome to them. An unconscious gesture. Daisy raised her hands and touched her short silky curls with her beautifully manicured nails. What Rachel had to work hard to achieve—that put–together appearance—Daisy carried with her like standard equipment.

Women like Daisy didn't need ridiculously expensive red suits.

Daisy moved forward slowly, more quietly than Rachel had ever seen her move. They were shadowed in the short hallway between the central hall and the dining room. There was something in her movement that alarmed Rachel. Was Daisy the gazelle or the cheetah?

Rachel's fingers curled into fists. She stopped short of hissing, suddenly embarrassed. Jealousy did not become her. She relaxed her hands, flexing her fingers.

Daisy's elbow caught Rachel in the arm. She reacted by stepping back. Daisy half-turned and grabbed her firmly by the forearm.

"Rachel, my friend," she whispered. "You've been holding out on me." She shook her head. "And I don't blame you a bit."

Chapter Fourteen

Jack looked up, eyes narrowed as he stared into the shadowed hallway. "Rachel? Is someone with you?"

She stepped forward, practically shoving Daisy behind her. "Hi. I'm sorry we disturbed you. I didn't realize you'd come home." She entered the open doorway and gestured to Daisy to stand beside her. "This is my friend, Daisy Medina."

"Your friend who owns the restaurant?"

Had she told him that? She could easily have done so during one of their chats.

Daisy stepped into the picture. "That's me." She put her hands on her hips and did a little wiggle. "I can see we've interrupted you, but I can't apologize because I'm not sorry. I've never been in a house like this. I'm thrilled I got to see it. I hope you don't mind."

Jack smiled. "Not at all. Make yourself at home."

Daisy said, "We'll let you get back to your painting."

She grabbed Rachel's hand and tugged her along. Rachel cast one last glance at Jack and saw surprise on his face. As they entered the kitchen, Rachel whispered, "What are you doing?"

"Getting him interested, that's what."

"In you?" Her jaw practically dropped to the floor.

"Me?" Daisy touched her hair again. "Only if you don't want him."

Rachel stammered. "He's not a side of beef or a head of lettuce. He's a man."

"If I were a lesser person, I'd make something out of that statement, but I won't."

Daisy looked over Rachel's shoulder and smiled.

Rachel spun around. At a loss for what to say, she asked, "Hungry?"

"I am," Jack said.

She tried to read his half-smile and couldn't. "Daisy and I are going to have a casserole. We'll set a place for you."

"Not tonight. I have something else planned."

"Oh, sure." Something else planned. Not with her, of course. She wanted to turn her back and hide her face, but if she did, she'd be staring straight into Daisy's eyes. She felt trapped.

"For us. I'm having something delivered."

"Delivered? Out here?"

He smiled more broadly. "It's a celebration. I hope you like Italian."

Daisy said, "I've barged in, I can see."

"Not at all. The food should be here in about an hour." He looked at Daisy. "I hope that won't interfere with your travel plans."

"Not a bit. It's sweet of you to include me."

"You're welcome to stay the night."

Daisy gave Jack a slow smile. "I don't think so although it's tempting, I admit." She leaned against the table and put one hand on her hip. "But I'd love to do supper."

Rachel didn't dare look at her friend's face. Jack was doing enough of that. Suddenly, she felt invisible.

"I'll wrap up in the studio, then wash the paint off," he held up his hands, "and meet you both back here."

"Great," she said with a total lack of enthusiasm. He'd already left the kitchen. It took a visit from Daisy to merit a special dinner? Forget him. She should decline to attend. In fact, she should let the two of them–

Daisy pinched her arm.

"Hey!" She yelled. "That hurt."

Daisy hissed, "You were about to say something stupid, weren't you?"

"Excuse me?"

Daisy left, and Rachel followed. She caught up with her on the stairs. Daisy talked as if there'd been no interruption.

"Don't be a bad sport. Take advantage of opportunities. Unless you really aren't interested."

"Interested? I'm not."

"Right. So, that's why you look like someone popped your balloon and stole your lollipop."

"Don't tease me, Daisy. Be a friend, not a jerk." Rachel unlocked the door, and they walked through the sitting room to the bedroom. "Understand I'm staying here with this guy. How could that possibly work if I was mooning around, pursuing him? I don't need the masochism of unrequited love. Not that there's love or anything like that going on. It's just a phrase."

"Hey, come here," Daisy said. She took Rachel roughly by the shoulders and planted her in front of the bureau mirror. "Look at yourself."

What did Rachel see? A woman who was prepared to lose before she'd even had the guts to try. She turned away.

"No, you don't. Listen to me. I've been watching you for too long—watching you come into the diner alone, leave the diner alone, eat alone unless I barge in. I never see anyone, guy or gal, going up the stairs to your apartment, at least not since Jeremy left, and brothers don't count anyway."

She turned Rachel back to the mirror. "You're an attractive woman and it's beyond me what kind of 'keep away' signals you must be sending to men, but stop it. Stop it now. Fall in love now. With Jack? Not with Jack? That's not the point. But if it's not Jack, then move on. Go somewhere else. Not here and not at home. Somewhere where there are living, breathing men."

She stopped for a breath. "Rachel, invite people into your life."

****

Brendan pulled up. The headlights of his truck cut the twilight. It figured he would be the delivery guy. Rachel went out to help him bring in the food. Daisy followed and waited on the porch to hold the door.

His gaze slid past Rachel, straight to the porch. "Who's that?"

"My friend, Daisy. She stopped by on her way to Myrtle Beach."

When they joined her on the porch he said, "Hello. Daisy. I'm pleased to meet you. Now I see why Jack called and told me to bring extra and even invited me to stay to dinner. I think I have you to thank for that." He handed her a bag. "Let's get the food taken care of."

Daisy accepted the package and gave Rachel a quizzical look. Brendan passed, and Daisy stopped her with a touch. "You've got yourself a real interesting place here, Rachel. Never mind the house."

****

It was hard to stay in a bad mood when sitting around a chipped Formica kitchen table with the soft (ever-dim) bulbs casting a gentle light that muted the garish yellow walls—sitting across from Jack and with Daisy and Brendan at the ends of the table. Brendan's jokes lightened Jack's more dour moods, and Rachel flattered herself that Jack gazed at her more than once. Had she mistaken his interest in Daisy?

Brendan shared his charm equally, except that Daisy got an especially equal portion.

What had Brendan said on the porch? Jack had called him and asked him to bring more food. *More.*

Daisy was saying, "I wouldn't want to have to clean it, but the house is amazing. I've never been inside a place like this. The Newport mansions are all pristine. They don't hardly look like real people could've lived there. But this house—gosh, it feels almost like they're still around."

Brendan made an 'oooo' sound, a sort of spooky noise, and lowered his voice. "Like ghosts?"

Jack threw out, "Nothing ghostly. The vandals and looters are real. Right, Rachel?"

Daisy asked, "What does he mean? Vandals? Like people breaking and entering?"

She jumped in. "They steal the copper pipes and downspouts and rip the paneling from the walls." She turned to Jack. "But we fixed that, didn't we?"

"Not entirely, but we made a good step forward in discouraging them."

Daisy said, "When I arrived, if not for Rachel's car, I would've thought this place was empty. You need to make it look lived in. Put rockers on the porch. Nothing says someone lives here like a big fern in a pot on the front steps."

"Have you and Rachel been conspiring?"

She said, "I was telling Jack the other day that he should bring some of the furniture down from the attic. If someone peeks through the windows, it should look lived-in."

Daisy asked, "And?"

Jack shook his head. "The only reason the furniture is still here is because it's locked in the attic."

"But you're here now...or are you planning to leave again?"

He shrugged. "Undecided. Rachel is helping me figure it out."

"You're lucky to have her help."

Jack smiled at her. Not at Daisy. Not at Brendan. He cast those dark, yet warm eyes upon her and reeled her in over a plate of ravioli.

Chapter Fifteen

Rachel went up to the attic and through to Helene's side. She pulled the light string, switched off her flashlight and set it on the vanity. Silence. Gentle house-creaking noises. Warm air settled around her.

What now?

The treasure trunk was near at hand, but she resisted pawing through the clothing again. No time for dress-up today. Jack was away from the house and she was paying a visit.

A white rattan loveseat peeked out from under a rose-colored cotton blanket. The blanket was draped across one end as if left behind when its user left, intending to return soon.

Rachel ran her fingers along the exposed arm and examined them. No dust.

Is this where Helene sat? Not in the heat of the afternoon, surely. Was she relaxing here in her strange hideaway while Rachel was on the other side, listing the furniture?

Helene could've visited her any time she wanted. Everything Rachel had seen indicated she had free reign of the house, and outside of the house, too. Her seclusion was self-enforced. Knowing Helene was making her own decisions relieved Rachel of any legitimate concern for her, of any excuse for interfering in her life.

Rachel folded the blanket and left it on the loveseat, retrieved the flashlight and headed for the door.

From behind her, a whisper-soft voice said, "Hi."

Helene stood in the half-light near the small, dirt-covered gable window. The overhead bulb Rachel had forgotten to extinguish couldn't reach that far and served only to deepen the shadows. With the window at her back, Helene's face was unreadable.

Did she wave her hand? Rachel couldn't be sure.

Rachel stepped forward, and in that instant Helene moved toward the stairs like a startled deer. Rachel stopped, and Helene did the same, their eyes locked.

"I'll leave the door to the other side of the attic unbolted in case you'd like to visit." Rachel turned and walked away.

When she reached the door, she looked back and couldn't see Helene. Either she was gone or had hidden. A brief visit, yet Rachel was pleased. It was a beginning.

****

Rachel emerged from the attics blinking. It was easy to forget it was day while working away up there. After the encounter with Helene, she'd stayed on her side for an hour making additional notes. As she reached the central stairs, she heard snippets of conversation.

A man said, "...a place. You weren't kidding."

Another voice, Brendan's, answered, "I told you....every penny. You'll get it...."

She followed the voices and realized the two men were in the foyer. The front door was wide open, and they were doing something to the hinges.

"Hey, there."

Brendan spun around. "Rachel." A pause. "Sorry we disturbed you." He nodded toward the door. "Have to reset it. Some trouble latching. Doug's giving me a hand."

"I noticed that. Every other door in this place is locked as tight as Fort Knox, but the front door seems to unlock itself."

The other man had turned away.

Brendan's helper wore some sort of worker's jumpsuit. Blue. The sole of one sneaker faced upward as he knelt beside Brendan. She took in the details, and then ignored him since that seemed to be his preference. Rachel reached up and touched her nose. Strangely, it was as if something smelled bad. Not literally, but something bothered her and she couldn't pin it down. She shook it off and turned to leave.

Brendan called out, "When we're done with the door, I have to check some pipes in the basement. If you hear noises, don't be alarmed."

Rachel laughed, but it felt hollow. An odd mood seemed to have descended upon her.

"Thanks for the warning."

She continued to stand on the landing. Almost waiting. But for what? Whatever thought lingered just outside of her consciousness, remained elusive.

Time to move along.

She wanted to speak to Jack again about moving furniture down into some of the empty rooms on the second floor. She felt strongly about it, and Brendan and his helper would be perfect for the job. As soon as he returned she'd tackle him again. She'd catch him before he got in front of the easel. That morning Jack had barely noticed her. By now, she understood. He wasn't in a mood—he was in the mode.

When he donned his painting shirt and shut those dining room doors, she might not see him for hours or until the next day. The timing seemed to depend on how his work progressed, as did the quality of his mood.

In the meantime, she'd run her own errands. Trotting back up the stairs to grab her keys and purse almost felt like she was shaking free of whatever that strange feeling had been. When she came back down, the two workers were gone, presumably to the basement. Better them than her.

Rachel settled in the car, fastened her seatbelt and checked the rearview mirror as she backed out. In the mirror she saw a figure at the library window. The view was blurry, but clear enough. Helene.

Out and about during the daylight? Downstairs and standing at the window? Where anyone could see her?

Rachel's first thought was one of amazement—that Helene would come downstairs with the two men in the house, one of whom was a total stranger. Her second was of David Kilmer. A protective instinct she'd thought was reserved only for Jeremy rushed over her.

She slipped out of the car and scanned the grounds. No faces in the shrubbery, no shadows to give away a lurker.

Helene no longer stood at the window.

Rachel opened and shut the front door with care and moved rapidly, but carefully, through the foyer and into the central hall. She didn't want to sneak up on Helene and alarm her.

Maybe Helene had good reason to be wary of people. Maybe she, Rachel, wasn't doing Helene a favor by encouraging her to make contact. She looked at the dining room doors. They were shut tight.

After a minute or two of silence, Rachel decided Helene had returned to…wherever, and no one else was in sight. She might as well go.

She'd like to ask Jack for details about Helene's condition. She should also confess about David Kilmer.

Confess? No, not a confession. Merely tell Jack about having met him.

As she drove through the gates, she

decided she'd tell Jack about the encounters. Jack would be justified in asking why she hadn't told him sooner.

When she returned later that day, she saw Jack at his easel, the dining room doors standing open as if he was expecting her.

Chapter Sixteen

"Jack, can we talk?"

"What?"

She'd surprised him. The face he turned toward her showed annoyance. He saw it in her eyes. He forced his frown to ease and consciously relaxed his facial muscles into a friendlier expression. Or he hoped it was.

"If this isn't a good time, maybe we could...."

He interrupted. "Now is fine."

"I'd like to move some of the furniture items down."

"No, too much risk."

"Not on the ground floor, but into the empty rooms upstairs. I want to get a better view of the groupings, plus, while it's not fully climate controlled, it's still a better environment than the attic."

He laid his brush on the palette with the paint-covered end dangling over air. "I don't have time right now."

"I didn't mean you, literally. Hire a couple of guys. I can tell them what—"

"No."

"No?"

"I don't want any outsiders seeing the attic."

"You didn't mind Daisy seeing."

"That was different." He rubbed his forehead

and left a streak of red behind. "It's too big a risk. One will say something to someone else, and before you know it there'll be rumors all around the region, and probably on the Internet, that there's treasure hidden up there among the hoard of furniture, and then we'll really be in for it."

"Well, then, what about treasure? Maybe there's something to the rumors. Maybe we should search for it ourselves."

"Don't go there, Rachel. I don't want to think you're one of them." He regretted the words as soon as he said them.

"One of *them*?" Her voice was cool. "You know better than that, Jack. I only want to help you and Wynnedower, and Helene, too."

He moved close to her, wanting her to understand how seriously he regarded this danger, yet annoyed that she didn't appreciate the reality because she focused on everything except the negative.

"No, you don't know. You haven't thought it through. You encountered intruders once. You don't understand how crazy these people can get, how they lose all sense of proportion. I won't take a chance on hidden treasure rumors springing up again. An appraiser is risk enough, but that's it. When I have time maybe I'll move some of the pieces down. Maybe I'll get Mike or Brendan to help. Maybe. And it'll have to wait until I have time.

"I'm sorry, Rachel. I appreciate your intentions and the work you've done, but no, not yet." He touched her arm. "You understand?"

"Yes, but...."

"I know you don't agree. Just understand. That's all I ask." He shook his head. "The reality is that Wynnedower has few assets. Forget the talk of treasure. If it's going to escape the bulldozer, it has to pay its way. It hasn't been doing that, but I haven't given up hope yet. After the showing, we'll sit down and go through those estimates, deal with the furniture, and look at some real numbers."

"What about the realtor you were speaking with the day after I arrived? Are you still considering—"

"Selling? Yes." One more time, he'd try to make her grasp the reality of the situation. "I can't afford not to consider every option, including selling the house and the estate to a developer."

A small noise. A gasp. He looked up and saw May standing in the doorway.

It was unfortunate that she'd overheard, but facts were facts. In the end, maybe it was just as well. May, perhaps more than anyone, needed to understand and accept the likely future of Wynnedower.

Chapter Seventeen

Nearly mid-morning, Jack's voice echoed up the stairway and resounded down the hall and into her room. "Rachel! Rachel!"

She raced to the stairs. "Jack? What's happened? What's wrong?"

"I need your help."

"On my way."

"No, wait." He came up the first few steps. "I need you to pose. Put the dress on and come down. Quickly, because the light is passing."

"You want me to pose? *To pose?* You scared me. I thought it was an emergency."

"It is. The light is passing. It's perfect now, and I need you in the garden. Now. Hurry."

Annoyed, she was tempted to ignore him or to delay, but as he said, the light was passing. No time for argument. She tossed her shirt and shorts onto the bed and pulled the dress over her head. It floated down around her hips and legs. She grabbed the shoes she couldn't wear, and ran down the stairs to rescue Jack because he needed her.

May was in the central hall. Madame May. She gave Rachel a look that should've squelched any enthusiasm, but Rachel didn't care what May thought and passed her without a word.

"Here, Rachel. On the bench."

He posed her again, arranging her arms, her legs, the tilt of her head. Then he disappeared behind the canvas. Within minutes her body parts objected to the awkward, enforced posture.

She preferred posing indoors—or rather, she disliked posing indoors less than posing out of doors. It was hard to sit immobile when a gnat was trying to inspect one's eye or a fly was buzzing in your ear.

The cement bench bit into her hip. That poor hip bore most of her weight thanks to Jack's arrangement of her limbs which made her envision a floral arrangements of arms and legs—which made her lips twitch as she fought a giggle.

"Don't move."

No more of that attitude. She looked him in the eyes while trying not to disarrange her body. "I'm doing you a favor here. Did you forget that?"

"I apologize." He laid his brush on the palette and came over. He dropped to his knee and gently touched her chin. In a soft voice, he said, "Turn that way, please."

"I'm re-thinking this whole gig."

"Please. I know I've been curt. I'm focused on painting. Single-minded, I know. That's why I appreciate you so much."

Ego stroked, she asked for more, "Why do you appreciate me?"

"Because you work so well without supervision." He grinned. "And you do it so beautifully."

He whisked away, back to his feet, back at the easel, retrieved his brush, and it was as if they'd never had A Moment. Did they have a moment? She stared straight ahead at the leaves.

"Do you wonder what your great-grandfather would think of this? Of you painting? And out here in the garden. *En plein air*. That's what it's called, right?"

She waited. No response. "Did I step on some toes? Or are you concentrating?"

"Neither. I was remembering."

"What?"

"Stop moving."

"Then talk to me. Or can you not paint and talk at the same time?"

"I never knew Griffin, but my grandfather idolized him. He talked about him like he was a celebrity, about how he liked the fast life and hanging out with that set."

"What set?"

"Other artists. Bohemian. Rich dilettantes. Some of them visited here. Old Griffin Wynne never worried about money, so that ended up being what his son and grandson, my father, had to worry about all the time."

"Other artists? Famous ones? That must have been such an exciting time."

"He was involved in an exhibition in New York City in the early 1900s. I have photos of him with his artist friends somewhere around here. You might enjoy them. In fact, it feels kind of full circle with me about to have my own showing, doesn't it?" There was a long pause. "Might be useful for marketing. I'll mention them to Amanda. See what she thinks."

Amanda. Her annoyance flared, but only briefly. It was reasonable that Jack would talk about such things with his agent. In fact, Jack was full of chit-chat today, but it took a detour she wasn't expecting.

"That dress fits you like it was made for you."

She resisted preening and held the pose. "You think so? It's a beautiful gown. I've always had a weakness for old clothing. Rather, vintage clothing."

"Playing dress up. Helene enjoyed that when she was a kid."

"Same here. It's probably a universal pastime. Aunt Eunice had a trunk in her attic, too."

"The aunt who raised you, right? I'll bet you couldn't stay out of it." He grinned.

She returned his smile, while trying not to move. "There wasn't this kind of expensive finery, but some women's dresses and other odds and ends. Shoes and hats and such. I don't know who they belonged to. Probably Eunice. I liked to pretend they were my mother's and grandmother's."

"You strike me as someone who hangs onto stuff. I'll bet you still have those dresses."

"Oh. Well, no. Aunt Eunice worried about me going up to the attic. Climbing the pull-down ladder. Maybe falling through the part of the attic that wasn't floored. She worried, too, that Jeremy might try to follow me and get hurt." After one particularly difficult day in middle school, she'd gone up to the attic and discovered the trunk and its contents were gone. "They're long gone. She donated them."

Somehow her hands had moved from her lap to the bench and her body had shifted.

"I lost the pose. Jack, why didn't you say something?"

He didn't answer. She looked up. He was hiding behind the canvas, back at work. Had probably lost interest. Typical. She re-assumed the pose as best she could and decided to give him fifteen more minutes. After that, he was on his own.

****

Brendan was due mid-day. Jack had volunteered him to help her move some items around up in the attic, but definitely not down from the attic.

"Show me what you have in mind."

She unlocked the attic door, and he preceded her up the stairs. He gave a low whistle when they reached the top.

"You haven't been up here before?"

"No. Jack keeps the attic locked up tight."

"There are some boxes behind that furniture, and a cabinet is blocked."

"Anything good in 'em?"

"That's what I'm going to find out." She pointed to the far side. "Over there."

They each took an end of a table and shifted

it over a couple of feet to clear floor space.

"Could you move those boxes away from the wall? I don't want to bang my head on the low eaves. Actually, I'm glad I found this stuff. It'll be fun going through the boxes."

Brendan half-lifted and half-pulled the boxes into the floor area. "These are heavy." He yanked some flaps open.

"Still looking for treasure?"

"Very funny. I bet I'd remember some of this stuff from when I was kid. If you want, I'll help you empty the boxes."

"No need. You do a lot for Wynnedower already—repairs and caretaking and all. You probably know as much about the house as anyone."

"Hard not to. It's the local 'elephant in the room.' Is that the expression? My father's an electrician and my grandfather was a carpenter. When he was a kid, he did some work here for Mr. Wynne. Or rather, gramps was a kid and sort of an apprentice or helper to his dad."

"Which Mr. Wynne?"

"Old man Griffin. I heard stories about him. Some people are bigger than life. You know what I mean? Plus, the house is well-known around here, and we lived just down the road."

"Like David Kilmer."

Brendan gave her a funny look. "Why'd you mention him?"

She brushed a cobweb away from her face, thinking. She hadn't intended to mention

Kilmer. His name had just popped out. "No reason. I met him one day when I was outside. He said he lived nearby."

"He knows better than to come around here. Did you tell Jack?"

"No." She shook her head. She waited for him to ask 'why?' but he didn't.

"Good thing. I wouldn't mention it. You'll get him worked up over nothing."

His approval didn't comfort her. Instead, it made her feel silly and immature. She changed the subject. "Did your grandfather help build the house?"

"No. It was built before he came along. He did carpentry work. Kind of hush-hush. He'd never say much about it."

"Bigger than life tales and a famous house. Maybe that's what gave you a taste for treasure hunting."

"That was just being a kid." He shook his head. "But if you run into any secret rooms or passages, let me know."

Rachel knelt and peeked into one of the boxes Brendan had opened. "Ah, here we go. Now this is treasure."

Brendan was immediately on the floor beside her. "What?"

She held up a vase. "See this green glass? I need to look this up. I know it has a special name."

"Yeah. Dust magnet."

"I guess treasure is in the eye of the beholder."

****

Early the next morning, Rachel unlocked the attic door and ascended the stairs. Business as usual. When she switched on the light, she saw a visitor.

Helene had pulled back some of the sheeting. Seated on a striped settee, looking a lot like a shopper resting in a furniture store living room, she waited. Helene's dress, hair and skin were fair and picked up the nearby light, seeming to absorb it and glow with a faint luminescence.

Helene had sought her out—had accepted her invitation?

Speaking almost in a whisper, Rachel asked, "May I sit with you?"

Helene nodded, but kept her eyes averted.

How old was she? Jack was in his late thirties. Helene had to be close to that. Probably only a couple of years older than she was.

Rachel joined her on the settee. "I'm glad you came to visit me."

Again, that soft nod, but almost no eye contact. Her dress had a delicately smocked bodice, and tiny buttons glinted with reflected light. The skirt was longish, reaching halfway down her shins. Her feet were bare.

While Rachel was considering what to do next, Helene smiled at the floor, stood and walked down a furniture aisle to the attic door, the one that led to her side.

The light patter of her going-away footsteps,

not much more than the wispy sound of flesh against wood, made Rachel think of fairies and elves.

She got up and drew the sheeting back over the furniture. At first, it was hard to shake the surreal feel of Helene's visit. It felt significant despite the lack of conversation.

Soon Rachel was back at work, tweaking the inventory and adding more detail. In a dim area between the back wall and a massive dining room sidebar, she found a large black piece of cardboard. No, not cardboard. A portfolio. About three by four feet.

She slid it out and carried it to where the overhead light shone more strongly, untied the ribbon that held it closed and opened it wide, balancing it across the sheeted furniture.

Tissue papers, cracked and brittle, were front and back of a poster. The condition was pristine but fragile, and she didn't touch it. It might be a collector's item. No doubt it was connected to old Griffin Wynne's activities, but it was also ironic to find it at this time, given Jack's present activities.

Rachel appreciated a well-balanced, tidy fate.

The lettering read, "International Exhibition of Modern Art." The date was 1913, and the exhibition had been held in New York in an Armory. News clippings peeked out from under a flap. Rachel closed the portfolio carefully and re-tied the ribbon.

She could hardly wait to tell Jack what she'd

found. Should she mention his sister's visit, too? About that, she felt reluctant. The visit felt private between the two of them, something for her and Helene, at least, for the time being.

That night, awake in bed and ready to drift off, she heard raindrops hitting the roof. The light, dancing patter made her think of Helene.

Suddenly the patter changed to a deluge. Lightning lit the room, and thunder rumbled right on top of it.

Now, that was Jack all over.

Chapter Eighteen

The next day, Rachel stayed in the attic later than usual. The weather system that brought the rain had swept in with cooler air and she was making good use of the break in the heat.

On her hands and knees, half-under a dust shroud and searching for her lost pencil, a noise stopped her. She took a quick peek. Helene or Jack? No one was in sight. Only mounds of sheet-covered furniture. Jack was in the house, of course, but he usually stomped, except for those times early on when he was getting used to her being around and thought he was sneaking up on intruders.

Was it her imagination? If so, then why did goose bumps rise on her arms and why did she stay in hiding?

Because her brain stem tingled, and she paid attention.

A creak. A bump. Not her imagination, then. Someone was here. Why didn't they call out? Why didn't she?

Carefully, Rachel maneuvered her body under a sheet until she was hidden beneath the body of a high sofa. Dark, awkward pathways twisted between chair legs and around low aprons on bureaus, so she didn't try to go further.

Not Jack. Jack would know she was here

somewhere and would have bellowed as he usually did. The happier Jack was, the louder he was.

A nearer noise. Heat rushed up her chest, neck and face like a sudden fever.

She held her breath. Dust tickled her nose. A speck of it caught in her throat.

No coughing. Rachel squeezed her eyes shut. *No sneezing.*

Not Helene. Back on that first day when she'd been trapped in Jeremy's room, someone had paused outside the door. That had been Helene, she was sure of it. But this wasn't. What about those looters and intruders Jack was always warning about? Could this be one of them?

The rubber toe of a large sneaker pushed under the draped sheet only inches from her arm. Sweat broke out around her hairline. She was paralyzed by a fear she didn't understand.

No one had reason to harm her. Someone was merely looking for something. She should call out. She lifted her face, trying to breathe without making noise. She'd look foolish if she spoke now, but this was ridiculous. Still, she stayed low and quiet.

The shoe moved on.

She heard the wooden squeak of a step. Something brushed against the furniture drapes. The intruder was moving away, hopefully toward the stairs.

She detached her fingers from their death grip on a chair leg. Foolish, that's how she felt.

Probably, the man hadn't even known she was here.

The light went out.

She stopped breathing.

No more creaks. Was he waiting, thinking the dark would flush her out?

She held back, but heard nothing more. Cautiously, she put her head out, then her shoulders, and tried to wrench herself around soundlessly. Finally, out from under the furniture and in the aisle, she trembled. There was no choice. She had to turn the light back on.

Heart pounding, she crawled until she was near the overhead light, then stood and grabbed for the string. She pulled it, prepared to defend herself immediately.

No one.

Someone had come upstairs and, not finding her, had turned off the light before leaving? How tidy. Why hadn't he called out?

David Kilmer?

Her stomach flipped. She gripped a chair back so hard her fingers hurt.

Why not? He was a strange character.

But in the house?

Who else?

She moved softly but quickly to the stairs.

No one lurked in the stairway or hallway.

If Kilmer was the culprit, then he would have one goal in mind: Helene.

A stalker, that's what he was.

Rachel reached the nursery door. She

paused to drag in a calming breath, then knocked. Could he have gotten inside Helene's rooms?

She whispered, "Helene?"

The wood was rough against her cheek as she pressed her ear to it, straining to hear. Was Helene in danger?

Was she, Rachel, over-reacting?

The subtle groan of the stair treads from the main staircase warned her, but not quickly enough for her to move away. That's how Jack came upon her knocking on his sister's door after he'd been very clear about leaving her alone.

He glowered. Dark emotion transformed his face back to the rude, abrasive bully she'd first met. She didn't feel anger in return, but bereft, as if she'd lost something precious. Guilt, too. Not for this, but because she deserved to feel guilty for so much more.

"I asked you to leave her alone. How complicated was that, that you couldn't respect such a simple request? I answered your questions, I invited you to remain in my home, not only as a guest, but out of respect for your wishes, I arranged employment. You wanted a place to stay while you waited for your brother." His face was a rich maroon. "But you couldn't respect my request about my sister."

Of course, he was angry; he didn't know that Helene had already reached out to her. She could explain. "You might be surprised, but your sister makes decisions. She decided to–"

"My sister has made her decision, with my full support, which is more than I can say for you and your brother."

He moved as he talked, walking quickly down the stairs. She'd been judged and dismissed. She followed him.

"Jack, please wait. Let me explain."

He stopped abruptly. "It's time for you to leave."

"But…but–" she stammered. "What about the inventory? What about your trip?"

"I apologize for making it your concern."

His sudden calm, the regret in his voice, alarmed her more than his anger had.

"I did lean on you. I'm sorry for that." He walked back up a few steps. "I didn't do you any favor by letting you wait here for your brother. My mistake. Let him live his own life."

He turned and was gone. He left her on the stair landing, abandoned, embarrassed and ashamed for feeling that way. What had become of her independent life? When had she ever needed anyone except Jeremy?

If she did as Jack ordered, she was going back to it—to that self-sufficient, but lonely life.

Back to Baltimore? Really?

Chapter Nineteen

In the end, it was simple. She'd been uninvited.

Rachel threw her suitcase on the bed. She stomped around her room sweeping her belongings out of the drawers and tossing them onto the bed where they landed helter-skelter.

Ingrate. Hot-headed brute.

She was re-folding the garments she'd scattered across the bedspread when she realized she was missing an important point— the whole reason she'd been knocking on Helene's door.

The intruder.

Not only should she tell Jack about the intruder in the attic but also about David Kilmer, even if the delay made her look bad. She could hardly damage Jack's opinion of her more than she already had.

Half-hearted packing finished, Rachel zipped the suitcase and set it on the floor. She could manage it down the stairs, but before she left Wynnedower she had a few things to tell Mr. Jack Wynne. He was going to listen whether he wanted to hear it or not.

He was in the dining room, but he wasn't painting. The easel was turned away. The brush lay idle on the palette alongside the drying paints. Jack was staring toward the far windows, away from the gardens, across the green expanse of lawn which stretched to the edge of the woods. His arms were crossed and his shoulders appeared slightly hunched. His painting smock was on the floor where it lay entangled with the disarranged drop cloth.

Regret tugged at her heart. "Jack," she whispered.

His arms uncrossed. One hand went to his thigh, the other combed roughly through his hair. Without turning, he asked, "Are you still here?"

"It took me a few minutes to pack." Whispers were gone. Her temper tried to hijack her voice. It didn't quite succeed because sadness outweighed it. "You didn't expect me to leave my belongings behind, did you?"

He stood and faced her. Despite his rigid posture, his voice was soft and polite, as if to a stranger. "No. I'll carry your suitcase down."

"I can manage my suitcase. I wanted to thank you for helping me out when I needed it and there's something I need to tell you before I leave."

Beyond the three walls of windows the sun was setting in a final blaze of gold. It cast the distant trees into dark silhouette. The sunset touched Jack's hair and brushed his shoulders. It passed him with the speed of light and warmed her face with its last rays. Jack followed in its wake, crossing the room.

Rachel waited, paralyzed by the swift change in Jack's mood. As he moved toward her, she stood her ground. His eyes pulled her in, then left her, drawn to a point behind her.

May said, "Mr. Wynne, I need you. Something's wrong with Miss Helene."

Jack touched Rachel's shoulders. "Don't leave," he ordered, and followed May.

Stunned, she didn't move, and in the waning light outside she saw a dark figure running across the lawn into the black area of trees.

She walked into the central hall. She paused.

The air felt different. A gentle current brushed her face.

Rachel ran through the central hall, past the library, through the vestibule and into the conservatory. The cardboard patch lay on the floor. She stopped and turned slowly back toward the French doors. Wide open. An unlikely oversight in this house.

Rachel shoved the cardboard back into its spot, flipped the door lock closed and vowed to return with the appropriate key to lock the French doors, but first she had to get upstairs.

The nursery door was open, and voices drifted through to the hallway. The room was empty. The trio was in the next room, and that door was also partway open.

This room was furnished with comfy furniture, a flowered overstuffed chair, a rocker with a ruffled padded seat cushion, and a table covered with a cross-stitched cloth. Framed family photos hung on the wall. A row of dolls sat on a shelf. These were quick impressions of the room as she moved through it directly to the next.

Helene was sitting on her bed. Jack and May blocked most of Rachel's view.

Jack said, "What upset you? You need to tell me."

Helene wrung her hands while casting repeated glances at the window.

"Jack, I think I know."

"How could you?" He turned to face Rachel. His expression was as guarded his voice.

"I met David Kilmer."

Everything stopped. She took the next step.

"He's been here on Wynnedower property. Helene may have seen him."

May gasped.

Facing Helene, Jack asked, "Did you see David Kilmer?"

Helene did nothing for a very long moment, then nodded at Jack. She placed her pale hand on his cheek and nodded again.

"I didn't know, but now that I do, I'll make sure he goes away, that he stays away from here. Do you believe me?"

"Yes." It was a thin sound. She reached her arms up and put them around his neck, laying her cheek against his chest.

"Feel better now?"

She nodded.

"May will stay here with you. I'm sorry Kilmer bothered you tonight."

Helene frowned and started to shake her head, but before Rachel could puzzle it out,

Jack had ushered the two of them smoothly from the room. If Helene had worries, she'd have to share them with May.

"Come with me," Jack said.

He moved fast. She slowed. No need to rush only to be yelled at again. To be fair, her fate was her own fault, but she wasn't a Ping-Pong ball subject to his whims.

She came to a halt in the central hall. "Jack, stop."

He did.

"I'm sorry. I should've told you about David Kilmer before. I told him to go away, that if he didn't I *would* tell you. But then other things happened, and I didn't. I just didn't."

"How did you meet him?"

"He came to me soon after I arrived here. He claimed to be Jeremy's friend, but all he really wanted was to know where Helene was. He said he wanted to know she was safe, and he'd go away."

"And you told him."

"I told him to go away and stay away, and that's all. When I realized Helene was actually here, I got worried. I was checking on her earlier today when...well, when...you know. You came along."

"Checking on her?"

"Something happened in the attic. Someone was up there with me."

Jack shook his head, impatience in the quick movement. "Someone? Not Helene or May?"

"No. I think someone was...." Saying it aloud

made it sound silly.

"Did you see someone?"

"Not exactly. Part of a shoe, that's all. I hid."

"You hid." He frowned.

"Must you repeat what I say?"

Jack stared at her, examining her face and causing her heart to race.

"So, you were concerned because something happened in the attic and you went to check on Helene because David Kilmer has been coming around looking for her."

"Yes, that's it exactly." He made her actions sound reasonable. She felt the worst of the tension leave her.

"Alright. Come with me."

"Escorting me from the premises?" Rachel blinked back tears. "You don't trust me to leave on my own?"

"I don't want you to leave. Come with me."

He no longer seemed angry. Which made her angry.

"Wait a minute. A short time ago you were kicking me out. Now you're not? It's too much for me. I need an explanation."

He took a breath. "Earlier, I thought you were satisfying your curiosity at my sister's expense."

Rachel bit her lip. She knew he expected her to explode. She wouldn't.

He brushed his hair back from his forehead with one striking gesture. "I understand now. Angry? No, I'm not angry anymore. I don't understand why you kept Kilmer a secret. Then again, you didn't know me any better than you knew Kilmer. You didn't know you were being used."

True, she hadn't known at first, but she'd figured it out pretty quickly. She bit her lip.

"Satisfied? Don't keep secrets from me about things that concern me, my family, or Wynnedower, okay?" He took silence for assent. "Good. Then come with me."

He led the way to his quarters. He pulled a cardboard box out of a morass of jumbled books and stuff in the corner. He put the box on his desk and lifted out some black frames. Old and chipped, they were similar to the kind used to frame certificates and office awards.

"See?"

She accepted one of the frames from him. It was a group photo of several men in suits and a woman. The woman's mode of dress fixed the timeframe for Rachel. Her skirt was long, and the fabric was draped with no crinoline. She wore a shirtwaist. Her hair was piled on top of her head. The men were arrayed along the stairs in various poses, even lounging, certainly nothing stiff as one might see in formal antique photos. There was an air of noblesse oblige to the photo that made her think of long ago when the rich could afford to flirt with unconventional lifestyles and dally with new ideas. She tore her attention away from it.

"Jack, what about David Kilmer?"

"I don't know. I have to think about it." He shook his head. "But not right now."

"You aren't angry?"

"Angry? At Kilmer, yes. Not at you."

"Oh." She couldn't help smiling. She hid her expression by looking down at the framed photograph.

Jack pointed a finger, touching the glass. "The man in the middle, with the goatee, is my great-grandfather."

"The others?" She turned it over. Names were scribbled on the back in a tall, looping hand. "Is this correct?"

"What?"

She pointed to the names, faded and scribbled. "These. I can barely decipher them, but is that...Sloan? Kuhn? Those names are familiar. I'm going to research them and see if I can tie the names up with the faces."

Her brain was galloping. She was positive she recognized those names. This could be the heart of his renovation, of marketing Wynnedower.

Griffin Wynne—artist and patron of the arts—the poster from the 1913 Armory Show she'd found in the attic—tales of visiting artists—the photographic proof of high times at Wynnedower. There was value to be mined here. Perhaps they could play on the myth of the hidden treasure? Why not? Slogans bloomed in her head. *Myth and History and Treasure. Or maybe Myth, Mystique and Roaring High Times.....*

She took the next framed photograph from his hands. It showed women in Greek togas—

very short ones. Ivy was wrapped around their heads, and they were smiling and posing. She picked up another one.

"Who's in this photo?" Excited, she tapped her finger on the glass. "Oh, goodness, Jack. I don't know who's standing next to Griffin, but this is your stairway, Wynnedower's staircase, and that's a Manet on the wall behind them."

Jack sat on the arm of his sofa. "When I found the photos, it brought back memories. Things I'd forgotten. I remember these from the library. They hung in there when I was a kid. I knew you'd get a kick out of them, but then I found you upstairs at Helene's door. You should've come directly to me. You know that, right?"

She sat the framed photos down on his desk. It was difficult to come back to an awkward topic, but important.

"He told me that he and Helene fell in love and you paid him to go away."

Jack checked out the view, now pitch dark, before answering. "He was using my sister."

"He said he loved her. If he was using her, then for what? What did he hope to gain?"

"A fortune that no longer existed? Maybe this house?" He looked at the ceiling molding, then around the room. "Something this house represented to him, maybe." He added softly, "He grew up not far from here. As a child he came with his grandfather to do work around here. He was about the same age as Helene, a little younger than me. He wanted to be one of us. He wasn't one of us. He wanted a way in, maybe."

He shrugged. "More likely, he wanted the wealth that didn't exist. Hasn't existed since old Griffin Wynne partied hearty with his artist buddies and threw his fortune into their various schemes and dreams."

Had Kilmer mentioned growing up in the area? Knowing Jack and Helene as children? She didn't think he had…or maybe it was just a lack of specifics and she'd assumed. Had he done that deliberately? No matter, Jack had taken care of him before and would again.

"One more thing. After you and May went up to Helene, I felt a draft and realized the French doors to the conservatory were open and the cardboard patch in the exterior door was on the floor."

He stared. "That's how he got in?"

"He. Or someone else. We need to get that pane fixed. It's glass, so it's no more than a psychological barrier, but better than cardboard. We also need a locksmith to put a better lock on the door."

He nodded. "A glazier and a locksmith. That's beyond Brendan's skill. Can you arrange it?"

"I can." Now they could move on to more important things. "Jack. You know I have a weird kind of brain, right?" She didn't wait for an answer. "This is none of my business, except you did invite me in and pay me to apply my skills to this house and its contents, so, as you said earlier, you did make it my business? I'm not a marketer, not a business person in any sense. I count things and collect extraneous information along the way. I can't help it."

"Get it over with. I think you drag out explanations and questions to torture me into doing what you want."

She did a quick check of his face. He was smiling. She picked up one of the framed photos and turned it to face him. "This is the answer."

Confusion clouded his face. He shook his head. "To what?"

"To the renovation question."

"The renovation or sale question?"

"If you move forward with the renovation, yes. If you decide to sell, a certain amount of renovation, plus this." She waved the photo. "This could only help the price. That is, unless you sell to someone who only wants to knock it down for an office or a subdivision."

Visions filled her head. She paced as she explained. "The concept of the birth of modern art, the mystique of the bohemian lifestyle, the gilded age into the roaring twenties, there's so much we can go with. Build upon. It's real. It really happened here." She closed her eyes and dramatically drew in a deep breath. "It's still in the air. The atmosphere here is steeped in it. And what about you? You're having your own exhibition."

"A small gallery showing."

"In New York City. Don't downplay it."

He shoved his hands in his pockets as he paced slowly with short steps, thinking, absorbed. Finally he stopped and shook his head, perhaps hoping to dislodge thoughts he wasn't ready to deal with right now. On the other hand, he hadn't laughed at her or gotten angry.

She spoke softly. "It might be interesting to get some good copies of some of the paintings that were at the Armory show. It was a seminal event and remembered in a lot of quarters. In fact, someone at the University of Virginia did a big thing about it on the anniversary of the exhibition. It's on the Web. I found it when I was preparing for the interview with Mr. Ballew. I did a lot of surfing and reading, brushing up for the interview."

Jack said, "Maybe replicas, maybe some biographical stuff of some of the artists, reflected in the public rooms and in the guest rooms. Wait." He held up his hand as if directing traffic, as if he could thereby direct their thoughts.

"This deserves thought and I don't have time. I don't have time to deal with Kilmer either, but I have to make time for that, for Helene's sake." He put the framed photos back into the top of the box.

"Wait," Rachel echoed. "I understand you can't be side-tracked right now, but do you mind if I keep the photos in my room? For inspiration? I'll have ideas for you when you return from New York."

He smiled. She read appreciation in his eyes. Admiration. Well, that was probably pushing it too far. Attraction? Maybe, but it and everything else came in third or later for Jack. Everything stacked up behind Helene and his painting. And Wynnedower.

She understood. They both had responsibilities. For her, everything had come second to Jeremy.

A shiver took her. To consider shoving Jeremy out of the top priority spot felt like anticipating a gravitational shift of the poles. Why? Because then her choices would all be about herself and accountable to her, with no 'Jeremy' in the equation.

Jack handed her the photographs. "What's wrong?"

"I was thinking about my brother." She traced the circumference of one frame with a finger. "I have to let him go. To live his life, I mean. But it's so sudden. One day he was a child and our worlds revolved around each other. Everything I've ever done was for him or because of him. I've spent my life worrying and planning for him. Now my worry is what happened to change him so suddenly? Has he gotten in with the wrong people? I don't know."

"Was it sudden? Really?"

"He talked about wanting to be independent." She shook her head. "But he's all set to go back to college to get his advanced degree—I don't want him to throw it away because he's suddenly gotten touchy about taking money from me or found the wrong crowd or...."

"Or the wrong woman?"

He made it sound like jealousy.

"I want the best for him. As you do for Helene."

The conversational atmosphere switched off.

Jack said, "I've got to get back to work." He left.

Why did she bother with him?

He came back and stuck his head through the open doorway. "Thanks, Rachel." And then he was gone again.

She put the frames back in the box, turned off the light and closed the door to his quarters. While carrying the box up the stairs, she admitted once and for all that she wanted to stay. It wasn't about waiting for Jeremy or about saving money or finishing a job.

She wanted to stay at Wynnedower. Jack and Helene needed her.

Chapter Twenty

"Rachel?"

Startled, she jumped and the measuring tape snapped back into its case.

"Sorry. I scared you."

It was the tone of his voice that scared her and his expression. Subdued, almost depressed.

"Not scared. I was focused, checking the measurements the carpenter made." She rattled on, watching his face. "Not that I don't trust him, but the numbers didn't line up with the other estimates."

"I've seen some of them coming by. I appreciate your efforts. May mentioned it, too."

"Should I translate that as 'complained'?" She tried to keep it light. It had been a short two days since their exciting conversation about art and ideas for marketing Wynnedower. Just today a carpenter and a general contractor had come by, so eager to get inside the mansion that they were practically drooling. "This is what you wanted, right?"

"I was thinking about all of the work you're putting into this. The decision about this place is still open, you know."

She echoed, "Of course." Inside, a patch of emotional quicksand stirred, but this wasn't the time to argue the fate of Wynnedower. "As a matter of fact, I've contacted a general contractor who specializes in restoration. That might be more expensive, but still the best way to go."

His expression didn't change. She asked, "Are you okay, Jack?"

He took the measuring tape from her hands, pulled and snapped the thin metal strip of inches and feet. "Kilmer will stay away. I spoke to him, to the police, and my attorney is obtaining a restraining order."

"A restraining order. The police?"

"He leaves me no choice. He avoided me because he knew he was unwelcome, but he continues coming onto Wynnedower property."

"Jack, this sounds more serious than I knew. He is a nuisance, a jerk. But the police and the courts?"

"There may be more to him than you realize. You were sufficiently scared to hide from him in the attic and then to try to warn Helene. He says that wasn't him. That he was out of town. But who else? Had to be him."

"My instinct told me something was wrong with him. I thought it was my lack of patience with his creepiness." Goosebumps popped up on her arms. She rubbed her skin briskly. "Will the police and a restraining order keep him away?"

He handed the tape measure back to her and walked off.

Once again, she was left hanging.

Jack, the great communicator.

Frustrated, she snapped the measuring tape herself and yelped when it pinched her finger.

****

He didn't ask for additional sittings. Rachel continued the overall inventory, including building the list of work needed. She hadn't yet attempted the let's-get-this-business-up-and-running list, but it all churned exhaustively through her mind.

In the days following Helene's episode, Rachel saw her more often, usually from the corner of her eye or lingering nearby.

Rachel carried the portfolio case down from the attic. She brushed off the thin layer of white dust and untied the black ribbon. She sneezed, and then opened the case to get another look at the poster. The colors were strong and the lettering was clear. She'd do her part to preserve it by keeping her hands off of it. She closed the portfolio, re-tied the ribbon and slid the portfolio between the dresser and the wall, much as it had been upstairs, but now in her room.

Her brain was percolating about the Armory Exhibit theme. Everywhere she went in the house she saw possibilities. For instance, the clothing in the attic was perfect within a decade or two of the time period, and she hadn't even seen most of it. They could display the clothing, perhaps on mannequins, a museum effect—a wax museum? But not overdone, not brassy. And there were likely other textiles. They could be framed or used as wall hangings. The possibilities went on and on.

Inside her head, Rachel saw an image of herself, gowned in silk and lace, with the green peacock shawl draped in careless folds from her arms. She stood on the stairs like the woman in the photo.

She itched to share her ideas with Jack, but the dining room doors stayed firmly shut.

"Miss Sevier?"

May stood in the doorway to the conservatory. "I have an appointment and Mr. Wynne is busy. Would you mind taking Miss Helene's tray to her?"

To say she was surprised was to understate her reaction. Rachel set her papers aside immediately. It was a relief to no longer pretend she didn't know about Helene. At Wynnedower, everyone seemed to know everything— everyone except her—and it was good to finally be 'in the know.'

"I'll be happy to, Mrs. Sellers. Is her meal ready now?"

She shuffled her papers into a neat stack and placed them in the folder. Leaving the pen, pencil and eraser neatly aligned on top of the folder, she followed May and her blue peony dress. The large peonies undulated in a slow rolling motion as May walked.

They reached the kitchen, and she pointed to a tray covered by a white cloth.

"She may want you to sit and keep her company. Perhaps not. She'll let you know."

"Does she ever come down to eat?"

Red suffused May's face. Her round cheeks darkened to an alarming purple. "No, Ma'am, she most certainly does not." She stepped quickly over to the counter and straightened the already straight cloth. "Perhaps I should take this to her after all."

"You can trust me, Mrs. Sellers. I asked a question, that's all. How else am I to know what's customary?"

"Well, I suppose. She'll already be waiting for her meal. This is her main meal. She only takes a light snack in the evening. I'll be back before then." She plucked her sweater from the back of a kitchen chair. "Miss Sevier, exactly how much longer will you be at Wynnedower?"

"Time will tell." Rachel smiled sweetly and maneuvered around her. "Excuse me."

Would she need magic words to induce Helene to open her door? She didn't have the key, and Helene hadn't responded to her knock before, but maybe it would be different this time. After all, she had her food.

"Helene?" She leaned closer to the door. "It's Rachel. Mrs. Sellers had to go somewhere, so I have your lunch."

Little scuffling noises came from the far side. The lock made a gentle thunk as the key turned, followed by the opening of the door. Helene stepped back quickly, but she stayed and didn't retreat into the next room. Rachel kept her eyes averted. In the animal kingdom that was the trick, right? No direct eye contact.

Non-threatening. She tried to keep her eyes on the tray and the table as she set up Helene's meal. Helene wore a filmy lavender garment—ultra feminine.

Done, Rachel turned toward the door.

Helene whispered, "Stay?"

Rachel smiled. It was what she'd hoped for. She sat on the flowered couch. Helene floated the napkin onto her lap. Finally, she looked directly at Rachel, and her lips curved in a slight, shy smile. The light filtered through a nearby window laying bands of light across her. Ethereal.

The same quality Kilmer had mentioned? It shook her to think of him.

There wasn't a piece of pasta in sight. A thick slice of meatloaf, a mash-up of potatoes with gravy, and green beans filled the plate. Unexotic and hearty. Had she expected Helene to dine on watercress and cucumber sandwiches?

"How are you, Helene? The meatloaf smells good."

A nod and a smile was the only answer. Helene ate with enthusiasm.

"Have you seen your brother's paintings?"

Again, a nod as she nibbled on the green beans. She held them like pretzels. Her expression had become lively and there was a glint in her eye that suggested she might actually express an opinion. Certainly, there was intelligence in her light blue gaze.

"He's very talented." Rachel cast about in

her brain for something more interesting to say. "I wore the dress you left on my bed." After a few minutes of silence, she tried again. "I'm sorry David Kilmer scared you the other night."

Helene tilted her head and looked puzzled.

"I mean, when he broke into the house a few days ago?"

Helene's eyes opened wide and she breathed the words, "Did he?" She took the napkin from her lap, carefully laid it over the used dishes on the tray, and pushed the table aside. Rachel stood, not sure what to expect. Without a word or wave, Helene went into the next room and shut the door.

Rachel closed the hallway door behind her. She didn't lock it because then the key would be on the wrong side, and Helene would be locked in versus locking the world out. Rachel carried the tray down to the kitchen, thinking about their strange interlude as she rinsed the dishes and set them in the sink for later, for Madame May.

****

She'd been trying to sketch a rough layout of the house, wanting to work some of her ideas into the reality of the house, but this place was such a maze of rooms that it was difficult to make comprehensive drawings that made sense.

Wynnedower needed to pay for itself. Jack's words.

For the umpteenth time she'd explained to a contractor that she was taking estimates for the home's owner—who was not her. For the umpteenth time, the contractor had looked at her, wanting to know who controlled the purse strings—again, not her.

This long-legged man in saggy jeans, t-shirt and a baseball cap yanked the paper from his clipboard. "Are you his wife? No? You're his assistant? Like a personal assistant?"

He did a slow, creepy scan of her legs, moved upward, stopping somewhere south of her face. She considered slamming her clipboard into his face, but opted for a higher road.

"More like a general assistant." She scanned the estimate and asked a few questions for clarification. After all, by now she was getting a good feel for ballpark, for too high or too low or for what was being omitted or glossed over.

"I could use an assistant like you. Anytime you want to change jobs, give me a call."

"Not likely, Mr.–" She scanned the paperwork as if searching for his insignificant name. "I won't call you for any reason whatsoever; however, the owner will contact you if he's interested in your estimate."

After Joe or Bob or Hal or whatever this one's name was, left, Rachel went to the dining room door and pounded on the wood. Enough was enough.

"Jack?"

"Coming."

"Jack, it's time to go through these. Or at

least take a look at them with me so I'll know I'm on the right track."

"But—"

"Jack, what's the point in painting right up until you leave? Are you really going to exhibit wet paint?"

He opened the doors. "No. The paintings for the show are already at the gallery."

"Your hair is crazy wild, and you're dressed almost as badly as the day we first met. What's your plan for that? You're leaving in two days, right?"

"Alright, alright."

She grabbed his sleeve and pulled him toward the kitchen. "You have to eat. You sit and go through this stack of papers. I don't expect decisions, but you need to understand what I've done, or how will you manage when you return?"

"How will I....?"

"When I leave after you get back." She hoped the sudden twist in her stomach didn't show on her face. Would he perceive this as a dare or a challenge? She hadn't intended it that way.

"You won't have to leave immediately, right? We have to take time to.... You know, what do you call it?"

"Transition?"

"Yes, you have to transition all of this to me. I can't remember all of it now." He leaned toward her, lowering his voice. "Right? You'll stay for a while?"

She wanted to say yes, but reality was reality. She had a huge imagination, but her dreams had never survived reality. "Jack. I've already been here a while. I don't want to lose my job at Stillman Inventory."

"Your first plan was better. Get a new job. You have more to offer than counting."

She shoved the clipboard and papers back at him. For some reason, his words angered her. Really ticked her off.

"Clean your brushes and pick up the paint tubes. It's time to pack up and move out of the dining room."

The shift in subject silenced him for the moment.

"If you need a studio, the conservatory is a better location. If you're going to stay here indefinitely, then I recommend you build a proper studio instead of taking up space in what should be the guest areas."

She turned to leave the kitchen, then spun back around on her heel. "Also, while you're gone, I plan to encourage Helene to come out and take an active interest in the project. Encourage only. I won't force anything. I want you to know so you won't think I'm going behind your back."

"She won't."

"We'll see. Now, that you've sent Kilmer on his way, it's safe. We'll keep things locked up properly and we won't take any chances."

He didn't answer.

"No objections? Trust my judgment on this.

Helene needs more than what she's getting in those rooms. If she didn't, she wouldn't be roaming at night, and now, during the day, too."

He waved his hands as if wanting to make a point, but no words came out. Finally, his movements stilled. "Be careful of her, and for her. I don't think it's fair to put this responsibility on you, but if you're signing up for it, then so be it. Remember, this is the way she is. It isn't a choice or trauma. She's always been like this to some degree, but anything that worries her adds to it. Cumulative, I guess. If she's pushed too far...well, if she's pushed too far, she'll retreat back to her rooms."

"Which is where she already is." She touched his arm. "I promise I'll be careful."

"Rachel, you can invite her out of her rooms, but don't get her involved in plans for restoration. If I decide to sell Wynnedower, I don't want it to hurt her more than it would already."

His hand slid over hers. She tried not to read anything into it. Dreaming had tripped her up in life more than once. Not dreaming. Fantasizing. Pretending something was going to be different instead of accepting it 'as is.'

She'd spent years taking care of herself and Jeremy and planning their future only to awaken one day and discover that, no matter how well-intentioned and how valuable her actions were, the motivation had grown up and wanted to be on his own. Even Aunt Eunice.... She tried to help Eunice, too, in the later years, but no matter how many times Eunice said she was thankful for Rachel's help, Rachel knew her aunt considered her bossy and high-handed.

Naturally a man like Jack would be interesting to a bossy wallflower bookworm inventory specialist. But she'd done a solid job of not imagining more in the relationship than there actually was. In fact, and in reality, Jack was far, far away from what a reasonable woman would consider good sweetheart material.

****

Tracing the broken brick paths with her feet, visualizing the garden, resting on the concrete bench and evaluating the view…while the path at her back, May's path, promised a mystery and tantalized as it vanished into the forest. Not just a mystery about May. What about the dark figure she'd seen the evening of Helene's distress? Whoever had gotten in…. Kilmer, right?

No one had actually seen him well enough to identify him except Helene, right? And she seemed vague about it.

Jack was away. May was in the kitchen. Rachel walked beneath the overgrown arbor and headed toward the woods.

The path was wide between the tall trees, more than sufficient for a car to pass. It didn't look like that happened often.

Bird song. Fluttery leaves. The noises were like little snatches of music. Clean air. She breathed deeply, sending thank you thoughts to the trees for their gift of oxygen. She felt like a nature girl despite what Jeremy said about her and the outdoors. A nature girl, but a savvy one. She avoided branches and tall weeds, hoping also to avoid tiny hitchhikers. Problem avoidance was mostly about proper management.

As she walked, the wheel tracks became more obvious. This must have been a wagon path long ago, but it wasn't rutted like the dirt road leading to Wynnedower. Unused. No litter.

She came to a stop. A fork in the path. Now what?

Take Robert Frost's advice? Follow the road less-travelled? But then that wouldn't lead her to May's house, would it?

She was about to move forward when a shoe print caught her eye. Captured like a stamped mold in a slick patch of red mud, the treads had hardened as the print dried. A man-sized print. Heading away from her.

When had it last rained?

The evening before Helene's intruder and the open conservatory door?

Rachel stared at the print, thinking it must surely belong to the figure she'd seen running away. Kilmer? Something bothered her, but she couldn't pin it down. She looked around. The only print she could see was that one captured in clay.

The path curved again, and she saw May's house.

A small, charming house. Trim and neat. A tin roof and wood siding, but painted and solid looking. Not a house for mysteries.

Rachel sat on the trunk of a fallen tree. What had she expected? A haunted house with bats circling above? Wynnedower was far more mysterious, even sinister, in appearance than May's cottage.

It was a civilized clearing in the woods. Bushes and flower beds showed May's activities when she wasn't at Wynnedower. The path, barely a road, continued beyond.

The setting hinted at a May who was pretty basic. Lacking in imagination, certainly, else how could she have spent her days ranging between this trim house and Wynnedower? The car, an older model mid-size something or other, was parked discreetly next to a Crepe Myrtle. Pink blossoms littered the car's roof and hood.

If Wynnedower had a future, it could include May. *Should* include May. Rachel made a mental note to speak to Jack. He might not want Helene involved in renovation plans, but what harm could it do to let May see that Wynnedower had a chance to survive, and that its future could include her, its most devoted supporter?

Her curiosity had seeped away. She stood and brushed the bits of bark from her shorts and started walking back. The distance seemed much shorter returning.

Near where the woods ended, the imposing

wings of the dining room and Jack's quarters loomed toward her.

Wynnedower, from the back, from this distance and despite being neglected, was impressive. The lawn looked lush and green, again from a distance, because the distance disguised the bare patches and weedy invaders.

From this angle, the faint telltale marks of vehicle traffic turned left and followed the edge of the tree line, curved around and passed by Jack's car parked at the east end of the building. Jack's car, Jack's wing, the neglected garden, then the dining room wing.

Beyond the dining room, near the wide wooden doors at the west end of the house, was a pickup truck. A man was doing something to the doors. Must be Brendan because she was pretty sure that was his truck.

She angled across the yard. As she got closer, she could see Brendan was working on the doors. He stood, moved over to the truck and put something in the truck bed. He looked up, saw her and smiled.

"Hey, there."

She stared at the freshly cleared earth at the entrance to the doors. "They'll open now?"

He kicked a tire to dislodge the dirt clinging to his scuffed boot. "They always opened or would have if the key hadn't been lost to the padlock." He lifted the long tool, the bolt cutter, from the truck bed. "Fixed now."

She nodded at the freshly exposed earth.

"The grass blocked it before. It looks neater now."

"Does that bother you?"

"No, well, yes, just thinking about security. Anyone trying to enter this way couldn't be seen from inside the house, except maybe from the dining room. These doors were blocked before, but not now."

Brendan turned to the doors and rattled the shiny new chain looped through the iron door handles. "No worries. I replaced the old rusty hardware with nice new shiny hardware."

Which was a rather pointless remark, she thought. Rust didn't make it weaker and might actually have made the lock harder to open. "I'm heading inside. Do you want me to take the new key to Jack?"

"Nope. He already has it." Brendan leaned against the truck. "You seem preoccupied. I don't think it's only about security."

"Thinking about May."

He nodded toward the woods. "Did you walk back to her house?"

"Yes. Can she drive out some back way?"

"Probably, unless it gets blocked by downed trees or the road gets washed out by the creek—the site of my infamous car jump. May can come and go by the dirt road out back or out this way." He waved at the perimeter of the open area. He flashed his disingenuous smile, but his eyes looked away. "Unless you're planning to chop wood, I can't think why anyone would bother trying the back way."

She was nearly back to the house and thinking about something else entirely when she thought of Brendan's boots and then the rubber toe of the shoe she'd seen in the attic. The wearer supposedly was the same person who'd disappeared into the woods. Kilmer, right? But Kilmer wore loafers, or had every time she'd seen him. His loafers had a smooth sole like Brendan's boots. But the print in the woods showed sneaker treads.

Chapter Twenty-one

Jack preferred to stay in the dining room, painting. Absorbed in his painting, the rest of the world ceased to exist. He didn't think about Wynnedower, about his sister, about the million nagging things that pulled at him, draining his time and energy. And he didn't get caught up in worrying over the coming trip and the showing. Anywhere other than being firmly in place in front of his easel, was nothing more than a landscape of duty and decisions.

Before Rachel.

She was aggravating, but not a drain.

So here he was, instead of painting, he was in the kitchen sharing a meal with her.

He watched as she sat across the table from him, spooning beef stroganoff casserole onto her plate. She looked up, saw him and smiled. He smiled back. He couldn't help himself.

She pushed the casserole dish across to him. "I found some interesting papers in that box."

"What box?"

"The one with the framed photographs?"

"Right. You found what?"

"Papers. Receipts. Amazing receipts. We should frame them."

"What's got you so excited about receipts?" Typical of Rachel to get excited over some slips of paper when the whole world was in turmoil and his own world was full of distractions and he had this art show looming and who knew how that would go...but he liked that she did. She had a way of focusing and shutting out the raucous noise of life.

"They're receipts for paintings. Paintings your great-grandfather must've purchased. Guess what? They name the paintings and the artists. Like Van Gogh. *Cottage Sunflowers*."

"Old news. I told you Griffin spent a small fortune dabbling in his art obsession. Whatever paintings he bought, however valuable, are long gone, sold to pay off debts. Griffin was a dreamer and an idealist whose head was turned by the fame of others."

"It's part of your heritage, Jack. Don't be so dismissive. Griffin wasn't perfect. No one is. I went to the Goochland Library this morning and looked up the paintings online. There is no *Cottage Sunflowers* painting. Lots of Van Gogh sunflowers, but none with that name. Same for the others listed on the receipts."

"So the name was changed. Or wrong. Or Griffin sold it to a private collector who didn't share his inventory."

"But the receipts themselves are like holding a piece of history in one's hands."

"The painting is the only thing that matters. The artist, too, I guess. The rest is just–" Her excitement enlivened him, but it also worried him. He didn't want her to be disappointed, or feel used, or....

"Oh, why do I bother? You really are a humbug, aren't you?"

"No, I'm not, or I would've dumped this place long ago." He scraped the last bits of pasta onto his fork. "But reveling in dusty receipts won't pay the bills."

"Someday, someone might be holding a receipt for one of your paintings in his hands and feeling like he's touching history."

Jack didn't answer. His brain had suddenly stopped and something electric started in his arms and went through his chest. She'd done that. Made it feel real. The possibilities. The future with the possibilities realized. He took a quick look at her face, almost expecting that she was making fun, but no. Her face was flushed; her amber eyes were flashing.

On the edge of a precipice. Where had that thought come from? Change the subject. He said, "I never asked about your parents or even your aunt. We always talk about Wynnedower."

She stared at him blankly.

"You and Jeremy. Did you always live in Baltimore?"

"No. Yes." She shrugged. "We moved there when we went to live with Aunt Eunice, but that was so long ago, and we were so young, that it might as well as been 'always'."

"You said your Aunt wasn't…what did you say? I forget how you phrased it. But she wasn't up to raising kids?"

"She was a gentle lady. Never married or dealt with children. Left to her, we would've spent every waking hour in front of the television. Anything that would keep us quiet and still, might keep us safe."

"Like couch potatoes?"

She laughed, but the humor didn't reflect in her eyes. "She wasn't mean or anything, but it was as if she had no frame of reference for living. Everything was either safe or it wasn't. She didn't want us to play outside because we might get stolen. At the end of each school day, everything we told her either alarmed her or worried her." Rachel clapped her hands to her cheeks in mock drama. "What? Jeremy only got a C on his spelling test? Had I spoken out in class too much and offended the teacher? Did Jeremy have another bruise? Had he hurt someone? Had someone hurt him?" She shook her head. "We'd just lost our parents, yet each day, I felt like Aunt Eunice was going to topple over from a heart attack over something I'd done, or hadn't done."

He tried to keep his face non-committal. "That was a difficult way to live, always having to watch out for landmines."

"She did the best she could, and so did I."

He tried to speak without inflection. "But she got rid of the trunk in the attic."

She sipped her tea before answering. "Again, she meant well. Maybe in addition to physical danger, she was worried that I was holding onto the past." She paused, then added, "I continued going up there anyway, mostly in the fall and spring when the weather was good, just to show…well, just to show her. It was a cozy place to read."

Jack couldn't hold back a short laugh. "Stubborn."

"Takes one to know one." She joined him in the laugh and started to gather the plates.

"With a much younger brother to worry about, I can see why you took on so much responsibility."

"True, but the responsibility was also a blessing. When we lost our parents…without Jeremy, I don't know what would have happened. He gave me purpose, something worth–"

He interrupted with a snort. "Your own life wasn't worth living for? Working for your own dreams?" His voice softened. "Did you ever wonder what it would have been like to be the younger one? The kid sister instead of the responsible one with all of the headaches?"

Chapter Twenty-two

Jack was shut away in his painting studio. Rachel knelt on the bare floor of the library with her notes and other papers spread around. She was hunched over her crude attempt at a floor plan, and wishing for a cushion for her knees.

May appeared in the open doorway. "There's someone here to see you."

"See me?" Another workman for an estimate? "I can't think of any appointments scheduled for today."

"What do you have there?" May leaned over, and her apron nearly brushed the floor. "A drawing of the rooms?"

Rachel remembered she'd resolved to include May. "A poor attempt, I'm afraid. Perhaps we could sit down and go over it together."

"Hmmph." She straightened and put her hands on her lower back. "Your visitor's in the foyer." She walked away.

So much for thoughtfulness.

She stood, found she'd been sitting too long, and shook her legs to get the blood flowing.

"Nice dance."

She stopped. Everything stopped.

"Rachel? I know you're angry. I hope you're still talking to me."

Her body and brain felt split in half. She wanted to yell in rage and also in joy. She spoke, and the word sounded brittle. "Jeremy."

"Sis?" He moved forward, his arms extended as he crossed the room. "I'm sorry I worried you. I thought I'd be back in plenty of time before you arrived."

His blond hair was longish and mussed. Lean as always, he stood tall. His jeans were faded and worn. His shirt was wrinkled.

She asked, "Are you okay?"

"Are you asking because you're going to jump me and pound on me if I say I'm okay? 'Cause you look…well, kind of crazy just now." He stared down at his worn jeans and grimy sneakers and added, "Not that I blame you."

Cajolery? They were way past that. "Don't think you can tease me out of being angry. Do you have any idea how much worry and inconvenience you've caused me and other people? All because…. Why? Why did you run away?"

Judging by his red-rimmed eyes, she suspected he'd come here first, perhaps directly from the airport. The sharpest points of her ire smoothed a bit, but the hurt remained strong.

"Run away? I didn't. I told the management company I was leaving. Moving out."

"They said you didn't give notice."

"Well, I did. I'll straighten that out later. The more important thing is what I didn't do—I didn't tell you." He fidgeted his arms. "This place echoes like crazy and gives me the creeps. I always feel watched in here. Can we go outside? Maybe walk down toward the river?"

"This way." She led him past the library and they paused at the French doors. She unhooked the key ring from her belt loop and, from practice, deftly chose the correct key on the big ring and unlocked them.

Jeremy eyed her strangely. "You seem very comfortable here."

She preceded him into the conservatory and out to the terrace.

"Comfortable? Not really, but it's hardly surprising that I know my way around the place. I've been here a month. Day in, day out."

"Did you get that job you talked about? The one at the museum?"

She shook her head and watched her footing as she stepped down to the grass. "No, it evaporated. I stayed here anyway, waiting for you." *And you all but evaporated from my life, too. After everything I've done.* She stopped that thought.

"You've given up a lot for me, Rachel." He stared down the slope to the river beyond. "I'd give almost anything not to have this conversation with you. The last thing I ever wanted to do was disappoint you."

"That's why you didn't call? Not because you didn't think. You knew I was coming to visit. You were afraid to face me. Is that right?"

"Afraid? Maybe." He stopped and looked at her. "Not afraid of you. Afraid of *hurting* you. I don't want you to regret everything you've done for me. I don't want you to regret your life."

He reached out to touch her shoulder, and she moved away. He followed in silence until she broke it.

"So, no graduate school?"

"No." He stopped at the crest of the hill and dropped down to the grass. "Sis, I walked away from graduation knowing I didn't want to sit in another class for a very long time, if ever. The thought of it—but I didn't know how to tell you. It was what you wanted. What you'd always worked so hard for. I thought, once upon a time, I wanted it, too. How could I—well, it would be like trashing everything you did for me. All those years and all that money." He leaned over and took her hand. "I'm grateful, but I can't live your life and mine at the same time, and I wouldn't hurt you for the world."

But you would for another woman? She banished that thought, too. It was unworthy and unfair. She sat beside him and examined his face.

In his clear, golden eyes and gentle smile, she recognized the same Jeremy she'd cared for, bossed around, worried over, and sacrificed for. Somewhere along the way, things had changed. She put her elbows on her knees and grasped her arms.

"I want you to live your own life, but I don't want you to make mistakes. It's not easy, sometimes it's impossible, to go back and undo regrets—to make it right." She laid her head on her forearms and stared down at the blades of grass.

"Rachel." He drew in a deep breath and exhaled it slowly. "Let me put it his way: there are two scenarios. In number one, I go on to grad school and pass the CPA exam. I get a job and go to work every day and, hopefully, do well and get ahead. Or, in the second scenario, I stop my formal education for a while, maybe forever, and I propose to the woman I love. We take over the outfitting store her dad turned over to her, and live in the Rockies with the fir trees and the aspens. In our spare time, she pursues photography, which she's already pretty successful with, and I get to hang out where the sky is as vivid as a sapphire, the air is crisp and clear, and where I can feel the earth, not pavement beneath my feet."

Sapphire, indeed. *Bah.* Rachel kept her head down, squeezing the moisture back into her eyes, and let the silence draw out. The grass smelled good here, too, and the Virginia sky was a deep and forever blue. But Jeremy was in love. Without the woman he loved, sky was just sky; earth was just dirt.

"Okay." She lifted her head from her arms and stared straight ahead.

"No hard feelings?"

She scooted nearer, and he put his arm around her shoulders. She rested her head against him. Maybe peaceful, mostly spent—a simple surrender to the inevitable.

"Do I get to meet her?" She sniffled.

He pulled her closer in a hug. "Her name is Lia Drake. She's smart and clever like you."

"Flatterer. Only the facts, please."

"Her eyes are green, and her hair is short and white-blonde. She likes hiking and camping."

"You enjoy those things? You never did before."

"I never did them before. You were a great sister-mom, but not a nature or sports gal." He laughed. "Remember when you came to my soccer game? When they wanted to continue playing in the rain, you were outraged. Remember how you held that newspaper over your head, yelled at the ref and got thrown from the field?"

"I embarrassed you."

"Yes, but in retrospect, it's a really funny story."

"Brute." She punched him in the arm. "Have you made a joke of me to your true love?"

"Not possible. There is no one brave enough to cross you. And if that foolhardy person does exist and tried, I would take them apart. Rachel, what about you?"

"Me? I suppose I have to accept your choice. I did what I could. No, I don't mean it like that. We both did the best we could. Even Aunt Eunice." Her tone sounded forlorn, and she didn't want that. "We all did our best after mom and dad died." Rachel stood and brushed the loose grass from her shorts. "No more of that." She waved her hand at a fluttery insect hovering near her ear.

"That's not what I meant. I'm talking about you and your life. You put your dreams off to take care of me. Now what will you do? Please don't go back to that inventory job."

"Don't change the subject. I want to talk about you. Tell me the truth, Jeremy. When you told me you wanted to be independent and manage your own tuition and other expenses, you knew you weren't going back to school. Am I right? You did that so I wouldn't figure out you weren't going back, maybe not until it was too late to do anything about it. Would you have told me the truth then?"

"I didn't intend to wait until now to tell you. I did want it to be face to face. I thought I'd be back sooner. You got here early; I got here late."

"So when do you return to Lia?"

"Soon. When I believe you're okay. Why are you hiding away here in this big old house? Not waiting for me, I hope?"

She wrapped her arm in his. "Well, I had that vacation time I needed to use, and this is quite a tourist destination. Sun and fun at Wynnedower–On-The-James."

"Seriously."

"I was waiting for you, but after I knew you were okay, I could've gone home, although I did still have hope of that museum job at the time. I got involved with the house and with Jack."

"Jack? Involved?"

"Wynne. The owner. Your former employer

whom you left in a lurch? He had to return to Wynnedower sooner than planned because you left. I met him when I came looking for you."

"You say that a bit too casually. You forget how well I know you, Sis."

"That so? Then you should know I'm not a monster, and you should've been more up front with me." They walked back up to the terrace. "Speaking of monsters…well, not a monster…but I met your friend, David Kilmer."

"David…?"

"Yes, Kilmer." She sat on the brick wall. "You can't have forgotten him. He's memorable in his own way. He said he was a friend of yours. Well, sort of a friend."

Jeremy settled on the wall next to her.

"Kilmer? You mean the guy who came around with that crazy story about a lost love? I told him to get lost."

"He wasn't at least an acquaintance? He talked as if you two were friendly."

Jeremy snorted. "Not likely."

"Then I'm confused."

"Rachel, why would he tell you anything anyway? Is he still coming around here? Is he bothering you?" Jeremy's eyes narrowed.

Was he protective? Of her? She liked it. "He's been here a few times."

"I ran him off and forgot about him. He's been far from my mind for this past month."

"Been thinking of other things, huh?"

His smile turned sweet again. "Well, yeah. But what about you? Sounds like some strange characters are hanging around here. When you asked about Kilmer, at first I thought you were asking about the other guy. Younger than Kilmer, about my age. Works at the garage out on the main road."

"Brendan, maybe? He's Mike's younger brother. Why do you ask?"

"He was always showing up to do odd jobs, or so he said. Didn't seem very productive. More snooping than anything else."

"He works around the house and some house-sitting, too, for Jack."

"Jack, again. Did you notice your voice does a funny bump when you say his name?"

"A bump?"

"Yeah, like a little Ja-ack." He mimicked a flirty belle. "How sweet."

"Stop it. Between you and Daisy, you should open a match-making service."

"I'm off the market. For good, if Lia will have me." His smile spread across his face. "And she will."

Rachel stared down at the herringbone brick pattern. "Yeah, she will." She reached over and patted his leg. "She will."

He put his arm around her and pulled her close again. Her head rested below his chin. She'd raised him. Now he was about to belong to another woman. She placed her hand over her heart.

"You okay? You sighed."

"Did I?" Rachel moved away and sat up straight. "I'm fine. Colorado is a long way away.

I'll miss you."

"I want you to meet her soon. Her family, too. You raised me to appreciate the value of family. They've been great. There's something else...I feel a little odd about saying it...and I don't mean it as a criticism, but remember how we always talked about going to church, but didn't?"

He took her hand again. "They do, and I'm enjoying it."

He might not mean to criticize, but she felt the pang anyway. "Time and money. No time, and I couldn't afford the clothes to dress right for church."

"Things are more casual now." He lifted her hand and touched it to her cheek. "Anyway, it's new to me—like a lot of stuff right now—and I'll keep you posted. But, you have to come visit us, the sooner the better. I want you to be a part of it, too."

He'd added that last to soothe her feelings. He hadn't done it very artfully, but she appreciated his intent. They sat for a minute listening to the breeze ruffling through the nearby trees. A bird sang and a squirrel ran across the terrace wall on the far side, ignoring them, intent upon the business of living.

Jeremy said, "Are you going to introduce me?"

"To Jack?"

"Who else? My former employer, for that matter, and now someone who means something to my sister. But don't worry, I won't give you away. Unless you want me to?"

An errant strand of hair tickled her face, and she pushed it back behind her ear. "Don't do anything to embarrass me."

"Me?"

"I'm serious." She took his hand. "He's an artist, did you know that? He's about to leave for a week for his New York gallery showing, his first, and it's a big deal for him."

"He must be good."

"He is. He asked me to stay until he returned. To watch out for the house and stuff."

Jeremy frowned. "That sounds dangerous. Don't tell me you're leaving the inventory profession to become a security guard? Seriously, I don't like the idea of you being here alone."

"Oh, goodness, no. I won't be alone. May will be here. Did you meet May?"

"No—oh, wait. Sellers, right? She dropped by a few times like she owned the place. I did my best to avoid her."

"I'm not surprised. Anyway, Brendan will be here at night to watch the back of the house."

"Really?" He didn't sound pleased.

"Brendan's fine. A very nice young man and a happy antidote to May."

"He's not a kid. He's about my age, isn't he? Are you sure he's safe?"

She laughed. "You're funny. How have I managed while you've been gone for most of the past four years? I think I can take care of myself."

"Point taken."

"Then there's Helene. But we don't discuss her, so don't tell anyone she's here."

"What are you talking about?"

"It's a long story, but as you can see, it's quite a full house."

"May, who needs a happy antidote, Brendan, who's a 'nice' young man, and a woman we can't talk about. How does that sound to you? As bizarre as it sounds to me?"

And somehow she fit into that mix. What did that say about her?

They stood, but before leaving the terrace and going back to reality—the reality they had to share with the rest of the crazy world—she touched his arm and hugged him. Never mind that the top of her head barely reached his shoulder. She hugged him as if he was the little brother she was parenting for the last time.

Jeremy's arms stiffened, and his chest grew taut. She backed away. Someone had joined them. He was standing in the conservatory doorway, his face flushed and his expression angry.

"Jack? Is something wrong?"

"Apparently not?"

A delicious shiver raced up her spine.

"Jack, meet Jeremy, my brother." She touched her brother's arm. "And your former employee."

"Jeremy." He said the name, and it hung there for a second. "I'm glad to see you well and whole. Your sister was worried."

Jeremy left her side and stepped forward, extending his hand. "Mr. Wynne? I'm pleased to meet you. Yes, I have a lot to make up to my sister, but we've already discussed most of it. I understand there was some sort of miscommunication with the management company."

"You left without notice. They discovered you were gone when they found the envelope with the house key in the drop box."

Jack had his hands on his hips; Jeremy did the same. A face-off. *Showdown at the OK Corral.* Rachel bit her lip to keep from interfering.

"Betty. That's who I spoke with," Jeremy said. "I can't recall her last name. She told me to drop the house key off when I was on my way out of town."

Jack shrugged. "Then I'm sure there's an explanation. I'm glad to hear it wasn't as it seemed." He nodded toward the house. "Will you come in? There's some coffee left."

Jeremy smiled at Rachel, then looked back at Jack. "Thanks, but no. I came by to talk to Rachel, and I've got some running around to do before I leave town."

"Leaving again?"

"Yes." He turned to her. "I'll be back to see you before I do."

She reached up and patted his cheek. "You still have some things upstairs. Didn't I recognize that bedspread?"

He glanced upward, frowning, and then his

expression cleared. "Oh, sure. I'll get them when I return." He turned back to Jack. "If that's okay?"

"Of course, and I'm glad I got to meet you. Rachel's been helping me with the house and arranging estimates and all sorts of things. I don't know how I'd have managed without her."

He nodded. "She's special. Very."

"She is."

She followed Jeremy, but paused as she passed Jack and gave him a quick smile as if to say, 'see, he's an adult and I'm letting him live his life.'

The old worn-out items he'd left behind upstairs in his room had been truly left behind. He was a grown man, moving on. What did he need with a threadbare bedspread and an old Christmas-gift sweater? It wasn't the same as leaving one's sister. She wasn't worn-out and threadbare—not yet. But she wasn't needed either, not by him.

After his car had vanished down the dirt road, she sat on the front steps. Not thinking, not even teary, but feeling empty.

"You okay?" Jack asked.

She sat up straighter. "I'm fine. He is, too."

He surprised her and sat on the porch beside her.

"You did a good job of bringing him up, Rachel."

His voice brushed her skin and warmed her. She couldn't find any words and simply stared ahead, nodding.

Jack put his arm around her shoulders, awkwardly at first, as if not knowing where to settle, but then he did. His arm tightened and he rested his fingers on her upper arm.

"He's going to be fine. You will, too."

She wanted to rest against the warmth of him, enjoy his arm around her, but she didn't dare—her self-control would be lost and she'd embarrass them both. She kept her posture stiff.

"Thanks, Jack. I appreciate the kind words."

Jack withdrew his arm and patted her on the back.

"Let's get back to work. That's always the best thing."

Chapter Twenty-three

"Wait, I'll be right there." She called out as she crossed the bedroom with the portfolio. Her foot caught a chair leg, and she fell. She threw the portfolio aside rather than land on it. As she hit the floor, the portfolio slammed into the side of the dresser.

Heavy footsteps ran up the stairs. "Are you okay?"

"I'm fine. Only clumsy." She got to her feet.

Jack was already in the doorway. "Are you sure? I'm leaving now."

"Good luck. I know your gallery showing will be fabulous." She walked to meet him and they stood together into the hallway.

His expression remained serious. He looked down at a package he was holding. Blue paper with a bow. Rachel almost said aloud, 'that'll never survive the plane ride without getting crushed,' but was cut short as Jack said, "It's for you."

"For me?"

He held it toward her. "For you. A small thank you for everything you've done."

She felt it keenly—that cocoon of isolation—she'd called it independence once upon a time. It pressed in around her. The cocoon stretched and snapped as Rachel reached out and touched the paper. "Did you wrap the package yourself?"

Jack nodded.

"Should I open it now?"

"Now, yes, or I'll miss my plane." He smiled.

Standing there in the hall with Jack, Rachel broke the tape and pulled the paper from the box. The box fell open and dropped to the floor unheeded as she held the gift.

"Jack, you can't." Oh, no. Her eyes stung. Her lashes felt wet.

He took the peacock shawl from her hands. He stood close to her and draped it over her shoulders. He focused on the act of wrapping it around her as if he were sculpting a work of art.

She touched his hand. "Jack."

His arms enfolded her, pulled her to his chest, and his lips came down to hers.

His kiss swamped her utterly. Flushed with emotion, she was lost to good sense. She welcomed his embrace and the rough feel of his lips and gave back as good as she got until the first rush was past. Jack withdrew his lips. With his fingers in her hair, he eased her head back gently and met her eyes.

"Rachel. The shawl is a gift, a thank you. I hadn't planned to...to do more, but I won't apologize for the kiss. Please don't want me to." He searched her face with his dark eyes. "I'm only sorry I didn't do this sooner. Now I have to leave, and I can't if I don't have your promise that you'll be here when I return."

"No apology. Yes, I'll be here when you return." She touched his cheek, and her finger trailed down his jawline and neck as if of its own volition.

He shivered. His arms tightened. He asked, "Once more for goodbye?"

"No. Once more for good luck."

The horn honking broke them apart.

"Brendan's taking me to the airport. He'll pick me up when I return. Mike's going to do some work on the car. One more thing. I spoke with the management company. Betty went out on maternity leave prematurely. Probably right after she'd spoken with Jeremy."

Warmth surged through her again. In a way, Kilmer was right—Jack could be temperamental. He could be self-absorbed and rude. But the Jack she knew could also be tender and kind. Generous, too. She touched the soft silk of the shawl to her cheek.

As soon as Jack was gone, Rachel called Daisy and got her voicemail.

"Guess what? Jeremy didn't leave without notice. I'll explain more later. And guess what else…no, I'll tell you about it when we speak." She didn't know what Daisy would make of that message, but the giggling at the end might give her a hint.

When the portfolio had flown, so had the poster, but with no harm done. Rachel retrieved it from the floor, put the portfolio case on the bed, and saw thin white paper edges peeking out from the inner edge.

She ran her fingers inside the black interior pocket and the papers then gently tugged the papers out.

Floor plans. Architectural blueprints of the first and second floors of Wynnedower. Basement, too.

All of her clumsy attempts at drawing the layout of the myriad rooms, and here was the real thing exposing all the nooks and crannies and secret places.

She sat on the bed and walked her eyes through the lines and shapes of the house. The diagrams were clear. She'd covered almost every inch of this house, personally, at least once, except for the basement. This was a treat. Being extremely visual, her brain accepted this information in a way that walking around hadn't done. Seeing the detailed big-picture flow, it all came together in her head.

But it was hard to focus. She touched her lips. They still tingled. She flopped back onto the bed. A week. He'd be gone a week. It seemed forever.

Yet when he came back—well, she wasn't going to jump ahead of the facts. She would deal with his return when the time came, and it would work out.

Was she in love?

Suddenly, Jeremy came to her mind. Was he in love? He was barely twenty-two.

His choices, both the choice to travel with a girl and not to tell his sister and to forego grad school, didn't hurt so much now. She congratulated herself on moving forward.

She could appreciate a little bit about how it

felt to fall for someone.

Correction. Not quite fallen, but dangerously close to the edge.

Rachel carried the blueprints downstairs. They were large but thin and very old. She arranged them on the bare floor of the central hall.

The basement was unknown territory. The blueprints showed rooms in the eastern half and a large open area in the western half. The wide double doors on the back of the house were labeled as Carriage Doors. The carriage area inside the basement was blocked off from the rest of the basement by a wall with one door. That door was near the area of the central stairs.

On the first floor, there was the foyer with small rooms on either side. Next, the central hall. Library and conservatory to the left. Stairway to the right. Rooms were arrayed along the back, leading to Jack's quarters, like the kitchen and pantry. Facing the front of the house were the butler's quarters and a servants' area.

Rachel moved over to the second floor blueprint and settled herself on the floor. She didn't seem to have missed any rooms. She could've checked 'em off one by one.

"Those used to be her rooms."

May was standing behind her.

"What?"

"The room you're using and the sitting room was Miss Helene's suite. An intruder surprised her there once, and she would never go back. Jack moved her belongings into the nursery suite. Now they are in the same wing, if on different floors."

It clicked in her brain. That's why her rooms were better maintained. "I thought she lived elsewhere for most of her adult life. In England or somewhere."

"She traveled back and forth. For such a shy one, she travels well as long as she has someone with her to handle problems. Give her a book and a blanket. She finds those planes so chilly, you know. Not that I travel with her, but she tells me about it. She talks to me. Not to many people, but always to me. Like a mother to her, I am."

May was uncharacteristically talkative, but what was her point? To make Rachel jealous of her relationship with Helene? Not likely. She chose a safe response.

"I'm sure you are. I don't know how she'd manage without you."

"She confides in me, you understand. There's a special bond between me and the Wynne family."

Rachel swiveled all the way around, staying on the floor, but finally facing her fully. "And?"

"She's very vulnerable. Pushing her to do what she doesn't want is very distressing."

Distressing to May, certainly.

"I'll try to be more sensitive to her wishes." That should do it.

But no.

May continued, "Your interest in her brother, Mr. Wynne, is distressing to her and, I will add, unflattering to you. To your character."

Heat rushed up through Rachel. Anger. "Stay out of my business." She turned her back to May lest she say more and uglier words.

"It's smart to know about a person before getting involved. About his people and background. The Wynnes are an old and respected family."

She couldn't help herself. She said, "Helene should practice getting out more. If Jack sells Wynnedower...." She trailed off, embarrassed because she'd struck out at May deliberately.

"He wouldn't. He'd never do that to Miss Helene or to Wynnedower."

"Oh, really? You might be surprised what Helene would do." Anger had driven her words. Not just the words, but the way she'd thrown them at May.

May left. The sound of her footfalls receded into the distance.

Rachel tried to soothe her guilt. May was a snob who thought Rachel wasn't good enough. Or May was greedy and didn't want to share her setup here. Maybe May was like her and didn't have a real life of her own.

Rachel realized her fingers were back on her lips. She recalled the feel of Jack's kiss. What was between them was no one's business but theirs. Even they didn't know the extent of what was between them. Not yet. She was excited, and a little fearful, to find out. But find out, she would. Daisy would certainly approve of her determination. One day, with patience and more personal restraint, she'd make May understand that she, Rachel, wasn't bad or unworthy. It would just take time.

****

Rachel paused in the kitchen doorway considering the best way to phrase her request. Considering their earlier dust-up, she wanted to try to sweeten the request.

"Mrs. Sellers, I have a favor to ask."

"What?" She turned toward Rachel, an attitude showing on her face, and immediately shifted her attention to somewhere beyond her. "Miss Helene. Come in, dear. Are you ill? What do you need?" Flustered, May patted her apron absentmindedly, and then stretched her hands out toward their visitor.

A tiny smile played across Helene's lips, and she looked almost confident, like a watcher of long habit who suddenly appears, catching the watchees unaware and unprepared. Mischievous or just curious?

Rachel stayed back while May ushered Helene into the kitchen. May stood her in front of a chair and said "Sit here, dear. Careful now."

May spoke to Helene as if she were a half-witted invalid. She itched to slap May. She hadn't seen anything to indicate that was the case, nor that Helene was physically delicate. Merely shy and reclusive. Never mind May. Maybe she should just ask Helene.

May's attention was totally focused on

Helene. For May, Rachel had ceased to exist.

Rachel asked softly, "How are you today?"

Almost in a whisper, Helene answered, "I'm fine."

"I'm glad you came downstairs. Perhaps we could have brunch in the conservatory one day. Would you enjoy that?"

May interrupted, "I don't think...."

Helene spoke. "...would be lovely."

"It's a date then." Rachel tried to swallow the feeling of triumph. It wasn't about her or May, anyway. It was about Helene's best interests.

Helene nodded. "I'm ready to return to my room now."

May jumped forward. "I'll get you there safe and snug, Miss Helene."

"Thank you, Miss May."

****

It didn't add up, plain and simple. Rachel looked at the blueprint and then at the stair landing. She examined the blueprint more closely, then went to the kitchen.

Was it a duct? Did they have duct work at the turn of the prior century? Or was it simply a void between the stairs and kitchen? She returned to the blueprint and checked it again before climbing the stairs to the landing. She trailed her fingers along the wall.

The blueprints showed a door in this spot that opened onto a narrow stairway that led down to the kitchen. Probably some sort of servants' shortcut. There was no sign of a door now.

In the kitchen, in the corner where the steps should have ended, was the Welsh dresser with the lovely dishes. This dresser was a beautiful piece of furniture except for the uneven darkening of the finish from years of cooking fumes. It could've been a showpiece, but instead it was utilitarian. It should also have been free-standing.

The dresser was flush to the wall from a foot above her head down to the floor. It sat so close and tight against the wall that she couldn't get a finger behind it.

Yet the doors were on the blueprint, both in the kitchen and on the landing. This was the kind of mystery that would nag at her, but since the dresser was bolted to the wall, the question could have no answer. She resolved to ignore it and move on to other things. Like Jack's studio.

The paint materials were neatly tucked away, and the beautiful wood grain of the floor was no longer hidden. The patina was exquisite. The vast canvas drop cloth that had protected the floor had been folded and laid in a neat, large blocky square beside the wall where the paintings were stacked, upright and leaning.

This would be a beautiful room when restored to its intended purpose.

Never mind mystery, she told herself, but later, when she was going through the old documents and photos in Jack's box she found proof the door had once existed.

She stared at it intently, almost stepping in among the posers. The grouping was semi-casual and on the lower part of the stairs. A man in a suit and bowler hat was leaning against the stair rail. A woman in a long-skirted gown and a wide brimmed hat was standing a few steps directly below him. Several children sat on the steps. Behind them on the landing was a discreet but obvious door.

****

In the dark of night, in the quiet of her room—indeed, the silence of her room, the west wing and the entire second floor—she heard a noise, the kind of noise that made it into her room only by means of its vibration through the bones of the house.

Impossible to tell its origin. Feet bare against the wood floor, breath held, she listened for something more.

Stuff like this should only happen with Jack here. She didn't mind calling the cops if she saw a stranger outside, but an unknown sound from somewhere inside the mansion?

It came again, sort of a distant boom. Again the floor vibrated beneath her feet.

She pulled on her shorts and a t-shirt, muttering that she should've asked Jack for his gun.

Should she wake Brendan? Or May? No, not May. Brendan. But first she was going to tiptoe to the stairs and listen. Her pulse was beating so hard in her ears she couldn't be sure of hearing a stampeding herd of elephants.

She paused a few steps down.

No sound. No telltale gleam from the exterior motion lights filtered in through the windows, so nothing had tripped them.

Everything was fine.

Another noise, faint, came from directly below where she stood on the landing.

The basement?

Sound could be distorted and travel in unexpected ways. Might be mice. Or a rat. Revulsion raced the length of her body. No need to go down there.

Brendan was nearby. At the very least, she should wake him and get his opinion. He could check the basement while she guarded the main floor.

Stepping lightly, she moved down the stairs and then through the back hall to Jack's quarters. She knocked on the door softly. "Brendan?"

She knocked again. No answer.

The basement door was in the pantry. She eased the door open and stuck her head in. So dark and silent. No way on earth would she take a step down those stairs. She shut the door.

Had it been unlocked all along? May or Jack could've unlocked it recently and forgotten to relock it…no, that was farfetched considering how careful they were.

She could block the door. If someone was down there it would prevent them from gaining access to the rest of the house, at least through here. She placed her hands against a free-standing cabinet and tried to push it.

Brendan said, "What's up?"

He was standing in the kitchen. He was dressed in jeans and a t-shirt, but barefoot with his hair awry.

"I tried to wake you. I heard noises coming from the basement."

"The basement? Did you go down and check it out?"

"Are you joking?"

He scratched his head. "Scaredy cat. It's just a basement. Leave the cabinet where it is." He opened the basement door and reached in, fumbling for a light switch. The light came on.

"Stay here. I'll go down and check."

Barely through the doorway, Brendan yelped and stepped backward hastily. She jumped, and he laughed.

"You're mean," she said, trying to laugh with him though her attempt was a little weak.

He answered with a smile, then said, "I'll be back."

Brendan went down the stairs and passed from view.

She waited. One second. Two.

"Okay down there?" Rachel had visions of rats sinking their sharp little teeth into his bare toes. If he screamed for real, would she go to his aid? Probably not, but she could toss down a knife or something.

He called up. "Everything's fine."

A few minutes passed, then the basement stairs creaked.

"Nothing down here."

"But an intruder…could he have gone to one of the end stairways? He might be hiding down there, waiting to get upstairs."

"Rachel. There's no one down here. Trust me." He climbed the stairs. "What did the noise sound like?"

"Loud at first. Sort of a boom and then a vibration."

"Probably the water pipes. When air gets into pipes, it can sound like thunder." He put an arm around her shoulders. "Okay, now?"

She nodded, reassured. "Thanks, Brendan. I'm glad you're here."

"Why don't I walk you back to your room?" He tightened his arm around her in a companionable way.

"No, thanks. I'm fine now."

"Are you sure?"

"Yes." She stepped away and patted his arm. "Thanks, but I can manage on my own."

Brendan laughed. "Good night."

She waved and walked away, a bit uncomfortable, but not so much at Brendan's coziness. As unlikely as it seemed, she had the tiniest feeling that he might be toying with her.

****

"Mrs. Sellers, I think tomorrow morning is the best time for us to have brunch in the conservatory. I have my work table set up out there. We can use that." Rachel crossed her arms. "Well, I can see you disapprove. I hope you'll join us."

"Miss Helene will be uncomfortable with all those windows. Almost as bad as being outside for her."

"The conservatory is a step in the process. Not quite outside, but not shut away in these dark rooms, either. There'll be nobody but us around her."

"What if David Kilmer comes back? You saw what happened when she caught a glimpse of him."

"Yes, I did and why is that? I understand she might not like him and might get angry, but she was hysterical."

May pressed her lips together, thin like a ribbon, and then opened her mouth only to close it again. Rachel could see those words struggling to erupt, whether to tell Helene's secrets, or to hurl devastating insults at her for being nosey and high-handed. Rachel didn't know which, but she was amused by May's discomfiture at not wanting to blurt it out.

"Well, for heaven's sake, Mrs. Sellers, either speak or not. It's up to you."

"He's a snake, that one. Mind you, Miss Sevier, not to be too dismissive of him. He's a man with a will and no regard for the well-being of any other person. You'd do well to avoid him instead of...."

"Instead of what?"

"Meeting him out on the grounds. There's lots of windows in this house, missy."

She must have provoked May, indeed, for 'missy' to have escaped those lips.

"I don't meet him. On the few occasions when he has approached me, I tried to be courteous but not encouraging. He isn't my friend, and is barely an acquaintance, so do not imagine meetings that never happened."

"People think because I'm old that I don't see. I see how he waylays anyone who'll talk to him, even Brendan. He's thinking about himself. Only himself, and he doesn't care who gets hurt."

"Rachel? Is now good?" Brendan asked.

May looked back and forth between them.

Rachel explained, "Brendan's going to help me move some boxes and stuff around upstairs."

May turned back to the kitchen counter, dismissing them.

"Lunch at noon, then?"

They climbed the stairs together. Rachel thought he seemed less lighthearted than usual.

"Are you okay? Not coming down with anything, are you?" She resisted reaching up to check his forehead for fever.

"I'm fine. Fine," he added with emphasis. Brendan moved to the nearest mound and lifted the sheet. "It's like ghost furniture. And it's going to waste. I was a kid when they moved most of it up here."

"I assumed they moved it before that." I waved at a nearby settee. "See those? Can you put them with the other boxes?"

"Sure can." He hoisted a box. "I was a kid

back then. It was right after Jack got married. His wife wasn't about to live here. She preferred New York. Still does."

Rachel gripped the back of a chair with one hand and put the other to her own forehead. She felt light-headed.

He rushed to her. "Hey, what happened?"

"I think I'm ill, Brendan. Let's stop." The dim light was her friend. She pretended to cough with the dust. "Do you mind?"

He took her arm gently. "Are you dizzy? Is it your stomach?"

"I'll be okay. I'm going to lie down for a bit."

He assisted her down the stairs. "I'd offer to get May for you, but if you agreed to accept May's help, I'd be so scared I'd call 9-1-1 instead."

She managed a small smile at his sweet joke. She tried not to ask, but the words came out anyway, "What's her name? His wife?"

"Amanda."

"That's right. He mentioned her name, but I couldn't recall it." A lie to protect her pride—the façade of her pride. He'd called Amanda his agent.

"Thanks, Brendan. I'm going to lie down. Don't tell May."

"I'm going to take off for a few hours, then. Go into town. You sure it's okay to leave?"

"Yes, I'll be fine."

He left. Rachel lay on the bed and cried like a heartbroken teenager whose first crush asks some other girl to the dance. Tears trailed across her cheeks.

Hadn't she known it was all too good to be true?

Jack hadn't come looking for her; she'd put herself in his way. She'd been the one who drew him from friendship to that passionate kiss.

Now, he was in New York with his art show and his wife. She imagined them discussing the arrangement of the paintings, the lighting, the beauty and excitement of it. His arm would go around her. She would touch his shoulder as she laughed, sharing his excitement.

Rachel squeezed her eyes shut, but it didn't soften the image.

And yet, maybe there was an explanation. A wife. His wife. Brendan hadn't specifically said Jack was currently married, right? She dashed the thought. She wouldn't have accepted such rationalizing from Jeremy, and she couldn't accept it from herself.

Rachel allowed herself an hour for shock and self-pity, then rose from the bed and began to systematically gather the notes, materials and estimates she'd collected for Jack.

Her heart gave a wrench. How could a house get under one's skin as Wynnedower had burrowed under hers?

But the house didn't belong to her, nor did Jack. She could see the truth now. She'd fastened upon Jack because she was losing Jeremy. Jeremy was right to move on with his life. To make his own decisions. It would be too sad to think she'd raised a brother who couldn't separate his life from hers even if it did mean he was throwing away so much of what she'd worked for on his behalf and leaving a big, gaping hole in her life. That was her problem, not his.

She organized the papers by room, and then re-arranged them by category. Keep busy, she told herself. Continue as if nothing unhappy has occurred. Then leave.

Hadn't she agreed to stay? Well, agreements were made to be broken.

But brunch was already arranged. She didn't want to hurt Helene.

She'd put on a good face, one that would hide her hurt. She'd wrap up her notes and inventory and be ready to scoot out the door as soon as Jack returned.

It was all about business and that was all it had ever been about.

****

May scowled and muttered, but cooked brunch. As long as she kept her opinions to herself, there wouldn't be a confrontation. Rachel carried the plates and utensils out to the conservatory to set the table.

It was an exquisite morning despite her lack of sleep. A warm, gentle breeze swayed the trees tossing their foliage back and forth making the shadows move and creating whispery sounds.

Helene arrived with May and the food, and the aroma of bacon and hot, fresh cinnamon rolls.

"Here's your chair." Rachel gestured to the lyre back dining room chair, one of the items she'd brought down for convenience. "May, you are welcome to join us. I hope you'll reconsider."

"No." May dropped the food on the table and vanished.

Rachel arranged the food with more thought. "Juice, Helene?"

The late summer light was kind and made a halo of the fine fluffs of hair that escaped Helene's barrettes.

"Ladies, good morning." Brendan entered.

Startled, Rachel nearly jumped to shield Helene, then realized how casually he'd spoken.

"Do you two know each other?"

Helene gave him a quick, bright smile, then looked down at her hands.

"Sure do. I'm glad you're getting out more. What about you, Rachel? Feeling better?"

"I'm fine." It was clear that she, Rachel, had been the only one in the house who didn't know about Helene. Well, okay. Apparently, she, Rachel, was the only stranger at Wynnedower. The odd one out. The one who didn't belong.

"Will you join us?"

"I can't. My brother needs my help with a repo."

She detected tension in his voice and his smile seemed forced. "A repossession? Isn't that dangerous?"

"We use our brains, and we're careful. Most of the repos aren't a big deal." He smiled at her and winked at Helene.

"They blow everything up on TV. To make it more exciting, right?" Rachel suggested.

"Yep." He grabbed a roll from the basket. "Well, you ladies have a fun brunch, and I'll be back before supper." He mimicked a bow and left.

After the last croissant was consumed and while they lingered at the table, Rachel saw him.

They'd taken this big leap with breakfast in the conservatory, and who should come around skulking in the shrubbery?

Heat flooded her body in a hot rush of anger. If not for Helene's presence, she would've chased after him with her fork, or maybe she would've reached for her phone and called the police.

Call them before he can do harm. Even if the harm is no more than annoyance.

Helene's back was toward the area of shrubbery in question, and a screen of dead vegetation in the dry fountain helped shield her from view. She hoped so, anyway. When Helene stared at Rachel's hands, she realized her fingers were rat-a-tat-tatting the table.

All they needed to do was to wrap up their lovely meal, then she could escort Helene safely back inside. Helene would never know and thus couldn't be upset.

"Helene, are you done? I'm chilly. Let's go

in."

"Breakfast was lovely."

Rachel rose, pretending they had all the time in the world. "I'm so glad you enjoyed it. Go on to the kitchen. I'll be right there." She maneuvered Helene away from the exterior door and windows and practically pushed her into the house. "Will you ask Mrs. Sellers to make us some coffee?"

Helene nodded and went.

With a quick glance over her shoulder to make sure Helene was out of sight, Rachel walked briskly toward the exterior door. Kilmer stepped forward, apparently in haste to reach the door and perhaps assuming she was coming to join him, but instead she gave the lock a quick flip.

Something scary slipped across his face, flushed away by a good guy grin.

He spoke through the glass panels of the door. "Rachel? Is something wrong?"

"You aren't supposed to be here."

"What are you talking about?"

"Jack said so. He told you and spoke with the police, too. He got a restraining order."

"Rachel."

She stared at him. Was that pity in his eyes?

"Jack and I spoke, but it wasn't about me staying away. He was concerned about Helene. Talk to the police? I'm sure he didn't. Perhaps you misunderstood?" He appeared to consider, then shrugged. "Is he home now? Call him out here, and we'll talk."

"You know where he is."

"Where he is…. Oh, that's right. His showing. A fancy gallery in New York. Very impressive considering he only started painting seriously a few years ago. But talent's in the blood, isn't it? It's the perseverance that can be hard to come by. Was that Helene sharing lunch with you?"

"Leave this property."

"I understand. No problem. Jack will return soon. We'll work it out then." He didn't smile but tilted his head as if examining her face. "In any relationship there's give and take."

Despite the implied threat, despite him being unwelcome, it was on the tip of her tongue to ask if he knew Amanda…and what did he know about her and Jack? But shame kept it in. She shook inside and was amazed at the calm in her voice. "Go, or I'll call the police, and you can sort it out with them now and with Jack when he returns. And one last thing—you lied to me about being friends with Jeremy. I won't forgive that. Keep away from Brendan, too. You're nothing but trouble."

Rachel walked away, leaving the French doors between the conservatory and the house open to signal confidence that he would do as instructed. She intended to return and lock them as soon as he was out of view.

The table held the remains of their meal. She left it. It could wait until David was gone.

She was rounding the corner from the library to the central hall when she ran into Helene.

She was pale. She'd never gone as far as the kitchen.

"You saw him?"

She nodded, her blue eyes were opened so wide that they were nearly round, but otherwise she appeared to be okay.

"Wait here? If he's gone I want to gather the plates and stuff."

"Yes," she whispered.

David wasn't in sight, for what that was worth. She stacked the plates and utensils. Helene had followed her to the conservatory after all. Maybe that was a good sign.

"Take these to May in the kitchen and then meet me in the central hall?"

Again, Helene nodded. Their fingers touched as she accepted the plates. Helene left. Rachel locked the French doors. After a last look, a scan to spot unwanted guests, she joined Helene.

"You're okay?"

"I think so. I don't like him. Here." Her voice was soft, but steady.

"You're not afraid."

"I want him to go away."

"I told him to leave. Jack told him, too. If he comes back, I'll call the police. He doesn't have the right to pester you or loiter on the property. Do you want to talk about it?"

She shook her head 'no' but the words spilled out in a low, rushed flow. "He follows. Always follows. A nice boy when we were children. Mostly nice. He followed Jack around, but Jack was older and ignored him. I tried to be kind. I shouldn't have. He followed me to London once." She touched Rachel's hand. "You should always be honest in your dealings. Not do things out of pity or guilt."

"You were kind to him, but that was a long time ago and in no way your fault. Why does he persist? Do you know?"

"He said he loves me, but I don't think he does."

"Why?"

"Because someone who loves you doesn't do what makes you unhappy."

Was that true? Not altogether, but Rachel could agree in principle. "Sometimes we think we know better than our loved ones do, what's good for them, I mean." She rubbed her eyes. "Sometimes we don't mean it to be cruel. But, mind you, I'm not talking about David. There's something wrong with him. You're right to avoid him."

She took Helene's hand and patted it. "If you're alone and you see him, go to your room and lock your door, right? Don't get upset like you did last time. Be strong."

"Last time?"

"Yes. Remember how upset you were when you saw him?"

"Saw David?"

Rachel was confused. She decided she was confused by Helene's confusion. "That evening when you saw someone and got so upset? It was David Kilmer, right?"

"Oh, that. No, not him. Not that time. A stranger. To me." She moved her hand and returned the pat. "Brendan's friend. I was just surprised. You don't need to worry about me, Rachel."

Brendan's friend? That time of the evening, and without Brendan in the house? He had some explaining to do. On the other hand, it was no longer her business. He could do whatever explaining was called for, to Jack.

Chapter Twenty-four

"You should see this, Rachel. If this is even a small taste of what Griffin experienced, then I have a new appreciation for why he did what he did." There was silence, except for Jack's voice. "I slipped away, and I've got to get back out there, but this is so amazing and I have you to thank for a lot of it."

"Me? No, not at all."

"I couldn't be in New York, free of worry, if I didn't know you were there at Wynnedower with Helene. May is marvelous in her way, but, well, it's not the same as knowing you're there."

She bit back the question about his wife.

"I don't know if you've realized it yet, but Helene wanted you to stay. She likes having you around. I do, too."

"Jack." The words just wouldn't come.

"More than that, I want to tell you...."

Noises, a growing hum of voices, came through the receiver. One voice, a woman's voice, stood out among the others. "Hurry up. Why are you hiding in here?"

Jack said, "Rachel? I'm sorry. I've got to get back in there. I'll call you tonight."

But he didn't. And though she remembered Helene's advice about honesty, she wouldn't have indulged in it on Jack's big night. Jack had provided a roof over her head when she needed it, and she had performed services in return. Anything else was unimportant. Jack was due home in two days, and Rachel would be packed and ready to go.

The gift of the peacock shawl would go with her—a beautiful, bittersweet souvenir.

****

Standing in the central hall, Rachel stacked and restacked the information she was leaving behind for Jack on a small table. It was yet one more piece of furniture that had migrated down from the attic, not in direct opposition to Jack's obstinacy, but just because it was needed.

Distant voices caught her attention. She went to the window and spotted something truly strange—the tableau of May all but accosting a woman. May wasn't actually throwing blows, but every cell in her body seemed to be engaged. The woman she was berating had backed up against her car, a shiny blue SUV, and was fumbling to open the door. Rachel recognized the woman. May stood with her back to the house and watched until the realtor's car had vanished down the road.

Rachel scooted back to the table before May reached the door.

Moments later, she heard a swish of skirts, followed by May's voice.

"Are you going soon?"

She sounded combative. No doubt her adrenaline was still pulsing. Rachel tried to keep it cool. She kept her attention focused on the papers.

"When Jack returns."

"About what I'd expect from a woman like you."

Deep breath. Don't engage. Keep it light.

"Do you mind? Will you miss me?"

"Done your damage, and now you're gone."

Rachel released the papers and turned to face May. "I beg your pardon?"

"You've coaxed Miss Helene from the safety of her rooms. Out and about, but Mr. Wynne will be busier than ever with his art and she'll be more on her own and unprotected. But that won't be your problem, will it?"

Rachel gaped. Score one for May.

"Mr. Wynne will take her away again, perhaps. Perhaps he'll find somewhere else to paint. If he does, Wynnedower is done. Miss Helene loves Wynnedower. So, you see, either way she loses." She snorted. "Again, I say, very poor judgment on your part."

"Nonsense. Jack can still restore Wynnedower. He doesn't have to live here year round." She crossed her arms. "There's no reason Helene can't reside here without him."

"If Mr. Wynne goes...."

"Why not? Maybe with a companion or a cook. Seriously, why not? She's shy and maybe wants to avoid life and people in general, but that doesn't mean she can't live here without Jack."

"You've learned nothing about the Wynnes while you've been here. He would never leave his sister unprotected." May clasped her hands across her stomach. "Mr. Wynne has always watched over his sister. The one time he didn't, well, you've met David Kilmer. Miss Helene is such an innocent, so defenseless, that she can't manage on her own. Mr. Wynne understands that. Some things don't change. Shouldn't change."

A chill ran along Rachel's spine. It seized in the small of her back, and like a wireless signal it sent a message north to her brain, but the message fizzled before it got to the cells that could make sense of it. She couldn't think of anything more to say. Best to end the discussion.

"When it comes to Wynnedower, things will change one way or the other. I saw you talking to that woman outside. You know—"

"He won't sell. He'll never sell. Even if he decided to, Miss Helene will never allow it."

"Mrs. Sellers, I'm not your enemy. I have no power over Wynnedower. If you care about the house, then encourage Jack to renovate. Offer your help. Nobody knows Wynnedower like you."

May was as still and pale as a statue. Rachel felt a rush of sympathy for her. Of all the people in and out of Wynnedower, it appeared that the two of them were the biggest losers.

"I'm sorry for any aggravation I've caused you. I hope everything works out for you and Jack and Helene." Saying Jack's name out loud caused a pinch in her heart. She took a double-breath to erase it. The next words spilled out with no notice. "Do you know Amanda?"

Immediately she regretted asking because May's hand went to her own heart.

"Why do you ask?" Her voice sounded hoarse.

"Honestly, I don't know."

"Don't you? Well, I'll tell you. She and Mr. Wynne have a lovely apartment in New York. A lovely place. She doesn't care for country living, so he travels back and forth. They've had their troubles, that's true. One thing I know, someone like you hanging around making a fuss over him, doesn't help to work things out."

Rachel's temples began to throb. She wanted to shout that she wasn't a home wrecker. Instead, she said, "They're all adults and will have to figure life out without me. As for Wynnedower, they can torch it and bulldoze it as far as I'm concerned. If Jack's smart, he'll sell it and get what he can out of it."

Even as the words left her lips, she was appalled at her desire to hurt May. She needed OUT of this place. This situation. She brushed past a stricken-looking May.

Rachel was tired of worrying about people and things that were none of her business and would be out of her life very soon, but not yet, because within an hour May had tracked her down.

It was a different May this time, calmer and subdued, but still very pale. "I'm going back to my cottage for a while. Miss Helene is sleeping. Brendan is working for his brother."

They spoke with cool formality.
"No problem. Shall I check on her?"
"No need. I wanted you to be aware."
"Of course."
"I'll be back in time to fix supper."
"Lovely. Thanks."
"But only for us. Brendan won't be back tonight. His brother took him out of town. Last minute, for work. Very unhappy about it, he was. Not wanting to let Jack down, I believe. I'm pleased to see he's developing a sense of responsibility." She sniffed, then turned and left.

Rachel was relieved that apparently Madame May had decided to call a truce.

She went into the kitchen to get a glass of water. The basement popped into her mind. It might be worth a look at the carriage area, plus the blueprint showed rooms in the eastern half along a long hallway. Small rooms in a row. Servants' quarters. More echoes of *Gosford Park*.

It was none of her business. Still, it was the only part of the house she hadn't seen. As if confirming that she should do it, a flashlight stood on end on the counter.

She leaned in and pulled the light string. She hefted the flashlight in her hand. Just in case.

The wooden steps were steep with only one handrail to hold. She descended the stairs cautiously, half-expecting cadaver hands to thrust up between the steps and grab her ankles, but there was nothing frightening here.

It smelled old and musty. Not damp though. Bone dry and cool.

There was very little down here. A tool bench, long-forgotten. Some boxes stacked on the side. The floor was concrete right in the middle, but off to the sides she could see flagstones.

This area was relatively small and closed in. In one direction, there would be rooms, servants' quarters and such. The other way, through a door in a nearby wall, would be the carriage area.

A fine layer of dust and dirt covered everything. There was such a sense of stillness she felt foolish for having been afraid.

A ladder leaned against a support post near the center, the area directly below the stairs.

In the dust near ladder, a few marks stood out against the concrete. They were fresh-looking. Rachel went to stand beside it and stared overhead.

Between the floor joists above there was a flat piece of wood, more like a panel. It looked like the planks had been put together in such a way as to disguise it. A repair?

The rest of the ceiling appeared undisturbed and identical. This was different. Hatch-like. It reminded her of an attic ceiling panel.

She moved the ladder and placed it directly below the panel. Standing on the higher steps, she could easily touch it. She pushed up gently, not wanting anything to fall down on her head. It wouldn't do to get injured. No one knew she was down here. No one would miss her for hours, possibly not until Jack returned tomorrow.

The panel moved slightly. Bits of something filtered down. She brushed it from her cheek.

Up one more step. Now she could get a better grip. She held onto a joist and pushed up hard with her other hand. Balancing the panel on her fingertips, Rachel was able to shift it to the side and set it atop the joists.

The first floor should lie directly on the upper side of these joists, or would have except that this was in the area of the stairs.

It hit her like a bolt. Nearly knocked her off the ladder. The blueprint. The stairway door that was no longer there. A Welsh dresser where the door on the kitchen side should have been.

A hidey-hole beneath the first floor stair risers. For Brendan's treasure?

Correction. Jack and Helene's treasure.

Wynnedower's treasure.

Was she being silly? Maybe, but it was a secret place, and someone had been here recently, someone interested enough to bring the ladder over to this spot and disturb the dust.

She set the flashlight on the floor above and put both hands on either side of the opening to steady herself as she walked up the topmost steps of the ladder.

With her head inside the opening, she paused to allow her eyes to adjust to the gloom. This was an oddly-shaped space. She could see the form of the central stairs, but like a photographic negative—opposite to how she'd normally see it. She identified the underneath side of the steps coming off the large stairs. Maybe those missing steps from the blueprint? But a much smaller area.

With a little heave-ho and a push-off from the ladder, she was able to lift her body up through the opening until her butt found a seat on the floor of the mystery space.

She sat staring into the space as her vision sifted through the shadows, until she could sort out the shapes. It was very dry and cool. Almost a natural climate-controlled storage space between the cool, dry basement and the warmer house. As she stared, she saw a fine layer of dust on the floor boards, and then saw the area where the dust had been scuffled.

The location fit with the noises she'd heard most recently. So maybe someone had been here. Why?

Rachel pulled her legs up and got to her feet. She couldn't stand fully upright except for one small area. The other areas sloped down and were prime headache-makers for the unwary. She stopped short of the disturbed area and saw only a dark shadow at first, then realized it was a black cloth.

Leaning forward, she touched the cloth and found that it covered a box. She lifted the cloth. No, not a box. A trunk.

Brendan and his treasure? Had he been here? What about David Kilmer? He always seemed to be around. May? Hard to envision her climbing the ladder and shimmying up through the opening.

Rachel was here alone in the house except for Helene, and she wouldn't be coming down here. The dust on the floor had been disturbed, both below and up here, so if anything of interest had been here, it was likely gone now.

It was an old trunk, the kind ladies traveled with aboard steamships and trains a century earlier. Much like the one on Helene's side of the attic, but this one had a high, curved lid. Rachel knelt in front of it. She popped the locks and raised the lid.

Long, dark narrow somethings were stored in the chest lengthwise. She ran her fingers along the patterned edges. Frames. Stacked upright, one against the other.

Frames. Her breath stuck in her throat. Not Jack's. Old Griffin's artwork? Maybe old family portraits? What a marvelous addition that would be to the renovation.

The renovation. She wouldn't be here for it.

She shook off her disappointment. Her distress didn't matter. Her feelings for Wynnedower were separate from how she felt about Jack. Maybe this would be the key that convinced Jack to save Wynnedower.

She pulled at one of the frames. It lifted easily from among its fellows.

Color. She touched it. Thick. Oil. About two by three foot. She leaned it against the stair riser, sat back and switched on the flashlight.

It reminded her of Van Gogh's sunflowers. From what she could tell in this dim light, the coloring was similar, as was the composition. Griffin may have practiced his craft by copying a master. That was a pretty common teaching technique. Probably, someone had tucked away his paintings long, long ago and never thought of them again.

Even as a copy, there was skill here, obvious to her eye despite the poor light. She picked it up again and examined the signature. Had he copied Van Gogh's signature, too? She remembered the *Cottage Sunflower* receipt.

A slight shake in her hand echoed in her chest. Her mind went unaccountably blank as if her brain knew something it dared not accept.

She put the sunflower painting aside, grasped another frame and removed it from the trunk with great care.

A young girl with blonde hair in a blue overcoat was sitting next to a fountain. She had a big red ribbon in her hair. She knew she'd seen this girl before but she'd been standing— in a masterpiece at the hands of Renoir. Here the girl was sitting, not standing.

Suddenly overwhelmed, she wanted to run, to be at her small apartment over Daisy's diner where there were no decisions to be made, where she needed only to earn money to keep Jeremy in college and a roof over her head. Where her heart wouldn't race and her limbs wouldn't go weak with indecision and falter with the fear of making the wrong decision.

Why was it her problem, anyway?

It didn't matter why. She couldn't leave these unprotected. The disturbed dust told her that much. Why had someone come so close, yet left them here?

Because they were copies, and poor ones at that. She would see the truth clearly in better light. It was that simple.

One by one, she carried each painting carefully from the hiding place and down the ladder. Six trips in all. Studiously, she avoided examining them, keeping her focus intent upon transporting them as gently as possible.

She carried two at a time up the basement stairs being sure to touch only the frames. For a temporary refuge, she placed them in the lower pantry cabinets, one here, two there, until they were all upstairs. Then she made one last trip down to the basement to close the panel and return the ladder to its resting spot.

Now what? She had to keep them safe until Jack returned. They'd be his problem or his joy. Either way, it wasn't her business no matter how much she desired otherwise.

Until tomorrow.

****

That night, she tried over and over to envision how she could keep distance between them while she shared this exciting, but not yet confirmed as real, news. This was the kind of secret you told someone after laughing and throwing your arms around him and then whispering in his ear, "I have something to show you that you'll never believe."

It was that kind of news. It didn't mesh well with 'you never told me about your wife.'

Her fingers had touched works of art that might be—could be—masterpieces.

But her heart, if not broken, was sorely bruised.

You never told me about your wife.

It had an icy shower quality to it. An ice-pick shower quality.

Rachel spent a restless, sleepless night, her last night at Wynnedower, and never figured out how to deliver good news and bad all at one time. She tried in vain to sleep, awash in regret over that kiss—both that it occurred and that it hadn't happened again. Now that she knew the truth, there could be no more. Beyond that very personal concern was the question of who else knew about the paintings?

Someone did and had kept the information secret.

Chapter Twenty-five

Jack arrived home, excited and incredibly pleased with himself that he'd scored an earlier flight back. He had to rent a car, of course, since Brendan wasn't due to pick him up for several hours. He'd never been this eager to return home. Or, rather, to return to Wynnedower.

Amanda had been annoyed, arguing that he was missing some important networking opportunities in New York, but he'd blown it off. He couldn't wait.

She'd said, "I can see there's no holding you here. It's about that woman, isn't it? I hope you know what you're doing."

He answered, "For the first time in a long time, I can see it all coming together. I can see the future. I'm going to tell her about us. It's past time."

Amanda said, "Good luck, Jack." She placed her hands on his arms and reached up to kiss him. "I hope she's in an understanding mood."

"Rachel?" He paused. "Or are you talking about May?"

"Maybe both."

He'd grabbed a cab and rushed to the airport to catch that flight. About an hour and a half in the air to Richmond, then the drive out to

Wynnedower—it seemed forever. As he entered the house he yelled her name. "Rachel!"

He was ready to call her name again, but then there she was, already descending the stairs. He felt a shot of pride that she must've been waiting and watching for him to arrive. He ran up the first few steps, then saw her expression and his excitement faltered.

She straightened the collar of her blue jacket and smoothed the sleeves. She tucked her hair behind her ears. He noticed her hair had gotten longer while she'd been here. Her eyes seemed dull. No more than a sad light brown.

Jack searched his brain for some sort of safe territory—for something to say while he figured out what was going on with her. "Did I surprise you?"

"You're early."

His gaze moved beyond her. "Is something wrong? Is Helene okay?"

"She's fine."

"Then what? Tell me now, Rachel. I want to talk about great things. I want to tell you about the showing. I want to celebrate with you. If something serious has happened, I need to know now." He moved up to the landing.

She held out her hand. "Please stop."

He stared at her.

"I have things ready to turn over to you, and I need to talk to you about…something else."

"What?"

She paused and looked around, her

expression suddenly confused. "Not here. No." She paused before blurting out, "You never called back."

"What? When?"

"The night of your showing."

He saw indecision in her face, at odds with her words. As if they were saying these words, but talking about something else altogether different. Or, at least, she was, and he was struggling to figure it out.

Walking a wide arc around him, Rachel descended the last steps into the central hall. She pointed toward the table. "I've put the information I collected there. The appraisals and such, plus some ideas."

"You're leaving." His mind went blank for a moment.

"No reason to stay. Jeremy's situation is resolved. Your art show is over. It's time for me to return to real life."

"You came here for more than your brother. What about finding a different kind of job?"

"That was a silly dream, and I cannot impose upon your hospitality any longer." She turned back toward him. "There's the matter of employment, too—my part-time employment with you. I hope you don't mind that I'm not giving notice."

"I do mind."

"Jack, let's be adult about this, okay?"

He advanced toward her. "Are you behaving in an adult manner? Or are you trying to avoid the conversation we were going to have when I returned from New York?"

His question sucked the air from the room. Her face flushed.

She touched her cheek and he grabbed her hand. He pulled her fingers close to his face, touched her palm to his lips. Her hand was shaking. She waited one long, betraying moment before taking it back.

She clasped her hands tightly together, stared at Jack and said, "You don't have the right to behave this way."

Chapter Twenty-six

He frowned and shook his head. "What?"

"You heard me." She waited. For what, she didn't know. She received nothing from him but a blank stare. Unable to bear that stare any longer, she turned and ran back up the stairs, wishing that being righteous felt like sufficient reward, regretting that being right kept her from his arms. At her door, she hugged herself for comfort, or perhaps to keep herself from running back downstairs. To him.

She leaned her forehead against the wooden door. Smooth and cool, it offered small relief.

Why was she standing here? Because she was weak-willed and hoping to hear the sound of his footsteps following her?

No doubt he was already in his studio with his paintings.

His paintings. She slapped the wall. What a fool she was. She'd made her exit prematurely.

How on earth was she supposed to go back downstairs and force him to listen about those other paintings? How could she do that and maintain this chilly distance between them?

Because it was all about her? All that she'd done, everything she had invested her time and heart into, was as if nothing. The truth was she had invited herself in—looking for someone else's life in which to live. Anywhere, but in her own.

She hit the wall again, this time with her fists.

Experts must examine the paintings. They might be genuine or not, but at least Jack should have the opportunity to find out.

There was nothing left for her to do in her room. She was already packed. Her suitcase needed only to be lugged down the stairs and out to the car. It sat there, stuffed, zippered and upright, like a billboard message signaling 'time to go.'

Rachel decided to carry her suitcase down with her and tell Jack the news about the paintings as she was on her way out the door. Tell him privately, of course, so no one would be tipped off, and then she'd make a clean getaway.

She dropped onto the upholstered bench. Was she supposed to chase after him? Go to him after the scene they'd just endured and say, "Oh, and one more thing...."

Impossible.

No, not impossible. Merely awkward. Humbling.

Alright, then. She rose, tugged her sleeves back into place and brushed at her slacks. She drew in a deep breath. She was ready to go find Jack. Halfway down the stairs she realized she'd forgotten the suitcase and left her keys and phone on the dresser. Again. She paused on the landing. Should she go back and grab them before tackling Jack? It was called procrastination either way. Or maybe her subconscious was playing tricks to keep her here.

A rumble and a scraping noise vibrated the floor beneath her feet.

Not as loud as she'd heard it before, but unmistakable.

Was that a soft voice? Muffled words? A breath and a sigh? A bump, a slip?

Light-footed, she descended the last steps and flew to the dining room doors. She grasped the knobs and turned and they opened, but Jack wasn't there. In his quarters, then?

She ran down the hall.

Jack's door was unlocked. She went from room to room, past his living room and into his bedroom. A cursory glance took in the bed, night stands, bureau—nothing special, nothing fancy, and no Jack.

The basement, then, but with Jack missing, and knowing what she did about the paintings, no way was she going down there alone.

Jack's gun? Should she? Jack could be in danger. Her brittle nerves became steady, fed by a sudden rush of excitement.

Where would she keep the gun if she were Jack? Not the nightstand. Not the closet.

She walked back into his living room and stood quietly, thinking. The desk. She tried the top two drawers. No good. The bookcase. She pulled the chair over and climbed up. There it was.

His revolver was cold in her hand. She wasn't familiar with guns except for what she'd read or seen on television and in the movies, but she'd helped inventory a gun shop once. She could recognize a Ruger. She pushed the cylinder open, noting the gun was loaded.

If it was Jack making the noise, well, the paintings belonged to him and Helene—so no problem. If it wasn't Jack, well, then she could just about manage this revolver. Thank goodness it wasn't a semi-automatic. She put it into the pocket of her suit jacket. She and her pockets—she'd never expected to tote a gun in one. At least this jacket had a more substantial interior pocket.

A noise behind her caused her to turn and gasp.

"Helene."

Helene's eyes were wide, her smile uncertain.

Rachel touched her arm. "Where is Jack? I was talking to him only a short time ago, so he must be here somewhere."

"I don't know." She clutched Rachel's hand. "Is something wrong?"

"Wrong?"

"I heard you. You were angry."

What to say? "Everything will be okay." But as she was speaking, she was thinking. Right about now, someone could be realizing the paintings are gone. What would that person do next?

Helene flinched. Rachel unwound her grip.

"Go to your rooms and wait there for me, okay?"

Rachel watched Helene go, but her thoughts were on how best to get into the basement. There were at least three access points, the stairs from the pantry, the narrow stairs at either end of the house. And the carriage doors at the back—she'd almost forgotten them. But with Jack here, and likely downstairs, the direct approach seemed best.

She stood at the top of the pantry stairs and called down. "Jack?"

A shuffling noise, something scraped. A soft curse. She descended two steps.

"Rachel?"

"Brendan? You're down there? I heard noises again. Are you okay?"

"I'm fine. Fine." He stopped at the foot of the stairs, looked to the side and then back up at her. "I'm good. I heard a noise and came down to check it out."

"I did, too. Did you see anything? Is anyone down there with you?"

"Anyone?" He frowned.

"Jack."

"Jack?"

"Yes, didn't you bring him back from the airport? What's that smell?"

"Smell?"

"Like exhaust."

"The furnace. Sorry about that. I was working on it this morning."

"Is Jack down there?"

Brendan shook his head, saying, "I haven't gone to get him yet."

"He's back early."

"Oh? I'll be right up."

Rachel stepped back up into the pantry. Where was Jack? The last thought spurred her to return to the basement stairs. She had almost reached the bottom when Brendan was suddenly there in front of her. She did a small stutter step to regain her balance as she tipped forward.

Brendan grabbed her, wrapping his arms around her. "Steady. You okay?"

Jack's voice came from above. "What's going on? Rachel?" He was already several steps down and staring. His voice was cold, so cold, but hot, too, and sharp.

Brendan dropped one arm and shifted the other to rest around her waist. "Rachel told me you were back. Guess I don't need to drive out and pick you up."

She looked up at Jack. "I heard a noise."

"A noise." He didn't wait for a response, but turned and left. The floorboards above creaked as he walked away.

She pushed Brendan's arm away. The wooden stairs vibrated as she ran up.

The dining room doors were closed. She grabbed the door knobs.

"Rachel?" Jack stood in the hallway, near his quarters. "Were you looking for me?"

"I was. Where were you?"

"Getting my stuff from the rental car."

"Rental–"

"I was in a hurry to get here. Was. Now, I understand why you were so different when I returned. I'm surprised, but it's none of my business." He crossed his arms and shook his head. "You didn't have to sneak around. You're an adult and can make your own choices."

She swallowed her outrage and closed the last few steps between them. "Jack, I need to speak with you."

He held up one hand, palm outward, gesturing her to stop.

How dare he? Hair neat and a sports coat over a half-unbuttoned white shirt—his appearance more than respectable having come from Amanda—and he had the nerve to suggest her behavior was suspect.

He turned his back and walked into his rooms. He'd dismissed her. It ignited something deep in her core. She followed. Her vision turned blood red as words burst from her.

"Whatever is going on in that mulish, arrogant, self-centered mush that passes for your brain—well, it's wrong. It would serve you right if I left, just like that, but I won't. No, I won't, not until I've had my say." She put her face close to his even though she had to stand on tiptoe to do it. "Don't dare hint that you think there's something going on between me and Brendan. Don't." She waved her hands and did a lot of finger pointing. When the words ran out, she planted both hands in her hair and covered her head as if she were in danger of assault.

She was angry. Justified. Embarrassed.

His expression was hard, his jaw taut.

When she spoke again, she kept her voice under better control. "This will only take a moment of your time. Then I'll leave you and Helene and Wynnedower to figure out your future all by yourselves. Oh, and Amanda. I forgot about her, but then, you did, too, didn't you?"

"Amanda? What about her?" His arms dropped from their folded position, and his fists landed on his hips.

"It doesn't matter." She grabbed his arm. "I want to speak with you. Privately."

Jack's face turned maroon. She lost her grip on him as his hands wrapped around her upper arms. "It doesn't matter? I saw you two down in the basement, hanging on to each other and whispering in the dark. Don't play with me. I'm not some kid who falls for a new woman every few days."

His hold on her arm was harsh. She relished the pain because it felt real and memorable, not a wispy dream she'd doubt within a week of leaving this place.

Her heart hurt and her eyes watered. She averted her face. She was the same—not a kid and not someone who fell for every guy who came along. And she'd fallen hard.

The unseen Amanda danced in her head. "I don't have time for your temperamental flights of fancy, and neither do you. I have something important to tell you."

But Jack was stuck back at the beginning of the sentence.

"Temperamental? Me? Is that what you said?" He jabbed a finger into his chest. "I remember clearly that we shared two nice, if short, kisses before I left. But it's a different story now that I'm back. And you say *I'm* temperamental?" He put his hands on her arms again, and they kept right on sliding around her back. She gave up the attempt to argue when his lips touched hers.

His arms tightened, pressing her to his chest, his hands working against her back. She did the same, suddenly forgetting anything else mattered. But not for long. No matter how tempting his lips were, no matter how compelling the pressure of his hands, there was a wife back in New York and someone here who was trying to steal Wynnedower's treasure.

"Jack, I'm serious."

Her words were interspersed with heavy breathing. Jack barked a brief, rude laugh, before returning his lips to hers. Her arms found themselves tracing a path up his arms and to his neck and hair. Curls slipped through her fingers. His curls. Jack's curls. Some survival instinct, that brain stem, brought her back to reality. She pulled his face to her neck so she could speak.

"Jack, someone's trying to steal your paintings."

He stopped, suddenly serious. "My

paintings?"

So much for passion. "Keep your voice down."

"My paintings? What are you talking about?"

"Listen, there's something going on here at Wynnedower. I don't know who's behind it, and I don't know how...how dangerous it might be."

"Dangerous? What?"

Words weren't sufficient. They needed to go to the dining room. She opened the door for a quick look in the hallway. Brendan was standing on the other side.

"Hey, Jack. Welcome back." He walked past her into the room. Thumbs in his pockets, his hands hung casually as if nothing troubled him.

Jack said, still with tension in his voice, "Thanks for helping out here while I was gone."

"No trouble. It was quiet—well, except there were some noises in the basement a couple of times. Never figured out what it was."

"Or who," Rachel added, breathless.

Brendan shuffled his feet. "Not that I'm suggesting rats or anything. Maybe old house settling or an event in the pipes."

Jack's changing expression showed the progress of his thoughts—consternation first at the mention of noises in the basement, then considering possible explanations. "Is that why you and Rachel were down there?"

"She heard noises, too, although it isn't safe for her to go down there alone to investigate. I told her so."

Jack nodded. "Thanks for your help."

"Sure thing, Jack. I hope the showing went well."

"Very successful. Couldn't have been better."

"Great. How'd you get back? Aren't you early?"

"I rented a car. Wanted to surprise…everyone."

"Well, you did."

Rachel watched Brendan walk away, wanting to see him actually vanish around the corner. When he did, she turned back to Jack.

"I don't know where to start."

"Just start." Frustration showed in his sharp words.

"Okay. First things first. You're here, and you're fine, so I don't need this." She removed the gun from her pocket and held it out.

He was silent, aghast, and made no move to accept it from her.

"I thought you might need rescuing." She laid the gun on the desk and put a finger to his lips. "Quiet. Don't say anything. Promise?" She pulled him into the hallway and to the dining room. Once inside, she closed the doors and pushed him further into the room, away from the doors. She couldn't resist a quick scan of the windows.

"Well, there's good news. I found Griffin's paintings."

"Not good news. Old news. Griffin left his paintings stashed here and there. My father once said that his mother kept hiding them so

Gramps couldn't hang them. I've seen them, and they're pretty awful."

The windows made her feel exposed, but the upside was that she could see clearly along the three sides of the room. If someone was eavesdropping they wouldn't be able to hear her.

"What's the mystery, Rachel?"

"Griffin's paintings. Not the ones he painted, but the ones he owned."

Jack scoffed. "You mean the fabled collection? The vanished collection? Griffin sold it off long ago. Anything he didn't sell off, his son did. I'm telling you, he impoverished the family. House poor."

"I found something in the basement, but there were signs that someone found it first."

"Were you hunting for treasure, too?" Disappointment showed in his eyes and colored his voice. "You're wasting your time."

Her palm itched to slap him. "You can be so pig-headed. Shut up before you say something you'll regret."

He drew in a slow, deep breath, but stayed silent.

"Someone had already been there, and secretively, so I moved the paintings. I believe someone intended to steal them from you. I heard noises down there again today, and that's when I found Brendan."

"Steal what?"

"The paintings."

"Who?"

"I don't know, so I hid them."

"You took them from a hiding place to hide them?" He smirked. "Where are they?"

"I'm going to show you, but prepare yourself. Remember, the more valuable the treasure, the more dangerous the treasure hunters can be."

"Please just explain."

She surveyed the row of windows on either side and in the convex end of the room and saw no one. Casually, as if approaching Jack's own art work, she went over to where his canvases were stacked, leaning against the wall. His canvases varied in size, many quite large and in and among them were six newly-added works of art.

She grasped a painting and gently pulled it away from the ones before and behind it.

Jack stared. He dropped to his knees. He stretched his long fingers toward the thick impasto of the vivid golden flowers but stopped short of touching it. He drew his fingers back, pressing them to his forehead, lost in reverie. Or star struck.

"Nice sunflowers, huh?" she asked.

Chapter Twenty-seven

Jack reached out, grabbed her wrist and pulled her down to the floor beside him. His brain felt at war with his eyes. He whispered close to her ear, "Is this real?"

"It's very convincing at first look. You need an expert to verify them."

"It."

"Them."

Jack sat all the way down. "Tell me."

He stared at her. He was missing something. This made no sense. She urged him forward. He obeyed. They crawled a few inches, to within reach of the paintings further back. Gently, careful not to shift the whole lot too much, she lifted a large, blocky painting forward and motioned to him to peek into the gap.

"Ren–Ren–"

"Renoir."

"*Girl With–With–*"

"This girl is without a watering can. She's sitting on the edge of a fountain, see? The watering can is a few feet away."

Jack shook his head, then raked his fingers back through his curls. "They were in Wynnedower the whole time?"

"Apparently."

"Two paintings?"

344

He tried to keep the evidence of his eyes at a distance, to stay cool and think it through. Rachel leaned toward him, her eyes were almost round, the color afire. He felt her breath warm on his ear.

"Six. Jack, these were Griffin's paintings, and they've been hidden in a chest in this house since…well, at least for the past century. Sometimes artists practiced by copying the masters, and a part of me can't believe they are truly the works of the masters. All I know is that you have to keep them safe until you can get an expert to verify authenticity."

He started to ask, "Who was it.…" He stopped short.

She sat silently now. Was she waiting for him to catch up?

The fog began to clear from his brain. He spoke tentatively, "Recently, in France.…"

"That's right. Someone had a couple hundred Picasso works show up in their garage or something. There's some kind of dispute about ownership. But this is different, Jack. Not a crystal clear path of ownership, but those receipts…and, Jack, these are unknown works and yet so similar to known works. Artists often do variations on a theme. I think these are the variations, not the paintings that ended up in the hands of museums and clients."

Jack stood abruptly, lifting her to her feet. She weighed no more than a feather.

"Show me. I want to see where you found them."

"But, Jack, please listen. Someone else found them first, and I'm sure they plan to come back for them. I think they already did and didn't find them, and they're bound to be angry, maybe desperate.... It could be anyone. It could be a stranger. Or not." She stared down at the floor, as if hesitant. "It could be someone you know."

She touched his arm. "Jack, I believe the only reason the paintings are still at Wynnedower is because I found them and moved them before he or they came back again."

"Who else could have found them?"

"Brendan?" She said it softly, lightly.

"Brendan." He didn't want to doubt his friend or spend more time arguing the unknowable. Unknowable for right now, anyway, and the minutes were flying past.

"Maybe not." She waved her hand at the paintings. "But we have to do something with them."

"What? I can't just telephone someone and say, hey, can you come over and take a look at my Van Gogh and Renoir? I might as well place an ad in the local paper and say, 'come help yourself." He tried to think it through. "They've been safe here so far...how long?"

"Two days. I found them yesterday. I was waiting for you to return to tell you."

"Where did you find them?"

"In the basement, in the area of the central stairs." She put her hands against his chest.

"You know where the landing is on the stairs? Did you know there was a door there many years ago?"

"There's never been a door there."

"I saw it on the blueprints."

He frowned. "You have blueprints?"

"I found them after you left. Listen, the door opened onto a narrow hallway with a short set of steps that led to the kitchen. The door into the kitchen was located where the Welsh cupboard is now."

"Okay."

"Between the two doors—now sealed off— is the hiding place. You can only access it from below."

"Someone deliberately constructed a hiding place for the paintings?" It sounded absurd.

"Maybe Griffin was concerned about the safety of the paintings, too. In fact, now that I think of it, the trunk the paintings were stored in couldn't fit through the opening in the floor. Griffin must've put the trunk there before closing it off." She bit her lip, then said, "In fact, Brendan mentioned his great-grandfather or maybe it was his grandfather…but anyway they did carpentry work–"

"Many did over the years, including Kilmer's grandfather." Almost absentmindedly, he put one arm around her shoulders and pulled her close.

Chapter Twenty-eight

She didn't object to his arm around her, even if he didn't seem to be fully aware that he was holding her. She felt wanted. Needed, valued—someone who belonged. Surely, it was okay to pretend for a moment, before she had to go back to doing the right thing.

Jack muttered, and his dark eyes burned with excitement.

She asked, "What now?"

"Amanda. I should call Amanda."

Her heart dropped right out of her chest and plummeted straight to the floor where it landed, splat, like a bloody pulp.

Amanda.

She plucked Jack's arm from her shoulders and pushed it away, resenting that she had to. Resenting Amanda. Resenting her resentment. Jack eyed her strangely.

She wanted to speak, to say something clever and hurtful, but her lips were numb, and her jaw seemed locked. She turned her face away.

Jack's hand touched her chin and turned her toward him. "Now what's wrong?"

The softness of his voice almost reduced her to tears. Foolish. "Let's take care of these paintings. Or, rather, do what you need to do to take care of these paintings or you're likely to find someone else has helped himself, or themselves, to them."

She stepped away, but paused to throw back, "Oh, and while you're at it, give my regards to your wife."

He moved like a man caught between two powerful magnets—a step toward her, a step back to the stacked paintings, then forward again.

"Wait, Rachel." He caught her as she turned the key and opened the dining room doors. "What's wrong?"

"What's wrong? How about Amanda? Does she think something is wrong?"

She thought she could walk away coolly, but Jack had other ideas. A rude man with an ego and a hot temper, he swept her into the curve of his arm.

"Who told you we were married?"

"Not you," she accused.

"Who?"

She tried to stare him down, but then her heart gave a sad jerk. "I don't remember."

"I doubt that. Think again."

"Are you calling me a liar? I may be very…inquiring and imaginative, but I know the difference between reality and fiction."

"That's not what I said. Who?"

"Brendan. I asked May. She said your marriage had problems. She said my presence here wasn't helping." Or did she? "Well, she said something like that."

Jack stared. His eyes were dark and serious

and unflinching. There was no perceptible change in his expression, yet she received some intangible spark from the force of his personality, and the tension flowed out of her. Her legs felt rubbery. Her reaction made no sense. Pure emotionalism. No logic.

Falling in love had no logic. Had she been fooling herself, thinking she had the option of walking away with dignity?

He trailed his fingers along the side of her face, tracing her cheek and jawline. As her heart swelled and ached, he dropped his hand and stepped back.

"I'm sorry, Rachel."

And? Next? Was he done? Seriously?

"I can explain."

"Perhaps Amanda doesn't understand you." Her anger gifted her with the strength to push him away. "Give me a break."

Suddenly, she was back right where she'd been. Gently but firmly, Jack held her.

His cheek against hers, his breath warm on her ear, he whispered, "My marital state is no one's business—no one's but mine and yours. Am I married? No. But I do have obligations, and it looks like I've got some things to tidy up." He put his forehead to hers in a caress, and then stared into her eyes. "What I don't understand is why Brendan would bother saying anything at all. He hardly knows Amanda."

Why, indeed? "Well, May wants me to leave...maybe Brendan wants the same."

Could that have been his intent? She tried to remember what May had actually said.

"Trust me, Rachel. Can you do that?"

Her eyes answered for her. Jack nodded.

"I'll call...." He cleared his throat. "I'll make some calls and we'll get the paintings somewhere safe. We'll figure it out together."

Together. It was more than a house. More than people. It was the security of loving and being loved. Being needed and needing.

Suddenly, she understood. Home was in Jack's arms.

Jack was home to her in a way that Jeremy never was, never could have been. Rachel had made sure Jeremy would be prepared to not only dwell in the world but to succeed. His path had changed, but everything she'd ever done, ever sacrificed for the sake of his future, had been worth it. Including the outcome that he had changed his path and didn't need her anymore. He loved her, but he didn't need her. Without her, his world would go on.

Jack needed her in his world. She believed that.

It frightened her that she couldn't control Jack in the same, best-intentioned way that she managed Jeremy's life, and even Aunt Eunice's.

The ground seemed to tremble beneath her feet, and truth shivered up through her body.

"You're shaking. You're not afraid, are you? Trust me, Rachel. Will you?"

Home. Not necessarily a building, but a

place where, without you, it isn't home for anyone who matters in your life. For anyone who cares about you. It's the place for which you'll risk everything to keep it and them safe and sound and they'll do the same for you. She nodded, 'yes.'

He moved away from her and pulled an object from his pocket.

She stared. "What's that?"

He motioned with the shiny black piece of fancy electronics in his hand. "My phone?"

"Since when?"

"New York. Amanda convinced me." He paused, and his face flushed. "Away from home and all, I was cut off from…everyone. Everyone here at Wynnedower. You…." He gave up poking his fingers at the slick cover and shook it as if it might rattle.

"Oh, give it here." She snatched it and hit the button that restored it to life.

"How'd you do that? They showed me in the store–"

He moved close to her, to look over her shoulder, and his scent enveloped her, not perfume, but good old-fashioned soap and water and fabric softener. Despite herself, she leaned slightly backward, as if magnetized.

Jack said, "Amanda deals with things like this in her line of business. I'm not taking any chances. I'm staying with these paintings until they're secure—certainly more secure than here at Wynnedower."

"Call her, then. Call the police, too. I feel like

we're sitting ducks."

"Will you check on Helene? She should've been in to say hello already. I don't want to leave you here alone with these paintings. If someone is after them, I don't want to put you in more danger."

"She was here earlier. I guess it was while you were outside unloading the car. I asked her to wait in her rooms." Rachel nodded and touched her hand to his chest.

He held her hand between both of his. "It's all going to work out. Don't worry. Think of it. Here, all these years, under our noses...old Griffin's probably sitting up in his grave and yelling for his cane."

His excitement and optimism were contagious, but the feeling of imminent danger persisted. She captured his darkly warm eyes in her memory and took the image straight into her heart. She put her free hand to his cheek.

"Be careful, Jack. I'll come right back."

Out of Jack's presence, her unease redoubled. She ran up the stairs and down the hall. Helene's door was closed, but unlocked.

She eased it open and said softly, "Helene?"

No response. She peeked inside.

Helene's corner chair was empty. A book lay open and abandoned on the side table. Rachel moved into the room. The rooms felt empty, and empty they were.

She wasn't going to chase Helene around the house. She'd already been gone too long. She returned downstairs.

May was back. She stood in the entrance hall, her expression anxious. "Is there a problem?"

Rachel scrambled to figure out how much she should say and settled for, "Have you seen Helene?"

"I was going to ask you the same. Did Jack return from New York?"

"He did. A short time ago."

May frowned. It looked more like a squint. "I saw a strange car. Did he come back alone? I thought maybe Amanda...."

Rachel fought back a sudden, illogical urge to cry. Only being caught in the vise between sympathy and antipathy toward May kept her cool.

May glanced toward the upstairs. "Miss Helene's okay?"

"She wasn't in her rooms, so..." Rachel fidgeted. She should tell her what was going on, at least enough to keep her safe. "May–"

"I'll go check for myself." May grasped the newel post and started up the steps. She turned back. "I heard a noise in the basement. I hate to say this, but maybe we should get in an exterminator? Also, as I walked up the path, I noticed the carriage doors looked crooked. At the very least, they need to be fixed to keep out rodents and weather." She didn't wait for an answer but continued on up the stairs, muttering, "Brendan was supposed to have already taken care of that."

Grateful to return to Jack, Rachel was

unprepared to open the dining room doors and find him gone. A quick scan reassured her that the paintings were still hidden among Jack's other paintings.

She ran down the hall and looked in his quarters. "Jack?"

This made no sense. Jack's big ring of keys was missing from the wall. She looked out the window. His rental car was parked on the side. Her heart wanted to gallop. She willed it to slow. She needed her wits.

Back in the dining room she walked along the walls of windows looking for something, anything that might answer her questions.

Crooked, May had said. The carriage doors were more than crooked. They were open only a few inches and the viewing angle was narrow, but she could see the chain was off the doors.

Jack had left the keys in the dining room doors. She pulled the doors closed and locked them, dropping the keys in her pocket.

Whatever was going on, she couldn't take any more chances. She went down the hall to use Jack's phone.

The phone line was strung from poles outside and entered the house near the top of the first floor. It never occurred to her that the lines would be sabotaged, and likely they weren't, but the phone was gone.

The phone was gone. The little clip at the end of the phone line dangled in the air.

She needed her phone, and her car keys, too.

She ran up the stairs and down the hall. Her doors were open.

At first, all she saw was that her suitcase had been unzipped, and its contents were hanging out across the bench and down to the floor. The dresser top was bare, except for the doily. The ring of Wynnedower keys, her car keys and cell phone were gone.

She heard a click behind her and spun around.

"Rachel?" Brendan shut the bedroom door. "Where are the paintings?"

"So, it was you. How could you?"

"How could I? How could I what? Finders, keepers, Rachel. As simple as that. No one even knew about them. It would have, should have, been easy to take them out through the basement—no one knew so no one would miss them. Until you screwed it up by snooping around. You took something simple and turned it into a mess, a big mess."

"Me? Are you seriously trying to blame me?"

"They're mine, Rachel. I found them."

"They belong to Wynnedower. To Jack and Helene." She changed her tone. "Walk away, Brendan. I understand your excitement at the find. What I don't understand is how you thought it would be okay to spirit them away and dispose of them on the sly."

"It's complicated. I found a guy with an 'in' who's going to help me sell them. I needed someone who knew buyers, plus I owed him." He gripped her arm, and she winced. Anger mixed with fear on Brendan's face. "He isn't going to let anyone just walk away. I have to have the paintings, Rachel."

She tried to bring the tension down a notch. "Instead, let's figure out a way to handle that guy. Call the police." She grabbed his arm with her free hand, refusing to show fear. "Brendan, listen to me. What laws have you actually broken? I mean, really? We can arrange a finder's fee for you, but that only works if no one gets hurt. Where's Jack?"

He shook his head. "I don't know."

"Brendan, how dangerous is that man? If he has hurt Jack...."

"He's been here before, back before I found them. He was...he thought...well, he was curious. Didn't believe me about this place. He thought I was talking big. Now he's expecting the paintings."

"We'll call the police. When he sees the police cars, he'll run away. We'll put out some kind of press release saying the paintings are phonies....which they probably are. That'll get him off your back."

"You don't think they're real? They look real." He was truly pale and sweating.

She tightened her grip on his arm and shook him. "Counterfeit art is as old as art itself." She paused for emphasis. "Don't you feel it, Brendan?"

"Feel what?"

"The way out. Take it while it's available. Before it's too late. Help me find Jack."

"There's Kilmer, too."

She frowned. "What about him?"

"He knew work had been done in the area of the stairs, that doors had been closed off when his grandfather was a kid. He gave me some info that helped me find the paintings. In exchange, I gave him information about Helene."

Her heart ached. She put her hands in her hair and pressed her fingers against her head.

Think, Rachel. Think.

"So, it was both of you sneaking around Wynnedower. Or should I say 'three of you'?" She shook her head. "Is Kilmer in the house now?"

Brendan nodded.

"Find him. Tell him it's over. Get him out of the house while I call the police. Where's my phone?"

He put his arm around her shoulders. "I appreciate that you want to help me."

They were near the bathroom door. Suddenly he pushed, shoving her down onto the ceramic tile.

"I'm sorry." His words were muffled by the slamming of the door and the twist of the key from his side.

"Brendan, don't do this."

He didn't answer. She beat at the door, calling his name, knowing it was useless unless May or Helene heard her screaming. But Brendan had taken the key. If anyone heard her, how long would it take them to find a duplicate key?

Helene. David was in the house.

She sat on the edge of the bathtub and heard the gentle clink of the two keys in her pocket. Would they work? What was the likelihood?

She pulled the keys from her pocket.

No rhyme, no reason—hadn't Jack said? She closed her eyes tightly. In her mind, she watched the key fit. She felt the lock mechanism slide open. Breath held, she inserted the key and turned.

Nothing. Logic made the result obvious, but she tried the other key, too.

She slid to the floor, her head and shoulder against the wooden door, too discouraged to yell again. Even if she got free, what could she do?

What, indeed? She closed her eyes and tried to see it—what she could do if she escaped. No, not if, but when. It was hard to keep up the positive outlook. Resilience didn't matter if she was trapped.

Jack missing. Helene missing.

Jack had been with the paintings. Had he called the police before being interrupted? Interrupted, yes, because otherwise he wouldn't have left before finishing what he was doing.

Brendan, maybe? While she was looking for Helene. It would only have taken a simple, 'Hey, Jack, come see...or Jack, Rachel needs you.' Jack would be lured away. Down to the basement, surely.

That was all. The images ran out.

Why wouldn't they dry up? She was stuck here with no one to help her. If not her, then who would help Jack?

It felt like she'd been there forever when something touched her thigh.

She looked down and saw the metal stem of a key. Its little orange tag showed from under the edge of the door.

"Hello?" She pulled the key the rest of the way through and clutched it. "Hello?"

She bent and placed her cheek against the floor. Through the narrow gap she saw feminine fingers and the lavender fabric of Helene's dress puddled on the wood.

"Helene?"

A gentle shushing noise came from the other side. She blinked, and no one was there.

Rachel pushed the key into the lock, and the tumblers rolled.

Forehead against the crystal doorknob, she took a long drag of air into her lungs and held it for a few seconds to calm herself. She visualized herself going into Jeremy's room, then the hallway, then the three stairways. Which would be the best choice?

She didn't have her car keys or the keys to Wynnedower. Presumably Helene did, so if the doors in the stairwells were locked, that only left the central stairs. Once downstairs, she would have to go straight out the front door and run down the dirt track for a mile or so. And then what? Wave down a passing motorist? Or go to Mike's Towing and hope Mike wasn't in on the theft?

The gun. She'd left it on Jack's desk.

She kept low in Jeremy's room because she could see the bedroom door was open. She listened. No sight, no sound. No one.

Her first goal was to reach the east end stairs. As she moved through the hallway, it was unnerving to see many of the doors open. Jack's key ring had been missing, too. Brendan or someone must've been searching for the paintings. Had he tried the dining room? Even without a key, the doors wouldn't be that hard to kick open. The paintings, probably copies, were far down on her list of what to protect, but if Jack was already in the hands of these dangerous fools, then she might need them for bargaining.

She paused for a peek into Helene's room. Still no one, but now, on the table by the flowered chair, were her car keys. She picked them up and stared at them. No time to think, she put them into her pocket.

Now she could drive down that road instead of running, but so much time had already passed. She headed down the stairs.

Jack's door was open.

The gun was no longer on the desk. Maybe Jack had taken it with him or put it away? She searched in the desk drawers, on the top of the bookcase and in the night stand, and didn't find it.

That left finding Jack. She saw Jack's rental car through the window, still parked.

Jack didn't want to believe bad things about Brendan, but reality could be cruel, and wanting to believe the best made Jack vulnerable.

She checked the dining room doors on the way and found them still locked. Urged on by a sense of time running out, she went back down the hall to the east end stairs instead of choosing the front door. Where was the value in driving away to summon help, if her help was needed now? Right now. Right below her feet.

Moving down the stairs in the dark, her fingers trailed along the rough, wooden boards, nearly blind, afraid that the least bit of stray light would filter into the long hallway and give her away.

In the basement hallway, she kept the blueprint image of the hall in her head. She paused every few feet to touch the walls with her hands and to feel the floor with her feet. Servants' quarters and storage rooms lined both sides of the hall. The doors were closed and helped mark her passage. The pace was slow. When the sound of hushed voices reached her, she stopped.

The voices sounded disembodied, curling out from the far end of the basement.

"…everywhere. I can't find…."

Brendan's voice.

By now, her eyes were well-adjusted to the dark. Beyond the end of the hallway, in the area of the central stairs, the dark was less intense because the door to the carriage area was open a fraction.

She crept to the door and tried to see through the gap. At least two people were in there and moving toward her out of the deeper shadows.

The silhouetted figures walked into the open area which was dimly lit by the wedge of light that filtered in through the carriage doors. That light brushed the outlines of a truck. The side nearest to where Rachel crouched was a dark, amorphous area of shadow.

The smell of exhaust stole the oxygen even though the truck's motor was off. She couldn't see what lay in the shadows alongside the truck, but she sensed his presence so strongly, it was as if she could see every detail in his face.

"Too bad."

"The deal was that we weren't going to hurt anyone."

"Where's the woman and the sister?"

Brendan's words were murmured, too low to be understood.

"He's a freak. Is he in the house, too?" The man sounded angry and bad-tempered.

"No," Brendan said. "The women are gone, too. Ran off into the woods. They don't know anything anyway—"

A loud thwack stopped Brendan's words.

"You brought me into this. Don't go weak on me now."

A pause, then Brendan answered, "It's over,

Doug. It's fallen apart, and you knocked out, maybe killed, the only guy who has the answers. It's not too late to back out. No one can identify you."

"Except you." He made a noise that sounded like a twisted laugh. "You deliver, or I'm gonna be embarrassed in front of some people in a real unhealthy way, and that's not going to happen."

A long taut silence stretched out between them.

"I've been straight with you. If I knew where those paintings were, I'd be right in it with you, but the longer this drags on–"

"Then fix it."

In that deep shadow beside the truck, there was a thud, followed by a groan.

"Well, we're in luck. He's not dead. Grab that end. We'll wake him up."

"Wait, Doug. He's a big guy and a dead weight right now. I'll get a chair. There's one over by the wall."

She squeezed her eyes shut and tears dampened her lashes. The words wanted to burst past her lips, 'take the paintings and go,' but she wasn't that big a fool. Offering the paintings right now wouldn't save Jack, or anyone. But she had hope. Brendan had told the man that she was gone—not locked in the bathroom and conveniently waiting to be questioned.

Brendan disappeared. The man kept saying, 'Wake up. Wake up,' to the tune of a flesh hitting flesh. Each blow wrenched her own stomach.

The man stood as Brendan returned. She heard Brendan say, "Here it is," and he swung the chair, hitting Doug with a loud, crunching thud. The chair then flew from his hands and banged into the side of the truck. Brendan launched himself onto the staggering man.

Acting purely on emotion, Rachel opened the door wide and threw herself into the shadows beside the truck. She landed on top of Jack who lay sprawled on the floor. He groaned and moved in reflex. She pulled at him, insanely thinking she could pull him away from danger. His name slipped out. "Jack!"

Cruel hands grabbed her, pulling her to her feet, and a hard voice said, "Who's this?" He dragged her nearer the light. "Jack, did you say? Well, you're my jackpot, aren't you?"

"Brendan?" She resisted the hands holding her and tried to see into the area into which he'd disappeared. Maybe a figure lying on the floor? Hard to tell.

"He's out." He crooked an arm around her neck. "Where are the paintings?"

Rachel pushed against his arm. "Why should I tell you? You're going to kill us. I'm not stupid."

"You're down here, aren't you? So you can't be too bright." He dragged her back to where Jack lay. "Tell me, or I'll cut his throat. You're not dead yet, and neither is he. But he will be if you don't tell. He'll die right in front of you."

"Where's Brendan?" She kept her voice loud in case Jack could hear her, in case Brendan wasn't totally disabled.

"He's bleeding out right about now. He shouldn't have double-crossed me. Learn from his mistake."

It was only him—just the one. Brendan wasn't helping him now. Brendan's helper, who'd turned away from her that day when she saw them working on the front door. The man Helene saw. Oh, Brendan. Jack was right about bringing strangers into Wynnedower.

Her heart was trying to bang right out of her chest. She felt faint. No good. She couldn't think through the fear.

Remove the extraneous; identify the true need.

Calm began to slow her panic. She said, "You win. Come with me, and I'll show you."

He heard the jingle of keys in her pockets and searched them. "Car keys? Nice. You won't need these." He dropped them into his own pocket.

"Go now. Take my car. Get away while you can." *Please go. Please.*

"Oh, I'll get away and leave with what I came for, too, but I'll want the truck for that."

He pushed her toward the stairs. She put one foot in front of the other. Slowly, they moved forward.

He followed so closely his breath stirred her hair. The sharp point of a blade dug into her back. Thinking of Brendan's silence, the knife, and now Jack, again, over and over. Jack lying in the basement—was he also in an ever-widening spread of blood? Her feet felt like twenty-pound weights were attached.

Stumbling on the steps only succeeded in getting the point of his knife pushed more firmly into her side and probably a tear in her jacket. Thinking furiously, but with no really helpful ideas and no time for her to think it out in her head, they entered the pantry and heard voices.

Helene said, "I told you to leave me alone."

From a distance, Kilmer answered, "You know I love you. I adored you when we were children and that feeling has grown each year, each day. It consumes me, Helene."

Rachel realized she'd stopped moving when the man pushed up close behind her. The blade poked in her side again and his hand covered her mouth.

"I don't love you."

"Helene, please, you did once and you will again if they'll leave us alone and let us be together."

"You don't love me." Her voice was steady, not loud, but strong with certainty.

"Come with me. We're going to split the proceeds from selling the paintings. We'll be able to—"

"They aren't yours."

He sounded put out. "We'll have to go away for a while, but then we'll come back and fix up Wynnedower. It'll be everything we ever wanted it to be, like we dreamed years ago."

"We were six. I don't love you. Stay away from me."

Torn between the terrible events downstairs, the prick of the knife in her side, and the wounded voices floating out from the dining room, Rachel was mesmerized. The tragedy that had started below, continued to unfold around her with an increasing sense of inevitability. She was almost numb now and vaguely grateful for it.

The man spoke in her ear, excitement slurring his words, "They're in there, aren't they?"

She knew he didn't mean the people.

"Helene, I'll do anything for you. Let me. No one knows Wynnedower like I do. No one cares about it like me. Like I care for you. We'll take these. Just the two of us. But we don't have much time. They'll be up here any minute."

She and her captor had moved from the kitchen to the doorway of the dining room.

At about the same time that the man whispered in her ear, "Call them out," May spoke from behind them. "Miss Sevier, where is Miss Helene and who is this man?" Ahead of her, from the dining room, Rachel heard the click of a hammer being pulled back. That round was being chambered.

"I never blamed you, Helene. Never. In no time you'll be glad we did this."

The reverberation of the gun shot caused Rachel to step back. She nearly fell because the man was no longer behind her. He was choking, his throat wedged in the crook of Jack's arm.

Jack's face was dusty on one side and pale on the other and a trickle of blood had run from his black hair and into the corner of one eye. He sounded breathless. "Go see about Helene. Has anyone called the police?"

May was immobile, stunned into shock. Rachel pushed past her and rushed into the dining room. Helene was seated on the modeling chair, the gun in her hand, relaxed on her thigh. The bullet had gone somewhere, but not into David Kilmer. He huddled on the floor next to the box that had held Jack's painting junk. The stuff was now scattered on the floor. A couple of ornate frames rose above the open top of the box.

"Hello, Rachel. Are you okay?"

She gaped at Helene. "Did you shoot?"

"It was loud. It hurt my ears." A phone rang. Rachel's cell phone. The gun wavered as Helene dug into her skirt pocket. She pulled it out. "For you?"

"The gun, Helene. Please point it away. Down at the floor." Rachel took the phone. "Daisy? Sorry, can't talk." She disconnected and handed the phone to May.

"Please call 9-1-1."

Sounds of a scuffle outside the dining room overrode May's voice speaking in the background. Rachel ran out again feeling battered by too many choices, too many decisions of the life and death kind.

The man, Doug, stumbled into the hallway, knocked her splat against the wall. He ran toward the central hall, his feet slipping as he turned the corner, but he kept moving. Jack half fell out of the kitchen and into the hallway. His eyes hit on Rachel sitting on the floor with her back against the wall. He held one hand in front of his ribs as if to protect them and put his other hand on the wall. He slid down to his knees.

"He's running away," she said.

He said, "Let him go. The police can catch him later. My head is splitting. Are you okay? Who was shot?"

"No one. Helene shot, but didn't hit him. Didn't hit David, I mean. May called 9-1-1." It was so odd, yet felt so right, that the two of them were sitting and chatting on the hallway floor. They were bruised, but upright and breathing, and more interested in each other than in running down that horrible man.

"Brendan? He took me downstairs...said you needed me. That's all I remember. No, wait. His truck. I saw his truck before something hit me. You were right about him."

"He's injured. Badly, I think. Downstairs." She struggled to her feet. "I'll go check on him."

"No." Jack stopped her. "I'll go. Send May down if you don't need her. You said she called 9-1-1? Right. Please get that gun from Helene and put it away before she shoots someone. I don't want the police to see it and start shooting, either." He limped away.

Rachel went to the doorway. "Helene, can I have the gun now?"

"I'm taking care of this myself. I want to be sure David understands his visits distress me."

White and sweaty, David still crouched near the box.

"He understands."

"Okay, then." She pointed the gun at Rachel.

Brief alarm flared. "Point it that way, okay?" Rachel took it delicately. May was nearby. They exchanged looks when they heard sirens in the background. "May, can you put this away somewhere safe and then see if Jack needs help down in the basement? Brendan's hurt."

May took the gun, handed Rachel her cell phone and left.

There was nothing now to stop David from leaving except a body block and Rachel didn't care enough to try that. She cared about Jack. And about Brendan, too. They'd press charges against David—for trespassing, if nothing else. Beyond that, she didn't care what happened to him. Rachel stepped aside. David, his face white pale, his eyes wild, dashed past her as if she was invisible.

She went to the front of the house and ushered the police inside. Doug had run out that way. She was surprised to see her car still parked in the front yard. She didn't care about the car either.

The man who'd threatened her, who'd punished Brendan for changing his mind and trying to protect them, was tucked away in the back seat of the second cruiser.

****

Later, after all of the official questions had been answered and her brain was free to crumple, she sat with Helene at the kitchen table and explained she was going to the hospital to check on Jack.

"Do you want to go with me?"

"You said his head is hurt, but he's okay, right?"

"Yes. He'll be okay."

"Then I'll stay here with Miss May." She reached across the table and patted May's pasty white hand.

Rachel clutched her keys. They'd found them in the ignition of her car. Brendan's truck was still in the basement.

Almost to herself, Rachel asked, "Why he didn't drive away while he was in my car? Why did he take off on foot instead?"

Helene smiled her secret smile. "I heard you and Jack arguing on the stairs. I didn't want you to leave. Then I saw...." She blushed and giggled. "I saw you kissing and hugging, so I knew it was okay again, but by then I'd already fixed the car."

Helene. A serial battery killer.

May's face went dark. Her eyes glittered like hard, shiny marbles, and Rachel was scared. She rejected the fear. No more. No more drama. Done. She swept past May and went outside to hook up her car battery, hoping she remembered how to do it from watching Mike.

****

Jack stayed in the hospital overnight. He wanted to return home immediately, but Rachel reminded him that he'd be at the mercy of people with absolutely no medical training, and it was a long drive back into town and to the hospital. From long distance, Amanda arranged for a security firm to pick up the paintings. In the meantime, Wynnedower's treasure was in police custody.

Rachel dozed in the chair by Jack's bed. Thoughts of Brendan flitted in and out like dream seedlings that couldn't take root in bad soil. When had Brendan actually made his decision? First, to steal the paintings. Had his childhood game grown over the years into something real and terrible? And second, what about his decision to protect her and Jack even though it meant disaster for him? Had he chosen that course at the moment he pushed her into the bathroom and told the man she'd left? Or was it after he lured Jack downstairs and then realized people could really get hurt and might die as a result of his actions?

Brendan had committed acts of selfish stupidity. But when his eyes had opened to the reality of his actions, he had also committed acts of selfless courage.

Finally, giving into her need, she slipped out of Jack's room.

Mike was sitting at Brendan's bedside, his head back against the chair, looking dazed and stricken. They all felt dazed. Except Brendan.

Who knew what he did or didn't feel at this point? Somewhere between the blood loss, the internal damage from the knife, and a nasty head wound, he was suspended in no man's land. A coma.

"Any change?" she asked, knowing there wasn't.

Brendan's big brother shook his head in rough jerks, then pressed his hands to the sides of his face and leaned forward, shutting her out.

This hadn't been her first trip to his room during the long night. This time, before she left, she paused by Brendan's bedside. "Thank you for trying to make it right."

She touched his hand, then walked away. She hoped he'd heard her.

Chapter Twenty-nine

"We can get on with our lives now."

"We?" Rachel asked.

"We."

The grass itched her neck, but the shape of Jack's forearm was perfect beneath her head. She admired how the light played with his curls, his strong jaw and warmed his dark eyes. It was a lovely recipe and a perfect mix.

His fingers traced the turn of her cheek and jaw and along the length of her neck. She trembled. She grabbed his hand before he could cross into more dangerous territory.

"Who makes up this 'we'? I believe you were going to explain something to me. You asked me to trust you and I did. I do. But I'd really like to hear how you're going to explain away this Amanda thing."

He leaned over her, blocking the light, and kissed her before moving away. He detached his hand from her grasp and sat up.

"Okay." He stared at the leaves shifting in a breeze high above. "Amanda and I married young, at a time when I was trying to make a living in the city. In a suit. At a desk."

"You met her in the city?"

"No. I met her here. Amanda is May's daughter."

He paused to let it sink in, perhaps to see what her reaction might be. She kept her emotions reined in. She wanted details. Amanda and May? It boggled her mind to think of it. May was his mother-in-law?

"The marriage stopped working long ago. I didn't want to live in the city, and she wanted to live nowhere else. But neither of us met anyone, so we let it drift. It was easier, maybe just lazier. May knew we had marital problems and were separated. I guess, as long as we weren't officially divorced, she hoped we'd reconcile. In the meantime, Wynnedower was her consolation.

"When the divorce was final, I broke the news to her myself, but words are only as good as the people who speak them. And those who hear them, I guess. I think I said something along the lines of 'our marriage is over' but I believe May took it as just another degree of separation." He sighed. "I should've said it more firmly…something that actually had the word 'divorce' in it, but I thought I was being gentle and considerate. I only realized recently that she still had hopes for a reconciliation."

She reached up and caressed his cheek. "You and May never let on about your relationship."

"Not my choice. It's always been that way. May preferred it. She's old-fashioned."

Rachel bit her lip. Doubt wrapped harsh fingers around her gut. "Old fashioned? Are you kidding me? That would be old-fashioned for a century ago. Old family retainer. An unfortunate connection to be kept quiet." She sat up. "Jack, honestly, have you considered that she might be more upset about the potential loss of Wynnedower than a divorce?"

He eased her back down and toyed with her hair. "Have I told you how mesmerizing your eyes are?"

"Are you changing the subject?"

"I just don't want you to worry. Or to be suspicious." He kissed her forehead. "I had no idea you could be so jealous."

"Me? Seriously? You were the one who was jealous when you saw Jeremy hugging me."

"Do you blame me? I had no idea he was your brother. At least, until I saw his eyes. Yes, I know you said he was tall and blond. Brendan, too."

He went suddenly quiet. Rachel knew they were both sad, reminded of Brendan and the tragedy for his family. Loss seemed to live on the fringes of life. Ever present. Ever ready to engage.

"No time like now," Jack said.

"What?" She was startled. It felt like he'd read her mind.

"I'm going to clear it up once and for all. No more euphemisms. I have to speak to May privately. She deserves that."

Rachel disagreed, but couldn't form the words. It was a misty feeling—no, more like a miasma.

"Jack–"

He stretched alongside her from toe to nose and brushed his lips against hers, and won the argument.

Several minutes later he drew away and stood. "I won't be long."

"Promise?"

"Promise."

As soon as he left, Rachel sat bolt upright fighting the screaming need to call him back. She hadn't been this frightened of Brendan and Doug. Why was she afraid now?

The sight of him striding up the hill and crossing the uncared for yard in front of the house spooked her. Was it was the idea of May believing against all logic that her daughter and Jack would resume their marriage. That kind of single-mindedness was disturbing.

May, against all logic, clinging...because it all fed into her love for this house? May could believe what she needed to believe if it helped to support her greatest desire. Not so different from most people.

Thinking about May and Jack finished the work on her stomach and nerves.

May. They were so focused on the danger to the paintings and the related danger to themselves, had they missed the heart of the danger?

The back of her neck tingled, not as in feeling watched, but as if that doggone brain stem was trying to tell her something.

She closed her eyes tightly. She sees Jack as he enters Wynnedower. He goes through the hall to the kitchen. He says 'hello' to May as he's done over and over for many years. Unexceptional. He goes closer to her so that he can place a hand on her shoulder. He says 'May, I need to talk to you,' and he sees the sudden alarm on her face, especially after all they've just been through. To soothe her, he adds, "It's about Amanda and me." Then nothing. Rachel's imagination stops there.

There was nothing after that.

She ran toward the house. Her only goal was to find Jack before he and May reached the blank space in her head.

Rachel heard their voices as she entered the foyer. She tried to gauge their tenor.

Jack and May were beyond the double doors, talking in the dining room. She moved forward on cat's feet.

The dining room door knobs turned. She did a quick side-step into the central hall, back beyond where she'd be seen unless they walked this way.

May's footsteps went toward the kitchen. Rachel stepped out when the coast was clear and moved quickly into the dining room, easing the doors almost closed, not wanting to make a noise with the latch sliding home.

"How'd it go?" she whispered.

He gave her a thumbs up and moved toward her. "She wasn't happy, but she took it okay." He wrapped his arms around her. "Now, it's time for us. I want to take you away from here for a change of scene. We'll leave Wynnedower and go play in New York. I want to show you the city and then we'll–"

"Mr. Wynne?"

Jack stepped back. "May?"

They both saw the gun, Jack's gun, at the same time—just as May pulled the trigger.

Chapter Thirty

They never knew which of them she intended to shoot, but it was Jack whose knees buckled and he fell back onto his painter's cart. The palette sailed, and paint tubes scattered. Jack landed heavily on the floor, gasping, his fingers clawing at the wood.

The loud clatter of the gun hitting the floor broke Rachel's paralysis. She never looked at May, but dropped immediately to the floor beside Jack.

Blood ran from somewhere in his mid-section. It spread through the fabric of his shirt. She tried to think of anything she'd ever read about bullet wounds, but came up empty. First aid, even rudimentary first aid, failed her. It was black in her head. She could only flail, weak-handed, rubber-fingered, and futile.

She screamed, "Call 9-1-1. Call 9-1-1!" From somewhere, her hands found the minimal skill to press against his wound.

He never opened his eyes, but the lines around them deepened with pain. He was sufficiently conscious to murmur her name. She put her ear close to his lips in case he had more to say, but there were only thin, erratic breaths.

Helene appeared, dropping into her line of sight, to kneel alongside Jack.

Rachel yelled, "Call 9-1-1."

"May did. She's in the kitchen. Waiting." Helene's hands moved over Rachel's, becoming bloody. She ran her fingers along her brother's face, leaving red streaks.

"May shot him." Rachel bent over and kissed his forehead. "We need help now, Helene. Now."

Helene nodded. She stood and left. The front door slammed.

Minutes later—minutes in which Rachel felt like she aged a year for every drop of blood Jack lost—she heard running footsteps. A slim woman with white-blonde hair paused only a split second in the doorway and was then quickly on the floor beside them. Rachel didn't question it when the woman lifted her hands to examine the wound, then placed them again on Jack's abdomen. The woman slipped her fingers beneath his back. When she pulled them out, they were wet with blood.

The woman held his wrist, pressing one finger against his flesh to feel his pulse. She pressed the tips of the fingers on her other hand along his neck near his jaw.

Rachel's first thought was how odd that Amanda should arrive now, how ironic that her mother would've made her a widow if she hadn't already been divorced.

Her next thought was that this woman was too young to be Amanda.

Jeremy knelt on the floor beside them.

Unreality. Seeing Jeremy suddenly there

made it seem more unreal, yet more manageable all at the same time. Illogic cradled her breaking heart and kept her going.

Jeremy held a folded cloth firmly against the wounded area as he drew Rachel's bloody hands away. She was horrified by the abundance of blood, but encouraged, too, by the slower soaking of the cloths that had appeared beside them.

"The bleeding has slowed. That's a good thing." She told herself it *must* be a good thing. It couldn't be that the flow was slower because he was running out of it.

The blonde woman said, "His pulse is weak. Are the EMTs on the way?"

"I think so. Helene said May called 9-1-1."

"Where's the shooter?" Jeremy asked.

"May. May shot him."

He followed her gaze to where the gun lay. "May shot him and then called 9-1-1? Do you know where she is?"

"Helene said she's waiting for the sheriff in the kitchen."

"Helene? Is she the thin, shy woman?"

He lifted his head, listening. In the next second, she heard the first sirens.

Belatedly, she asked, "Where'd you come from?"

"Helene was running down the dirt road as Lia and I drove up."

They heard footsteps in the foyer.

Jeremy yelled, "In here!"

Rachel nearly sobbed in relief. Too soon for

relief. But Jeremy and his Lia were here, and now the authorities had arrived. They were trained professionals who knew more than only what they might have read or imagined—and in a true emergency, they didn't go blank.

****

Hope was the cruelest emotion of all. It was also the most uplifting.

Jack would be fine. No other outcome was acceptable to her. From the moment they were en route to the hospital, every cell in her brain sparked alive and focused on visualizing Jack well and whole.

If force of human will could direct the present and future, then Jack and she were going to be okay. She added a prayer, too, and wished faith and God was something she'd spent some time learning. Strangely, when she sent up that prayer, it felt 'received,' and hope began to seem reasonable. With it, her mind seemed to clear. With the clarity came regret.

Rachel sat by his hospital bed. Lia sat on the cushioned window seat with her legs drawn up and her eyelids drooping. Jeremy had gone for coffee.

Jack's eyelids fluttered, perhaps dreaming, loitering somewhere below the veil of consciousness. She touched his arm, and though she knew she should let him rest, she ran her fingers lightly along his skin.

Regret. It tasted bitter. Regret for whatever part she'd played in pushing May to the breaking point, and for thinking she could manage a deadly weapon, then treating it as if it was no more impactful than a prop in a story or movie. Irresponsible. It wasn't a word she'd ever expected to apply to herself.

"Rachel?" His voice was thin, barely a rasp.

"I'm here."

"Take me home, to Wynnedower."

His weak, murmured command was laughable since he couldn't keep his eyes open.

"All in good time."

"How's May?"

His question shocked her as did her own sudden rush of anger. She bit her lip. Now wasn't the time for bitter words.

A woman spoke from the doorway, "She's okay. She's sorry."

Rachel looked up, startled. The dark-haired woman, tall and slim, wore a suit far more stylish than she, Rachel, could ever have imagined wearing. 'Style' fit the woman. It took seeing it to understand. The woman walked fluidly and with the confidence Rachel had always wanted to show—the confidence that said she had every right to be here or anywhere.

"You must be Amanda."

She stopped within a couple of feet. "Rachel?"

The woman extended her hand, but Rachel kept hers firmly upon Jack's arm.

Amanda drew her hand back. "I'm glad to meet you. I'm truly sorry for what happened with Mother. Something like this never occurred to me." She gave Jack a long, slow look. "How is he?"

Rachel removed her hand from Jack's arm and stepped back. Jack's arm moved, following her, his hand seeking hers.

His words were breathless and slightly slurred. "Amanda. I'm sorry about May. I should've managed it better."

"No, Jack." She touched his arm on the other side of the bed. "It was her choice. Our mistake was in not being firm about the truth, however harsh." She laughed softly. "Once she had us all arranged, she didn't want anything to change. I think she loves Wynnedower almost as much as she loves me. More, really." She stared across the room, her eyes touching briefly upon Jeremy and Lia. "Mother says it was an accident, that she was returning the gun." Amanda dropped her gaze to the floor. "Thank you for telling the police you thought it was a mistake."

Jack didn't respond. Rachel thought he'd drifted off again. She doubted the accident story, but it was a moot point now. She spoke into the gap. "Wynnedower and the Wynne family were her life."

Amanda shook her head and sighed. "It was all Wynnedower. For her the Wynnes were only an extension of the house. I'm certain it's true. How else could she have been satisfied with living as she did? What will she do now?"

"She'll find something else to live for. People

do." Did that sound harsh?

Amanda sighed. "I don't know what the judge will say, but thank God Jack didn't die. We'll return for the hearing, but she won't see Wynnedower again. Ever."

"He's out again. Let him rest." She took Amanda by the hand and drew her to the doorway.

Jeremy was standing there, holding cups of coffee. They exchanged looks. He nodded, then continued past to where Lia sat.

Rachel said, "Jack's will be okay. As to punishment...."

"She'll never return to Wynnedower. Ironic, isn't it?" Amanda hugged her arms. "At any rate, let Jack know that Helene is coming home with me for a visit. When he's up on his feet again, he can come to New York to get her."

"Thank you."

Amanda shook her head. "Mother is terribly fond of Helene, as am I. Do you know what she kept saying to me? Over and over, she said Helene will never sell Wynnedower. Do you know what that's all about?"

Rachel shivered and was grateful Amanda interpreted the movement as denial.

"Well, maybe someday she'll be able to explain it herself." She looked across the room at Jack. "Tell him, too, that the paintings arrived safely. They are being evaluated now. So far the results are encouraging."

Encouraging? Half a dozen paintings, possibly from the brushes of some of the most famous artists of modern times, and she said 'encouraging.' Later, when they had all recovered, they could celebrate—not the authenticity of the paintings, but life itself.

"One last thing. The property management company has another caretaker installed at Wynnedower."

Amanda left. Rachel turned to the cushioned window seat where Jeremy sat with his arm around Lia. Her head rested on his shoulder, and both of them were silent and staring.

"Don't you two have a plane to catch?"

Jeremy shook his head. "We can't leave you like this."

"You can, and you will. I'm ready to move forward and you are, too." Rachel wrapped her arms around Jeremy first, then motioned to Lia to join the group hug. When she released them, she said, "Go now, but...."

"What, Sis?" Jeremy sounded anxious.

"Keep your guest room ready. You never know when I might show up for a visit. I'll expect you to be there this time."

They left and, despite her encouraging words, once they were out of the room, she had to dab at tears.

The window overlooked the parking lot. A few floors below, Jeremy and Lia emerged hand in hand, walking with renewed energy. Jeremy looked up and waved. Rachel smiled. He might not be able to see his big sister standing at the window, but he knew she'd be watching.

Her phone buzzed. She pulled it from her pocket.

A message notification. She hit the voicemail button.

"Ms. Sevier? This is Carina. I'm calling regarding the appointment with Mr. Ballew. He's back and asked me to contact you with regard to the interview. If you're still interested, please call, and we'll schedule a new appointment."

Jack whispered, "Are you laughing?"

Rachel leaned over and kissed his rough cheek. "I just got a voicemail."

"From your brother?" He sounded confused.

"No, that's old news. This, Jack, is a message about the future."

THE END

ABOUT THE AUTHOR

Stories of heart and hope ~ from the Outer Banks to the Blue Ridge

USA Today Bestselling and award-winning author, Grace Greene, writes novels of contemporary romance with sweet inspiration, and women's fiction with romance, mystery and suspense.

A Virginia native, Grace has family ties to North Carolina. She writes books set in both locations. The Emerald Isle, NC Stories series of romance and sweet inspiration are set in North Carolina. The Virginia Country Roads novels, and the Cub Creek novels have more romance, mystery, and suspense.

Grace lives in central Virginia. Stay current with Grace's news at www.gracegreene.com.

You'll also find Grace here:
Http://twitter.com/Grace_Greene
Https://www.facebook.com/GraceGreeneBooks
Http://www.goodreads.com/Grace_Greene

Other Books by Grace Greene

THE MEMORY OF BUTTERFLIES
(Lake Union Publishing)

Brief Description:
A young mother lies to keep a devastating family secret from being revealed, but the lies, themselves, could end up destroying everything and everyone she loves. Hannah Cooper's daughter, Ellen, is leaving for college soon. As Ellen's high school graduation approaches, Hannah decides it's time to return to her roots in Cooper's Hollow along Virginia's beautiful and rustic Cub Creek. Hannah's new beginning comes with unanticipated risks that will cost her far more than she ever imagined—perhaps more than she can survive.

THE HAPPINESS IN BETWEEN
(Lake Union Publishing)

Brief Description:
Sandra Hurst has left her husband. Again. She's made the same mistake twice and her parents refuse to help this time—emotionally or financially. Desperate to earn money and determined to start over, she accepts an offer from her aunt to house-sit at the old family home, Cub Creek, in beautiful rural Virginia. But when Sandra arrives, she finds the house is shabby, her aunt's dog is missing, and the garden is woefully overgrown. And she

suspects her almost-ex-husband is on her trail. Sandra needs one more chance at regaining her self-respect, making peace with her family, and discovering what she's truly made of.

Thank you for purchasing

A STRANGER IN WYNNEDOWER

I hope you enjoyed it!

Please leave a review wherever this book is sold. It helps authors find readers and helps readers find books they'll enjoy.

Books by Grace Greene

Stories of heart and hope ~ from the Outer Banks to the Blue Ridge

Emerald Isle, NC Stories
Love. Suspense. Inspiration.

BEACH RENTAL (Emerald Isle novel #1)
BEACH WINDS (Emerald Isle novel #2)
BEACH WEDDING (Emerald Isle novel #3)
BEACH TOWEL (short story)
BEACH WALK (A Christmas novella)
BEACH CHRISTMAS (A Christmas novella)
CLAIR: BEACH BRIDES SERIES (novella)

Virginia Country Roads Novels
Love. Mystery. Suspense.

KINCAID'S HOPE
A STRANGER IN WYNNEDOWER
CUB CREEK (Cub Creek series #1)
LEAVING CUB CREEK (Cub Creek series #2)

Single Titles from Lake Union Publishing

THE HAPPINESS IN BETWEEN
THE MEMORY OF BUTTERFLIES
www.gracegreene.com